BIZARRE BONDS

PACK OF OUTCASTS - BOOK 2

EVA CHASE

Bizarre Bonds

Book 2 in the Pack of Outcasts series

First Digital Edition, 2025

Cover design: Sanja Balan (Sanja's Covers)

Ebook ISBN: 978-1-998582-47-1

Paperback ISBN: 978-1-998582-57-0

I

Periwinkle

I may have made a slight mistake.

No, "mistake" is what you call grabbing the salt instead of the sugar or ordering the chef's special only to realize it's about ten times bigger than your stomach. What's the word for "my essence is doing some bizarro thing I didn't know I was capable of or what it even is"?

At least the strange effect I've unexpectedly produced doesn't seem to be *bad*. The energy streaming out of me is a warm glow that lights up the chests of the four men it's veered toward. Unlike the blazes that've surged out of me in a gush of joy in the past, there's nothing searing or blinding about my current shiny outburst.

But it's come with other unfamiliar sensations. Like the thud of four heartbeats echoing alongside my own.

The layered rhythm resonates down to my bones. I might actually enjoy the heady vibration if the four men those heartbeats belong to weren't staring at me like I've sprouted a third arm.

As I glance down to confirm that I haven't actually gained any extra limbs, the beams fade away into the regular afternoon daylight of the forest we were walking through. Amid the trees, all four of my teammates—two of whom have become my lovers, the other two I've hoped are something close to friends now—remain as rigid as the looming trunks.

Their heartbeats keep reverberating through my body. Alongside the uneasy pounding, four currents of emotion whirl into me, as if I've stepped into a river of flavors. Lemon-sour discomfort mingles with tangy-pickle confusion and moldy-bread anxiety.

I've never picked up on their moods so strongly before. It's like I've somehow opened a direct tap into their internal states rather than relying on the foam that spills over the top of the mug.

My mouth opens and closes and opens again. "Oops?"

I'm struggling to come up with any better word to address this unprecedented situation.

The men clearly don't have any more idea what I've done than I do. Jonah takes a tentative step toward me, his cedar-brown face tight beneath the fall of his wavy black hair. "What was that, Peri? What just happened?"

He hasn't put any of his sorcery or his teacherly authority into the question, but I know I have to answer all the same. Which would be easier if I had an actual answer.

I twist my hands in front of me. The eager rush of my delight that sparked the glow has faltered just like the supernatural light did. "I don't know. That's never happened before. I didn't *mean* to do anything. I was just so happy…"

Raze's eyes, the black basilisk irises hidden behind his conjured green contacts, widen. Tension ripples through his huge, sinewy frame. "I felt it—how happy you were. But you're… worried now. Why do I know that?"

They can pick up on my emotions too? Does the tap go both ways?

I don't think that's logistically possible with actual faucets, but with whatever strange brewing system I've spontaneously created, who knows?

Mirage tugs at his henley shirt. He peers past the collar at his lean chest and lets out a laugh that sounds much more awkward than his usual good humor.

With his nimble fingers, the fox shifter plucks at the buttons to part the fabric farther down. "The glow isn't all gone. It stuck to me."

A circle of the pale light about the size of a cherry pulses against the golden-brown skin of his upper chest in time with the heartbeat that must be his. I think the glowing spot might be right over his heart.

My breath catches in my throat. I put that luminescent mark there—I must have.

So why do I have no clue how?

Hail has been standing stiffly this entire time. Now, the winter fae yanks at his own shirt to check beneath it.

His pale, gorgeous face tenses even more than it had before with a flash of his dark blue eyes. "There's one on me too. What the fuck *is* that?"

All trace of the friendly warmth he's offered me recently has vanished from his voice. The look he shoots me is only accusing. I taste the bitter punch of his frustration.

I splay my hands in a helpless gesture. "I really don't know. I didn't mean to do anything at all. I've never left my glow on anyone before, even in the biggest outbursts."

Jonah and Raze are checking their own chests. Their expressions and flickers of uneasy emotion tell me they're seeing the same thing as Mirage and Hail.

It occurs to me to peek beneath my T-shirt, the black one with the pink flower print I thought was just the right mix of tough and cute.

Between the abundant slopes of my human-like body's breasts, a matching glow throbs alongside my own heartbeat. I guess it's a good thing I didn't leave myself out of this odd club I founded?

The two beings who've been leading our trek back to civilization move closer. Rollick, the demon who runs the academy we're meant to be returning to, studies each of us briefly before his gaze settles on me. "Why don't you explain exactly what you experienced starting right before those beams shot out of you, Peri?"

Rollick might not look all that imposing to mortal eyes with his tall-but-not-towering form and symmetrical-but-not-stunning face, but he has an aura of power so intense I suspect he could knock me over with a blink. If anyone can figure this out, he can.

I think back to the moments before the glow coursed out of me. "I was relieved that we finally stopped the sorcerer and that we managed to do it by working together—that we'd been such a good team. I was looking forward to seeing how much more we could accomplish. The thought made me so happy—and the light rushed out of me in those beams. I didn't aim it at anyone. That part happened on its own."

The demon cocks his head. "And then?"

"I don't know. I got the impression of their hearts beating. I can still feel that now. And I can taste their emotions a lot more strongly than before. But maybe that will fade too, like the light did? None of my outbursts have ever lasted very long."

"Except we can feel Peri too," Jonah says in a strained voice. "Raze just said— And I'm picking up on her emotions right now. I can tell that she really is confused, and nervous… and her feet are hurting."

Raze's brow knits. "They are. Why didn't you tell us they were bothering you?"

"I—" I don't know what to say. The ache from my past wounds—dealt by the cruel sorcerer who just kicked the bucket—is dull enough, familiar enough that it doesn't really bother me. I can never spend all that long on my feet in physical form without the old injuries waking up. "I guess I'm used to tuning it out unless it's especially bad."

Also, when I do mention it, Raze has a habit of sweeping me *off* my feet. Which makes me all giddy but also is kind of embarrassing when we have an audience.

"This is fascinating." Rollick rubs his chin, peering at Mirage's mark and then glancing over at Sorsha, the phoenix shifter who helped with the last stage of our mission. "It's almost like an opposite version of the first shadowbloods' marks. Except from what they've said, they only developed those through more… intimate entanglements."

Shame and guilt flare through my connection with Jonah. Not the kind of draft I'd like to have on tap.

He speaks hastily. "Nothing like that has happened between Peri and me."

My own cheeks heat with a different sort of embarrassment. I didn't realize I'd end up needing to discuss the details of my intimate fun with the school's headmaster. "I've gotten close with Raze and Mirage. But not today. Obviously not right when it happened. And nothing like that glow happened when we did. What are shadowbloods?"

Before Rollick can answer, Hail lets out a sputter. "The two of them? But you— This is fucking *ridiculous*."

An edge of resentment creeps through his uneasiness, like a bitter thread of baking soda that didn't get blended into the pastry right.

I didn't blend it right. This whole mess is my fault.

"We're still figuring out what this is," Rollick says mildly, and turns his attention back to me. "The shadowbloods are a small group of unusual beings who, like Sorsha, are hybrids, a mix of human and shadowkind. Only in their case, they were created by human scientists experimenting in labs. Their romantic involvement has led to dark blotches forming in a similar area on their chests. Not quite the same, though. And not lighting up."

Sorsha frowns. "And their marks don't seem to work like these ones. They can tell where each other is and there's that power-swapping trick they can do, but they've said they only sense emotions from each other when it's something extreme."

Rollick hums to himself. "Yes. I suppose it makes sense that a similar bond might appear differently when it's initiated by a being whose powers are focused on emotions."

"A *bond?*" Hail repeats, his tone even harsher. "I don't want to be bound to her. I don't want to be attached to anyone."

He rounds on me so swiftly my nerves jump—which maybe the men can feel, because Raze growls.

My reaction doesn't deter the fae man's anger, though.

Hail jabs his finger at me, an icy breeze that I don't think came from the forest rippling through his white-blond hair. "Why would you do this? What are you trying to prove? You didn't even want— I'm not going to *belong* to you like some kind of 'mate.' You can't just claim people or whatever the fuck you thought you were doing."

A burn of tears forms behind my eyes. "I promise, I didn't think I was doing anything. I didn't mean for any of this to happen. You don't owe me anything."

Mirage chuckles, his five fox tails that are the same bright red as his shaggy hair appearing for a quick swish. He speaks in his singsong voice. "All tied up, all the way through." But a shudder ripples through the emotions he's giving off at the same time: a splash of saltiness that tastes almost frantic.

Rollick clicks his tongue at Hail. "There's no need to have a tantrum about it. Very few shadowkind form permanent supernatural bonds. We *don't* know that what's happened here won't simply fade over time. Peri doesn't appear to have any more control over you than she would have before. You can simply ignore it. Unless a small bit of glow will put such a cramp in your style?"

Hail's lips pull back in a grimace. "She'll be looking right inside me even more than she could before. I can't stop knowing what's inside her, whether I care or not. She obviously thinks she owns us somehow or other. It was only us she hit with that light, not you two."

"The four of you are my team," I say quietly, hugging myself.

It's true that I was feeling particularly affectionate toward them. Did I set off some other dimension of my powers that I didn't know I was capable of?

Just when I think I've gotten a handle on my abilities, something new has to pop up and tip everything upside down.

Jonah swipes his hand across his forehead, guilt still trickling off him. Is he worried that he provoked this "bond" with the attraction he admitted to me but said he couldn't act on?

Mirage spins around, his mouth set in a stiff smile that jabs at my heart. I don't think he's actually happy about this development, as fond as he's acted toward me in the past.

Having a delicious interlude in the woods is a very different thing from being constantly tied to me.

Even Raze, for all the devotion he's shown, is feeling more uneasy than pleased. None of them wanted this.

Of course they didn't. Even triple chocolate cake tastes awful if someone forces it down your throat.

And I'm not sure I can say I'm triple-chocolate-cake amazing no matter how thoroughly I beat my fears this morning.

I inhale deeply, dragging whatever shreds of optimism I can out of my whirling head. "I'll try to remove it. Maybe it won't be that hard. If I did it, I should be able to undo it, right?"

Hail taps his foot impatiently.

Rollick shakes his head. "I doubt it'd be that simple. These sorts of things rarely are."

"I *have* to try. It's only fair."

None of these men should be bound to me if they don't want to be.

The thought sends a fleeting pang through my chest, but I dismiss it, focusing on the thump of their heartbeats. On the memory of the glow that streamed out of me.

It's lingering in them. Can I detach it, reel the light back into me, and snap the connection at the same time? Turn the tap right off and chuck it in the trash?

I picture the glow on their chests and clench my hands as if grasping hold. With all the mental strength I have in me, I yank at the light.

Come back to me. Be a good bond. Let go of them and come back.

Nothing happens that I can sense.

When I look into the men's faces, I can tell nothing's changed for them either. The glowing mark shines on where Mirage has left the collar of his shirt unbuttoned.

A sensation as heavy as a ball of lard sinks into my gut.

I can't take it back. We're stuck like this.

2

Jonah

At the base of the steps to his private jet, Rollick claps me on the shoulder. "I'm sure you'll be fine. What's a little glow? And I've met a lot worse beings you could be connected to, for however long it lasts."

I force a smile. I know the demon is trying to be reassuring, but his typical coolly casual approach doesn't do much to ease the uneasiness that's gnawing at me. He's already glancing off toward the horizon.

I suspect my problem is hardly the most pressing thing on his mind. It is *mine* rather than his, after all.

"Is everything all right?" I ask.

I hesitate to mention Quinn: the woman he's been dedicated to for as long as I've known him, the woman who saved my life as a toddler and taught me most of what I know about using my sorcerous skills. If her health is faltering again, Rollick won't want to have the fact rubbed in.

The demon's tone stays breezy. "Other than one rather puzzling rift? There's nothing to concern yourself with. I always have some concern or another to stay on top of."

He dips his head to me in farewell and strides up the steps into the jet.

I head across the dusty ground to the sprawling stucco academy buildings that stand just ten minutes' walk away from the small airfield. The rest of my "team" went inside as soon as we arrived, but I wanted to see Rollick off.

Maybe I was hoping he'd offer some actual advice. But I'm not really sure what kind of advice I need, so it's hard to blame him for failing to provide it. Mentoring isn't really the demon's style anyway.

Despite what he did say, I can't totally ignore the faint pulse of warmth from the glowing spot on my chest. It comes with the vague but undeniable awareness that not far away, Peri's heart is beating nearly as quickly as my own.

Alongside the rhythm flow the twinges of uncertainty and embarrassment that've trickled into me since we first realized that she'd locked us into these strange bonds—and that she couldn't remove the connection.

The awareness of her makes my gut twist. I simultaneously want to go comfort her and to stay as far away as I can.

I never wanted—I mean, I *did* want her, in all her dazzling, buoyant sweetness—but I never would have indulged those desires—

As I step into the building, the sight of Shanty waiting in the hall derails my anxious train of thought.

The siren tilts her head toward the other end of the pale-walled hallway. "The rest of the administrative staff would like to speak with you."

My stomach knots tighter. As I follow her, I can't help

making one pointed observation. "You waited until Rollick was gone."

Shanty shrugs with a rustle of her dark blue hair. "The headmaster had other matters to attend to. He's already spoken to you at length about the situation, I'm guessing."

And the rest of the board members know that the demon is vaguely fond of me. He might have overruled the idea of whatever this meeting is about before it started.

I did help lead a team of the academy's most incorrigible students to defeat a sorcerer who'd been harming shadowkind and humans alike for years… but it's hard to imagine they're calling me in just to congratulate me on a job well done.

When we step into the bright room with its curving table, I find one chair placed on the opposite side, across from the board of administrators. Normally I'd be sitting behind the table with the other board members, but today the interrogation spot is clearly meant for me.

If my stomach could sink any farther, it'd be dropping through the floor.

Shanty joins the four figures already waiting in their spots along the table. Pearl shoots me a dimpled smile, but the succubus is the only being who looks at all content.

Her wife, Toni—the only other human on the board—is leaning her wiry arms on the table, her posture stiff. Gnash the tiger shifter tips his burly frame back in his chair, his gaze narrowed at me as if he's considering pouncing. And Al's sallow face is set in an expression of distaste, but to be fair, that's pretty much always how the vampire looks unless we're discussing one of his favorite historical eras.

I take my seat and fold my arms over my chest. "What's this about?"

Gnash snorts. "I think you already know, kid. Rollick told us all about this special new mark you got. We'd like to know why one of your students thought it'd be a good idea to get all mate-y with you."

Pearl shoots him a chiding look and aims another smile at me. "It's standard procedure, to confirm that nothing untoward happened. So we can officially say we discussed the situation."

The others don't look so sure they'll get that confirmation.

Shanty sighs. "Why don't you tell us everything that's happened between you and Periwinkle?"

I swallow thickly. "There isn't much to tell. She's been in my Geography and Culture class. I've given her a little advice outside of that, nothing more than I've offered plenty of other students. I was assigned to lead the team of unstable beings she was a part of, and I directed her the same way I did the other three."

Toni arches her eyebrows. "So you had no interest in her beyond the professional?"

Another jab of guilt lances through me. I don't think it'd be wise to lie about this—Peri won't, if they ask her.

And if I lie, who am I to say I haven't done anything wrong?

"I've felt some attraction," I admit in an even tone. "I'd imagine you're all aware that what we feel isn't exactly under our control. I've never acted on those feelings. In fact, when I realized the interest was developing, I took steps to keep more distance from her."

Al's lips curl with more disdain. "Was *she* aware of this 'attraction'?"

Shame flares along the same line the guilt traveled. "Yes. I hid it as well as I could, but her main shadowkind power is picking up on emotions. When she indicated that she'd noticed, I was firm about the fact that nothing was going to come of those feelings. She never pushed for me to give in to them."

But maybe I should have put distance between us sooner, and then she wouldn't have noticed at all. Maybe I did indulge in my attraction farther than I should have let myself.

Why would she latch on to me this way if I haven't led her to believe it'd be welcome, one way or another?

How the hell can I expect any of my colleagues or students to respect me as an authority figure when I'm encouraging mating bonds with beings who should be off-limits?

The same concerns are echoed on the faces of the administrative board. If I can't convince myself I haven't screwed up, how can I expect them to believe it?

Pearl turns to the others with a bounce of her blond curls. "It isn't fair to expect him to keep his feelings totally secret when she has a power like that. Hasn't most of the trouble she's gotten into at the academy been because of her noticing her classmates' feelings when they'd rather she didn't?"

Gnash lets out a dismissive grunt and focuses back on me. "If what you're saying is true, why do you think she attached herself to you this way?"

"I don't know," I say honestly. "But it wasn't only me. It was all four of us who were part of the team. We'd just had a major victory—she dealt with a sorcerer who'd held her captive in the past—a lot of other emotions were running high. From what she's said, it mostly came out of happiness about what we'd all accomplished together, not romantic feelings."

Toni clasps her hands on the tabletop. "That does line up with what Rollick reported."

Shanty nods, her dark eyes trained on me. "We'll be

speaking with the team you were supervising for additional details. For now, I don't think there's any reason to enforce sanctions. You can return to teaching your regular classes tomorrow as planned."

She pauses, her gaze flicking to my chest where my shirt conceals the mark. "Take some time today to sort out your thoughts. I'm sure you have a lot to consider."

No kidding.

"Thank you." I dip my head respectfully and get up. I might be a board member, but that's mainly because of my sorcerous powers. I'm fully aware that even Toni has more than a decade of experience on me. The shadowkind members have centuries.

It wouldn't be much of a loss for them to kick me out if they thought I'd exploited my position to prey on a student.

As I leave the room, my innards feel just as tangled as before. Seeing Sorsha propped against the wall in the hallway outside loosens the tension just a little.

My foster mom offers me a crooked smile and motions for me to walk with her. "I heard the bigwigs ambushed you. I hope it wasn't too harsh a conversation."

I shake my head. "They asked the questions anyone would have asked. It's an unusual situation, without any precedent. I didn't know you'd stuck around."

"Not for long. I wanted to check on you before we left." She sweeps her flame-red ponytail back over her shoulder and peers at me from her nearly equal height. "You couldn't have been prepared for anything like this. Are you going to be okay?"

The phoenix shifter has never been particularly maternal, but I've never doubted that my well-being matters to her. She and the shadowkind men who helped raise me made sure I was comfortable, entertained, and protected, which is more than many parents by birth accomplish.

As I've gotten older, it's become more obvious that Sorsha is mostly winging the whole foster mom thing. All the same, it's nice to have someone looking out for me.

I shrug with feigned nonchalance, because there isn't much she can do if I say I don't know. Her phoenix fire isn't going to burn away this connection—and I'd rather not find out what'd happen if she tried.

"It's done," I say. "It might not last. Even if it does, it doesn't have *that* much impact on my life if I don't let it. Just one more adjustment."

"Well, if you need any advice on complicated matters of the heart, I'm not sure how much I could offer, but Ruse would be more than happy to weigh in."

A genuine chuckle tumbles out of me. I bet her beloved incubus has plenty he'd like to say about this situation and how I should handle it, but I suspect his attitude would be a lot more permissive than should apply in my situation. "I'll keep that in mind."

She ruffles my hair. "We're only a phone call away."

When she's gone, the mix of trepidation and guilt rises up inside me again. I wander toward my room in the staff quarters, but the thought of sitting still itches at me.

I end up heading outside and setting off across one of the hiking trails that winds through the dry New Mexico terrain toward the ruddy mountains in the distance. Normally if I wanted a workout, I'd go to the gym or the climbing wall, but I feel the need to get some literal distance from the being who marked me.

And the climbing wall reminds me of my conversation with Peri out there—when she attempted the wall herself and her fall led to us nearly kissing.

My feet smack the hard-packed earth with satisfying thuds. I pick up my pace to a jog, looking to work up a sweat under the late-spring sun. When my heart is pounding and my muscles are stretching, the exertion burns away the mental clutter for a sense of clarity.

At least, it usually does. I've only made it maybe a mile from the school buildings when a prickling sensation runs through the middle of my chest beneath the mark.

At first I ignore the mild discomfort. But as I lope onward, the prickling deepens into a full out spike.

I stop, peering down at myself, and the pain doesn't ebb. It pulses on alongside that distant heartbeat that isn't mine.

Fuck. It appears this link between us comes with a short leash.

With a shiver that's at odds with the warm desert air, I turn and start back the way I came.

3

Periwinkle

Shanty saunters from one side of the classroom to the other as she gives her lecture. The siren's blue hair sways with her sleek hips.

"If you're spending time in the mortal world, it's inevitable that you'll need to interact with humans now and then. That's why understanding the basics of politeness is so important. In your pairs, the more established student should demonstrate to the newer student how you'd ask a human for minor assistance."

I glance over at Vim, the being Shanty paired me off with. Politeness hasn't seemed to be one of her strong points in our past conversations.

Her scowl today is a little milder than usual, but I don't think that means she's softened to me. She's just less sure what to make of me after the news of my victory on a mission for the headmaster—and whatever rumors are swirling about the strange new power I've displayed.

Vim squares her broad shoulders ominously but then pastes a vacant smile on her face. "Excuse me. Could you point me to the nearest corner store?"

She's definitely better at being polite to me as an imaginary human than me as the being I actually am.

Shanty brushes past us with an approving pat of Vim's back. "Good. Now, the other partner should take a turn. Think of something you'd need to find or know if you're on your own in an unfamiliar setting. And experienced students, don't make it too easy for them."

I take a breath, and a ripple of emotion niggles at the back of my mind.

Part of me considers ignoring it, but a pang of guilt immediately follows that impulse. What if someone's hurt or in trouble?

I let my focus on the task in front of me relax and open myself so the feelings sweep through me.

Someone's irritated Hail, off on the other side of this school building. Jonah's working through a difficult problem that's making him stressed. He also has an annoying itch he can't quite reach.

Mirage—er, I think he's relieving himself in the bathroom, with some delight at the stream.

And Vim is staring at me with growing impatience.

I'm still getting the hang of balancing my own thoughts with the unpredictable flow of emotions from the men I accidentally marked. It doesn't seem right to neglect them— but it's awfully hard to concentrate on pretend scenarios for my schoolwork when their very real presence follows me around like four nagging ghosts.

I scramble to get back on track. What would I need if I was showing myself in the human world?

Good emotions to feed on. Happiness and excitement, but nothing too extreme.

I offer Vim a warmer smile than she gave me. "Hey there. What do people around here do for fun?"

I taste the pleasure she takes in following Shanty's instructions to be difficult. "Why are you asking me? I don't know you."

She starts to turn away, and my heart lurches. At the same time, a surge of mingled hunger and disgust smacks into me with the impression I know is Raze.

He's going on a hunt, and he's ashamed that he needs to kill to feed his body.

I can't help him with that problem from a distance—and being aware of his insecurity without him sharing it voluntarily feels like an intrusion.

I bury my connection to him as deep as I can in my consciousness and yank my mind back to the being in front of me.

Vim has raised her eyebrows.

"I—I'm new in town," I say hastily. "I didn't mean to bother you. You looked like you might know a good place to hang out and meet people."

"A decent start," Shanty says from right behind me, so abruptly my pulse jumps. I didn't notice her approaching. "You'll want to sound more confident. And it's usually better to let people know you're new right away, even to apologize for asking for help, before you get to your question."

As Vim's lips curl with a trace of a sneer, I nod. "Yes, of course. I'll remember that!"

Before we have to do any more mortal socializing practice, the bell rings to signal the end of class—my last class of the day. I start to relax, getting up out of my chair.

Then another burst of emotion jolts through my unintended bonds.

Mirage—he's restless. Some students in the courtyard are totally asking to have a prank played on them, and suppressing the urge is making him feel stifled.

My stance has gone rigid as the sensation ripples through me. I recognize it and set it aside, knowing the fox shifter probably doesn't want to be reminded of the ways *I've* inadvertently confined him.

Fen sidles up beside my desk. "Hey… Are you okay? You've seemed pretty distracted."

I have to smile at her concern. The water nymph is the only real friend I've made at the academy other than the men I'm now treading on uncertain ground with.

"It's just all the…" I wave my hand vaguely toward my chest, not wanting to talk about my unique situation out loud in front of our classmates. I told Fen last night what'd happened, so she'll be able to fill in the blanks. "I don't want to tune it out completely—and I can't really—but it's hard paying attention to everything at once."

"Of course it would be! I can't even imagine." Fen links her arm with mine as we head out of the classroom. "I was thinking—maybe we should look up mate bonds and all that stuff on the internet. There are computers in the library. A lot of the information on supernatural phenomena is pretty silly, but some humans have figured out useful facts. We'd at least get an idea of the possibilities."

My spirits lift at the thought of getting a better handle on the weirdness I accidentally created. "That's a great idea. You don't have to help—I could do the research on my own. If you were planning on doing something with Brine."

I think I've managed to keep any sign of jealousy under wraps. I shouldn't mind that Fen found another friend, someone who understands her unique challenges as a water-based shadowkind better than I can. And I don't want to overstep and take up all her time.

"Oh, that's fine. I want to see what we can find out! And we'll hang out with her at dinner anyway."

"Great." I aim a grateful smile at her.

Most of the reform building students are glad to be done with classes and have no interest in taking on additional work. All but one seat by the two rows of computers are free.

Fen and I sit down at a machine, and I stare at the screen and then the keyboard. "I, um, haven't actually used one of these before. I've seen people use them, but I'm not sure where to start."

"Oh! Here, I'll show you." Fen clicks on one of the little pictures on the screen, which opens up a big white square that takes up most of the space. She taps the keyboard to type a couple of words into the narrow rectangle at the top of the square. *Mate bonds.*

A bunch of text pops up on the screen. Who says humans don't use magic?

I peer at it avidly. "There's all kinds of information about them!"

Fen cocks her head. "I'm not sure what all this is referring to. Look, those two are talking about fae. This one mentions werewolves. It looks like some of the pages are lists of books —made-up stories. But then humans think that shadowkind are all kinds of made-up 'monsters', so something useful could come up there too."

She scrolls through the search results, clicking on one line of blue text and another so we can scan the write-ups they lead to. A lot of the "pages" include a whole bunch of words and names that I've never heard of before, so I'm pretty sure they have nothing to do with my powers.

The farther we go, the deeper the puzzled furrow digs into Fen's forehead. "Do you have some kind of special scent thing with the guys? Like their smell makes you feel… tingly or something?"

I remember Raze's tart but musky scent. It's delicious, but that's not the part of him that's really made me tingle.

No, that would be his hands… and lips… and tongue… and—

I can't restrain a giggle. "I guess I notice how they smell when we're close to each other, but there's nothing magical about it. And the impression I get hasn't changed since the connections formed."

"Hmm. It seems like a lot of these bonds supposedly happen with animal shifters. You can't shift into any kind of creature, can you?"

"As far as I can tell, I'm still human-ish looking even in shadowkind form, just shinier."

Fen taps her mouth. "Raze and Mirage are shifters, aren't they? And Hail is fae."

"Yeah, but Jonah is human," I point out. "And the bond marks came from *me*. I don't even know what I am for us to search for that."

"There's a bunch of talk about fated mates. Was there, like, a magical vibe that drew you to all of them before the whole marking thing happened? Did you feel a jolt when you first saw them or a zap when you first touched them?"

That sounds painful. Who would want zappy bonds?

I shake my head. "Before I got to know them, I was friendly with them for the same reasons I've been friendly with everyone else, as much as I can. Nothing different happened. I started to like them more as I got to know them. Just like with you. Except…"

My hair flickers with a brief ruddy glow.

Fen grins at me. "Except you want to cuddle up with them."

"Yeah. That part." I squint at the screen. "It seems like in most human versions of how magical bonds work, they can decide to talk to each other in their heads and things like that. That seems a lot more useful than just getting hit with emotions all the time."

"I guess it would be. Well, let's see if we can find anything closer to your situation."

A faint prickle spreads through my chest. I adjust my position, figuring it's an effect of my frustration. "Definitely. Keep going."

We read on through several more sites, none of which mention anything that sounds like what I've experienced.

"Did you have dreams about them before you met?" Fen asks in a tone that's already skeptical.

"Not that either. I don't dream much… When I do, it's usually about food." I grin despite the ache that's now seeping down to my gut. "Does that mean I'm fated for delicious meals?"

Fen laughs. "Let's hope so." She moves on to the next site.

The prickling sensation keeps intensifying, seeping deeper through my torso and up to my throat. I find myself rubbing my sternum as if that will push the discomfort away.

What's causing it? I don't sense any unpleasant emotions emanating from my men. They all seem pretty calm at the moment, other than Raze with his apprehension about his hunt, but my impression of him has faded with distance.

All at once, pain spikes straight through my heart. I gasp, and my lungs clench up.

Fen jerks around. "Peri? What's the matter?"

My voice comes out strained. "I… I don't know… Something… It hurts…"

The pain expands as if I'm being ripped down the middle. My breath stalls in my throat; my vision blurs. I have the vague awareness of my body tipping over on the chair—

And then nothing.

~

My mind swims up through the darkness. There's a soft surface underneath me. Voices murmur nearby.

It takes longer than it probably should for me to realize that it's dark because my eyes are closed. Gentle light glows through my eyelids.

Currents of anxious and stressed emotions whirl inside me like a noxious stew.

I blink and stare up at a white ceiling. When I take my next breath, filling my lungs with air, only a faint ache lingers from the pain that hit me before.

A female shadowkind with small horns on either side of her forehead appears over me. "How are you feeling, Periwinkle?"

"I— Better, I guess. What happened?"

"You fainted in the library. This is the infirmary, for students who are sick. Although I'm not sensing any illness or physical damage in you right now."

"That's probably because we're here."

That's Jonah's voice—flat and tense.

I gird myself and push tentatively into a sitting position.

I'm perched on a small bed in a bright room a little larger than the dorm bedrooms. It holds a few other beds along the wall, cabinets, and a sink.

Fen stands by the foot of my bed, her hands twisted together nervously. All four of the men I marked have clustered around the woman who I suppose is a being with healing powers.

I press my hand to my temple. "I don't understand. Everything started to hurt—just a little and then a lot."

Raze's voice comes out ragged. "I felt it too. I was running across the wild terrain nearby for my hunt, moving away from the school. It came up on me so suddenly I didn't realize— I raced back as fast as I could."

I frown at him. "You think I'm allergic to you hunting?"

Jonah clears his throat. "We think it's because of how far apart you and he were. I noticed the same thing briefly yesterday, when I went for a jog… This just confirms what I suspected. If we move more than a couple of miles away from you, it hurts both of us."

"Just fucking wonderful," Hail mutters under his breath, his gaze even darker than usual. "She's got us on a leash."

Mirage shivers. "Two miles is a lot of room," he says, but he doesn't sound as if he really believes that.

Misery rolls through me in the wake of the pain. It feels like more than one serving—I can't say how much of it is even mine.

"I'm sorry. I didn't mean for *any* of this to happen."

Hail glowers at me. "Lot of good that does us."

Raze whirls on him. "Leave her alone, you—"

At a squeak of the door, he falls silent.

Pearl has appeared in the doorway. After a glance at all of us, her usual cheerful demeanor dims.

"Hey," she says tentatively. "We just got a call from Rollick. Another one of those weird rifts has popped up. He wants the team back together."

4

Periwinkle

The first thing I notice when we step out of the car is the scattered high rises looming over a sprawl of lumpy urban architecture in the distance. Normally I like a thriving city atmosphere, but in this particular case, it seems non-ideal.

I hesitate. "The new rift appeared this close to a city?"

Rollick beckons the five of us away from the vehicle that transported us from the airfield, his expression unusually solemn. "And less than a quarter mile off one of the biggest highways in the country. It seems we got lucky that the first one appeared in such an out-of-the-way location. Come on, have a look."

I feel the rift before I see it—that squirmy, wobbly sensation its strange energy provokes under my skin, cutting right through the warm spring air. I shiver, already sure I'm no keener to dive into this portal than the one up in northern Canada that we investigated over the past few weeks.

As we approach, the smear of wavering energy appears like a vague blurring of the low, grassy hills behind it, hovering just a couple of feet above the ground and stretching at least twenty higher and across.

Rollick stops when we're still about ten paces away, and I can't say I'm upset to keep my distance. I can see just fine from here, thank you.

"Popping up here, popping up there," Mirage says, but his singsong voice sounds just as unsettled as I am.

Jonah glances at Rollick. "How did you find out about this one? Do you have any idea how long it's been open?"

The demon shakes his head in answer to the second question. "I'm guessing not very long. One of the local shadowkind stumbled on it and alerted me yesterday. Some digging turned up a few tales of strange beasts roaming the city streets over the past day or two, but nothing beyond that."

Hail grimaces. "The warped creatures are tumbling out of this one too? We won't be keeping the existence of shadowkind secret for very long if they're partying all through downtown."

"As I've observed time and time again, humans have an incredible capacity for pretending away anything they don't want to admit could be real." Rollick rubs his hand along his jaw. "But there are limits. And this rift poses a significant threat to the nearby mortals as well as to us."

The winter fae scoffs as if dismissing the idea that any human deserves our concern. A deeper twitch ripples through my skin.

What if that whole city found out creatures from a realm of shadows exist—and regularly travel into their own world? Would hundreds of thousands of them pick up shiny nets and laser whips to hunt us down like a few mortals already do?

I've met plenty of friendly humans in my explorations of the mortal realm, but most of them had no idea I was what they'd consider a "monster." I'm not sure gambling on their good will would be a very fun game.

Jonah considers the rift with his forehead furrowed. "Has anyone notified the Highest Ones about all this weirdness yet?"

I glance over. "The Highest Ones?"

Rollick clicks his tongue. "Ah, you're lucky enough not to have crossed paths with our supposed overlords or any of their minions in your existence so far. The Highest mostly lounge around way off in the deepest depths of the shadow realm and only get involved in other business if they think they personally might be threatened. And I'd imagine they're still licking the wounds to their egos after an unfortunate incident a couple decades ago. We're probably better off without them trying to interfere in their out-of-touch way. None of them has so much as peeked into the mortal world willingly in centuries."

Raze takes a step toward the rift, his shoulders flexing as he studies it. I taste his tension like a thick, peppery soup. "Why did you want us to come out here? We couldn't really do anything about the first rift."

"And that whole experience ended so wonderfully," Hail mutters.

The basilisk shifter's head jerks around so he can glare at the other man. When Rollick clears his throat, they both appear to tamp down their animosity.

An animosity they'd put behind them just a few days ago. An animosity *I* stirred up all over again with these bonds I never meant to form.

Our headmaster must decide it's better not to dwell on

that subject. He focuses on Raze's question. "To begin with, I was hoping the five of you could share your observations on this rift and how you feel it compares to the one up north. You spent more time analyzing that one than I did. Maybe you'll pick up on something useful that I've missed."

Mirage springs toward the rift, his ruddy fox fur rippling over his body, and then bounds away in a backflip that ends with a full-body shudder. "It's just as creepy. Creeping and crawling right into my being."

His agitation quivers into me, more potent with our new connection. He glances my way as if noticing me noticing him and quickly yanks his eyes in the other direction.

I'm constantly spying on them now, absorbing their inner states—not just the full-serving emotions they can't help emanating, but every little scrap of feeling in between as well.

I can try to do something useful here. I tilt my head to the side, peering at the rift. "It does feel the same to me. And it's about the same size. It makes me... want to get away from it. Nothing about it gives me the impression that the place on the other side is my home." Even though I've spent more time in the shadow realm than the human world.

When I ease closer, a thicker waft of the rift's energy washes over me. I frown. "It's almost like it's... pushing out at me. Pushing me away? But also dragging me in at the same time."

Raze's lizard tongue darts over his lips. "If anything, I think this one might be even more intense. The way the vibes come off it."

The unnerving impressions stir up memories of standing by the other rift in the forest. Of that first moment my former captor hurled his sorcery at us again...

My gaze darts around us instinctively. But that's silly. He's dead—he couldn't be here now.

Of course, I thought it was impossible for him to be *there* at first too.

A question tumbles out of me. "Once a human's dead, they stay that way. Always. Don't they?"

Rollick's tone turns droll, but he doesn't mock me for the question. "In every instance I've encountered, and I've encountered a lot over the millennia."

Okay, we should be safe from that one threat then.

"Are we sure this *is* a new rift?" Jonah asks abruptly. "What if the first one made a much bigger jump than before and got more powerful in the meantime?"

Rollick snaps his fingers. "One of the first questions I asked myself. I left a couple of associates stationed near the original strange rift. They report that it's moved a couple of miles, but it's definitely still up there. "

My heart sinks. "The protections Sorsha put around it— the steel and silver—they didn't contain it after all."

The demon offers me a softer smile than usual. "No, but it was a long shot. Sorsha's going to venture up there regularly to move the protections as needed so we can still contain the creatures and their possible misbehavior. Of course, if this new rift hops around the same way, it could end up in a much more inconvenient location." His smile shifts into a frown as he glances toward the city.

My gaze latches on to the tallest of the skyscrapers, standing at least ten stories higher than the others around it and glittering in the mid-day sun. Its brilliance shines through my nerves. "Maybe there's enough silver and iron there to keep the rift away. That building could be a shield!"

Rollick chuckles. "The humans here are very proud of their recently built Diamond Victory Tower, but it'll be steel and glass, not very useful to our purposes. Iron and silver are rarely used by mortals in large quantities these days."

Despite his nonchalant pose, Hail obviously cares what's

going to happen at least a little. He shoves his hands in the pockets of his slacks. "How often are the creatures coming through this rift?"

"I haven't witnessed any so far, only had my people round up a couple that were still making nuisances of themselves in the area. They seem to have a lot in common with their shifty friends up north." Rollick pauses. "But perhaps we're about to get a little more data on that particular subject."

The blurred surface of the rift has started to undulate. More erratic energy washes over my skin, shoving me away while also yanking me toward it, the conflicting impulses raising the hairs on the back of my arms.

Apprehension flows into me from all of my men. An orange sheen flickers in my hair, revealing my own uneasiness.

Current mood-ring setting: creamsicle. If only it tasted as good.

A dark gray shape wavers through the blurred space and then plops down onto the solid ground below the rift. It appears we've found ourselves a… blob. Of fur? Or are those quills? Maybe a mix of both. Its main characteristic seems to be a distinctive lack of distinctiveness.

After a moment, the blob pushes itself upright and demonstrates its sturdy legs. Six of them.

It's like a puppy-sized, furry-quilled insect.

I can't tell where its body ends and its head begins—or which end its head is even at, for that matter. I'm guessing the direction it starts to trundle off in, presuming it walks forwards and not backwards.

With the weird beasts that rifts like this produce, that might not be a safe assumption.

Raze immediately prowls over to block the creature's path. Hail stalks after him, his face tightening.

The fae man has complained more than once about Raze's bloody feeding habits, and he's been the most hesitant to hurt any creatures even when they're lashing out at us. I'm not sure what threat either of them think this puppy-bug could pose, though.

As far as I can tell, it doesn't even have a mouth, let alone teeth. Its legs are thick but clawless.

I focus on the stout, fuzzy body. "We can let it be for now. It's not feeling at all hostile—just curious and a little confused."

We all ease around so that we're forming a potential barricade between the creature and its apparent destination. If it hurtles into significantly faster motion, it isn't going to get very far.

But it seems content to amble along, its body swaying from side to side in a way that makes me wonder if it's sniffing the ground. Does it have a nose?

The question has just passed through my head when the beast's stout frame spasms. Two more legs shoot out of its abdomen, all of them lengthening, and a sharp appendage juts out of the spot that I guess is its face.

Jonah blinks. "It grew a *beak*."

"Along came a spider and sat down beside us," Mirage says with a burst of nervous laughter.

"How's its internal state, Peri?" Rollick asks.

I've kept my focus on the strange creature through its sudden morph. "More confused and a little nervous, but still no aggression."

"All right. I'd better see if I can collect this one too."

The demon strides off toward his own vehicle, an SUV parked next to the sedan we arrived in. Hail's gaze follows him. "Collect…?"

Rollick's meaning becomes clear soon enough. He opens the back of the SUV and retrieves a metal contraption that he unfolds into a cage with a jerk of his hands.

Even though I know he wouldn't be doing the creature any harm, the sight of the metal bars sends a chill over my skin. Hail's stance tenses.

Rollick walks back with the cage and sets it on the ground several feet from where the creature is currently poking at the ground. "Jonah, I may need a little sorcerous assistance to compel it inside."

The memory of having sorcerer commands digging into my brain deepens the chill inside me. F- experience, do not recommend.

I peer at the creature, searching for any alternative, and a pang of thin-gruel sensation seeps through me.

"It's thirsty," I say just as Jonah is opening his mouth. "It's looking for water."

Rollick clicks his tongue. "That might make for a less traumatic capture. Just a second."

He strides away again and returns with a bottle of water and a dish that looks like it's probably meant to be an ashtray. Hopefully the beast doesn't mind a smoky aftertaste.

After pouring some water into the dish, Rollick sets it at the back of the cage. Then he dribbles a little liquid on the ground in a trail that leads close to the creature.

It only takes a moment for the beast to pick up on the moisture in the earth. It veers in that direction, pecking at the ground along the trail until it walks straight into the cage.

Rollick grins triumphantly and reaches to shut the cage door.

As his fingers grip the edge, the creature shudders again. Its spikes expand, its beak jutting to a sharper point, and it whirls around with a harsh shriek.

A jolt of anger jabs into me, jalapeno hot.

"Rollick!" I cry in warning, but it's not as if the other signs screamed "I come in peace." He smacks the door shut with a clang.

Light flares from the panels above and below the creature. Metal panels that must be made of silver and iron drop down within the bars, trapping it completely.

Rollick lifts the cage by a loop on its top, his mouth twisting. "I'd mind the shifting moods less if they didn't always seem to cycle around to animosity."

Jonah lets out a ragged chuckle. "No kidding."

Hail is studying the cage. "What are you going to do with it?"

"I'm seeing what I can make of the warped creatures' unusual natures… and whether they can be somewhat tamed." Rollick's gaze slides to me. "Your talents are certainly useful for evaluating them."

I offer a bright smile, shaking off my lingering nerves. "I'm happy to help however I can!"

The demon hums to himself and turns to eye the rift. "We can't leave this portal unmonitored… It'll take more elaborate protections than the other one, considering the necessary subtlety. The people I can call on to help with that might also be able to advise you and your newly bonded men on your peculiar situation."

5

Hail

Ice surrounds me with its numbing chill. My conjured sculptures fill my entire dorm bedroom, crystalline mountains with glinting forests looming here, gleaming castles shooting intricate turrets up toward the ceiling there.

No one could say I'm not ambitious. Well, I suppose they could, since I never let anyone see just how big I'm willing to go with my art, but *I* know. That's what matters.

The fewer fucks people think you give, the less likely they are to hassle you with their own shit.

My spectacle isn't inherently permanent, though. I can feel every particle of the ice I created and shaped with my magic. Patches of my private gallery are starting to melt, as always happens with the warmth that seeps through the walls from the rest of the building.

It's hard to summon the enthusiasm to bolster the frigid surfaces.

No matter how much of the cool air I breathe into my lungs, no matter how many faint draughts waft over my skin, the stupid glow in the middle of my chest keeps shining. I've been attempting to freeze it out of me for the past several minutes—again, even though it didn't work the first few times I tried.

Add stubbornness to the list of my stellar qualities. None of which are doing me a speck of good at the moment.

When I tug open the collar of my shirt to check, the spot radiates just as brightly as before.

And it doesn't just glow. I can feel *her*. All her quivers of embarrassment and determination, pain and delight, trickle into me as she moves through the school.

I'm never going to *stop* knowing how she feels. I can't even walk more than a mile or two away from her without sending her into a fit.

I never asked to be responsible for that pipsqueak.

The thought provokes a wince that pisses me off all over again.

For fuck's sake, I can't even think of her as a pipsqueak anymore, not after the power she pulled out of that curvy little body just a few days ago. Not after she saved all our hides from being sorcerer-possessed.

But now she might as well have possessed me, in a way that shows no sign of fading. And because of her damned power, Rollick wants her input on the mystery of these insane rifts, which means *I* have to keep tagging along as if we're a real team. I have to help protect humans who've never given a shit about protecting us.

They always seem to want more excitement in their stupid mortal lives. A horde of warped shadowkind creatures would give them plenty. Why deny them?

An elegant knock filters through my door. You wouldn't think the rapping of knuckles against a hard surface *could* be elegant, but I know one being who can pull it off.

Gloss's equally elegant voice carries through the wood. "Hail, let's go take a walk."

I bristle automatically, even though the snow wraith hasn't exactly done anything wrong.

Leaning back on my bed, I shape my own voice much like I manipulated the ice of my sculptures, forming a blasé tone. "I don't really feel like walking."

Gloss switches to a more cajoling approach. "Oh, you've got to at least let me in for a chat. It's been too long. I've barely seen you in the past two weeks."

What does it matter to her? What does she really want from me?

Most of the time, even if it's obvious she has larger goals for our partnership, she's been content with the prestige of hanging off the arm of one of the most powerful beings at the school, one who doesn't kowtow to the teachers or act like I'm ashamed of existing, the way Raze does.

Most of the time, I've been fine with that. I look good with her hanging off my arm. Her prestige as one of the school's queen bees adds to my own in turn. I can deal with the hassle of turning her bigger aims down later.

But how can I care about any of that when my entire existence has been locked down by a glowing cream puff?

If I totally snub her, Gloss will give me the cold shoulder the next time I actually want some company that won't irritate me to death. So I push myself off the bed and slip outside through the shadow beneath the door without bothering to open it.

Gloss has always been curious to see the inside of my room. Maybe even to see what I might try to do with her in that room. But that space is for me and me alone. If I ever get up close and personal with Gloss, it'll be in *her* bed like all the other beings I've had a little fun with.

As I materialize in front of her, Gloss offers me one of her usual subdued smiles. She fingers the front of my shirt, coyly flirtatious, and hesitates at the glimmer of light that peeks from beneath my collar.

A shudder runs through her slender frame. "That's—that's what the tiny freak put on you. Haven't they found a way to get it off yet?"

With a grimace, I pull away from her. "The headmaster seems to think it'll wear off on its own eventually."

Gloss wrinkles her nose. "But marking someone is so... so trite." Her voice hardens as if it's iced over. "She can't just *claim* you like you belong to her. Can't you do anything to break this bond or whatever it is?"

Does she think I wouldn't have already tried? If I hadn't, why would she figure I'd do it just because she asked?

Because in Gloss's mind, I belong to *her*. She claimed me as the being she wanted to slink around the school with just a few days after my arrival, reform student or not.

I don't know where she got the idea that we'll have anything in common when we're out of this place. My goals are probably closer to Peri's than they are to hers. She just sees me as a means to an end, a powerful force she expects to pave the way for her ambitions.

An uncomfortable twinge passes through my chest and sharpens my next words. "If I could, it'd already be gone. If *you* know some way to cut off a magical connection no one's ever heard of before, feel free to get on with it."

Gloss frowns. "I'm only trying to help."

Yeah, help herself by getting back her arm candy. I glower at her. "Reminding me of something I hate isn't what I'd call helpful. Is this all you wanted to chat about?"

Before she can answer, a couple of my dorm-mates

shoulder into the common hallway. One of them catches sight of me and lets out a loud snort. "If it isn't lover boy! Does your pretty little *mate* know you're picking up other ladies?"

His sidekick guffaws. "I'd hate to think how she'll punish him if she finds out. Do you think she'll go for a rope and collar next time to really make a statement?"

As much as their comments prick at my skin, I roll my eyes as if I'm bored by their heckling. "It must be hard knowing no one would ever want to bond mark *you*. Feel free to continue working out your frustrations."

The nonchalant insult appears to roll right off them. They keep snickering as they make their way to their shared bedroom. "Out of all the girls in the place, can you imagine being tied to that pathetic pudgy shrimp?"

"Hey, it means there's more of the good ones left for the rest of us now!"

I ignore them, keeping my expression impassive, but my teeth set on edge.

The worst part is, something in me wants to snap at them not because they're mocking me but because they have no idea what Peri is actually capable of.

I used to think she was pathetic too. Maybe this bond is punishment for all my mistakes.

Does such a dire punishment really fit the crime, though? And what would Raze and the other two be getting punished for? Those bozos liked the cream puff all along.

Gloss sets a reassuring hand on my arm—as if I need reassurance. Her eyes glitter. "Don't let them bother you. She won't get away with this. Why don't we head over to the— "

I swipe her hand away. "I don't want to go anywhere with you right now. Get that through your head."

Then, with a flare of shame at the outburst, I stalk past her out of the dorm without looking back.

I have class in half an hour, but I find I don't give a shit if I'm late for it. Or if I miss it altogether.

Are they going to kick me out when Rollick's new star student needs me nearby to stay conscious? Ha.

I might as well take advantage of the few slim benefits this unwanted bond comes with.

I veer toward the outer doors and stride out into the glaring desert sun. It's not noon yet, so the beams are far from their full power, but the dry heat courses over my skin.

My flesh seems to tighten against the sensation, longing for shady forests and warbling winds.

Good. Let the beams blaze through the turmoil inside me. Maybe the scorching desert summer can burn away the damned glow on my chest too.

I set off at a brisk pace, pushing my legs hard enough that I start to sweat almost immediately. The uncomfortable heat feels right, searing through my body.

I tip my head back so more of the sun's rays strike my face.

Even as I propel myself faster, a niggling reminder at the back of my mind has me veering in a slow arc. I can't take a real hike away from this place. I'd rather not have the basilisk glaring his disappointment at me if the cream puff faints again.

Especially considering *his* glares can be fatal.

It turns out my caution isn't enough. I'm circling around the farthest outbuildings, my shoes rasping against the hard earth and tossing up bits of grit, when a short but shapely figure with unmistakable teal hair wavers out of the shadow beneath a shrub several paces ahead.

The sight of the being who's caused most of my current problems brings my temper surging up my throat before I can catch it. "I wasn't going to walk far enough away for anything to bother you. You didn't need to check up on me."

Peri blinks, her big blue eyes echoing the distress at my harsh tone that's already reverberating into my chest. A smack of guilt hits me, followed by a prickle of irritation that she's made me feel guilty.

She tilts her head to the side as she studies me, staying where she is. Giving me my space. So fucking *considerate* now that I can't really escape her.

"I wasn't worried about that," she says in a humiliatingly gentle tone. "I could taste—you're upset about something. But also, it hurts you being outside when the sun is so hot. Especially when you're walking quickly. Why are you staying out here when the atmosphere is bothering you like that?"

A sharper flare of embarrassment surges up, more searing than the damned sun she's fretting about. She can feel even those simple reactions, even when I'm not in the same building as her?

Is there anything I can keep from her, just for myself? Is she going to be watching every flash of insecurity and smattering of gloom that comes over me for the rest of my life?

My hands clench at my sides, but I cool my voice until it could be ice itself, flat and cutting. "I don't see how that's any of your business, no matter how much you've *tried* to make it yours. Maybe I don't want to feel good all the time. Maybe I don't want you deciding how I should feel. The last thing I need is a babysitter."

Shamed yellow flickers through Peri's hair. "I'm sorry. I didn't mean to upset you more. I'll go back to the school. But please look after yourself."

"What I really want is for you to get your ridiculous fucking glow off me," I snarl, but she's already leapt back into the shadows before I've finished my sentence.

I wave my hand in her general direction. "That's right. Run off now that there's a mess you can't fix."

She doesn't reappear. The sun keeps beating down on me.

A sickly sensation congeals in my gut.

I deserve this pain even more than I did a few minutes ago, don't I? And the only being who actually cares if I'm suffering is the one who put me in this position in the first place.

6

Periwinkle

Shanty cocks her head, peering at me. "So, you managed to get enough control over your powers to purposefully blast this prick of a sorcerer, but you still can't turn them on and off when you want to?"

That about sums it up.

I grimace and look down at my hands. We've been trying to stir up a flare of emotional energy for nearly an hour to no effect.

"It seems that way," I say. "When we were up against the sorcerer, I got pretty freaked out. It was easy to just... propel the power that wanted to come out anyway. But I *was* able to hold it in until I was ready to use it. That's some progress!"

The siren lets out a huff, but it sounds more bemused than frustrated. "It is. I'd feel better if you could figure out how to tap into your destructive energy without needing to be in state of high stress that makes self-control even more difficult. The more practice you can get, the better."

"For sure. That's why I'm here!"

I hesitate despite my cheerful resolve, grappling with the other feelings tangled inside me.

After all the work she's putting into helping me, don't I owe it to her to be honest?

Shanty is smart enough to pick up on the fact that there's something I'm nervous about saying. Her wry tone gentles. "What is it, Peri?"

I clasp my hands together awkwardly. "It's even harder than usual for me to try to bring out one of those blasts right now because I don't know how bad it'll get. Last time when I was happy, I pushed that glowy connection on my team without meaning to. I have no idea what other effects my powers might have. If I hurt someone even worse than before…"

Shanty pats my shoulder. "The fact that you're worrying about it shows that you'll avoid any harmful effects if you possibly can. We all know that you don't want to impose yourself or your powers on anyone, Peri. Anything you do in this sealed room shouldn't affect anyone except me—and I can look after myself."

Is what she said about everyone trusting my good intentions true? Hail seems awfully upset with me. Mirage has kept his distance since the end of our mission. Jonah hasn't spoken to me outside of class.

Even Raze, who's stayed fairly affectionate, has seemed awkward.

It's like I'm a bowl of soup with a fly floating in it, and any second they'll all call for a waiter to take me away.

But the more I learn to control all of my powers, the more chance there is I can undo what I did, right? Then they'll see they can still trust me. We'll throw out the fly, not the whole soup.

With the renewed rush of determination, I meet Shanty's eyes. "I'm ready to try again."

I won't think about the surge of joy that overtook me after we finished the mission. That emotion comes with too many uncomfortable associations now. The roar of fear and anger I directed at my former captor tastes much simpler.

Shaking off the anxiety that wants to wrap tight around me, I sink farther into my memories of the confrontation. The horror of seeing all the shadowkind creatures David Blaver trapped, knowing the sorcerer must be treating them as cruelly as he did me. The panic when I wasn't sure I could protect my teammates. The force of all that fraught emotion welling up inside me, ready to blare out.

An echo of the sensation ripples under my skin. I drag in a breath and focus on the sketch Shanty tacked to the wall of the small room—a rough image of the sorcerer who's a whole bowl of spoiled broth with chunks of rancid tripe on top.

He's dead. I'll never have to face him again.

But if I did...

I push, and a current of churning darkness heaves out of me. It races forward in a concentrated stream rather than a vast wave and smacks into the picture.

My vision hazes briefly. I blink, yanking a few lingering quivers of energy back into my body so they can't go astray.

The picture has blackened as if I've burned it to a crisp. Whoa.

"Yeah!" I pump my fist victoriously. I'm going to conquer this problem like it's a double-decker cheeseburger for dinner.

Shanty lets out a little whoop of approval. "Now we're getting somewhere. Wow."

I can't hold back the grin that stretches across my face. "I really did it." I pause. "Not that I'd usually want to be blasting anyone or anything like that."

My teacher is still staring at the blackened paper. "I never would have thought you had it in you if I hadn't seen the effects myself. You do come in a deceptive package."

My satisfaction dwindles. I hug my rather squishy chest. "I don't deceive anyone on purpose."

Shanty shakes herself out of her daze and shoots me a quick smile. "Of course you don't. And hiding powers behind an innocent-looking front is a time-honored shadowkind tradition." She laughs and motions to herself. "People don't normally look at a being like me and think I'd be singing sailors to their doom."

My eyes widen. "Do you drown human sailors *now*?"

Shanty waves off the question. "Only if they really piss me off."

With the ding of the bell, she shoos me toward the door. "That was an excellent end to our session. I'll let the rest of the administration know about your progress."

Of course. Because they're all still waiting to see if more strange powers will come leaping out of me unexpectedly. If they might need to banish me no matter what I did for Rollick.

I can look on the bright side there too. Shanty has good news to tell them for once. Wouldn't even Gnash be impressed if he saw me hurl out some of my searing power— at an appropriate target, not in a chaotic flood?

No more deluges from this lady!

I set off through the halls at an upbeat pace, wanting to share my success with someone too. My feet automatically veer toward the closest source of friendly emotions I notice.

Jonah is in his teacher's office nearby. He's in a good mood, pleased and a little proud.

I bet he just helped one of his students. That would be a very Jonah-type thing to be pleased about.

It's only when I'm a few steps from his office door that I remember he might not be all that pleased to see *me*. What if he'd rather not talk to me at all, no matter what news I have?

I stop in the hallway, wavering with indecision that emerges in a yellow flicker from my hair.

Before the bond mark thing happened, our compassionate sorcerer told me that I could come to him for guidance when I needed it. But he also told me that he had to keep a distance because of the tinglier feelings he'd developed when I was around.

It seems awfully unfair that we could both have tingly feelings yet not be allowed to turn them into more delicious enjoyment, just because there are a few things he can teach me that I don't know. I hate making him uncomfortable, though.

Before I can make up my mind about what to do, the office door swings open. Jonah appears on the threshold, escorting out a student who's barely half his height but has a puffy gray beard that makes him look more than twice Jonah's age.

"I think once you're finished with that, you'll have a much more solid plan for your next placement," Jonah is saying.

When he glances around and sees me, his expression stutters. A confusing waft of emotions hits me: toffee-sweet delight that turns sour with the anxiety that swirls through it.

I back up a step. "I'm sorry. You're obviously busy. I'll see you the next time I have your class!"

Jonah's jaw tightens, but he nods to the other student before fully emerging into the hallway. A vague sense of apprehension reaches me along with a twinge of relief. What is he worried about right now?

His voice comes out even, but I catch the stiffness in it. "It's all right. What did you want to see me about, Peri?"

When he's standing this close, the thump of his heartbeat reverberating into me alongside my own, all the reasons he told me we couldn't be more than friendly fade into the distance. So many eager glimmers light up in him as he takes in my eyes, my lips, the curves beneath my clothes.

I remember the firm warmth of his arms around me when I fell off the climbing wall in the barn. The jolt that quivered through me when our gazes locked with his face so close to mine.

He would feel even better if I touched his cheek right now, ran my fingers into his hair, brushed my mouth against his. I'd feel good too. Good compounded on good with the emotions flowing between us, like the endless river of a chocolate fountain.

Except tragically that's not actually true. The foul stew of guilt and shame is already seeping up through every tastier emotion that emanates from him.

It's not like with Hail, whose hostility crackles through any glimmer of affection or interest before I've caught more than the faintest whiff. But Jonah doesn't *really* want me around any more than the winter fae does.

I don't think there's enough chocolate even between both of us to overwhelm that problem.

I force my mouth into another smile. He'll be able to pick up on some of my own conflicted emotions, but from what I've gathered, the impact isn't as strong as what I feel from the men. I'd like to put him at ease.

"I just wanted to let you know—my session with Shanty today went well. I managed to use my power completely on purpose for the first time. And not let anything bad happen because of it. Or… unwanted, or anything."

Jonah's expression twitches. I can tell he's putting on his

own smile through concentrated effort, although a little gust of pride—for me, this time—glazes my tongue like maple sugar.

"That's really great, Peri."

Now that I've started, I find I can't stop myself from hurtling onward. "Maybe if I get even better, I'll be able to figure out how to break the bond connections so everything can go back to…"

I trail off as a couple of other staff members amble past us down the hall. They aim curious glances at me and Jonah, and Jonah's stance tenses alongside a smack of sharper uneasiness.

It's them he's worried about. The other people at the school—what they think of him?

Of him when he's around me. Of whether he's broken the rules and what that would mean about him.

Any embers of enthusiasm still shimmering inside me go dull. I dip my head and turn around. "Anyway, I just wanted to tell you that. I'll see you in class."

I hurry away, my heart heavy.

I accidentally inflicted my surprise power on Jonah out of a desire to be closer. What kind of fate did I offend that these supposed bonds have pushed him—and maybe all the men I care about—so much further away?

7

Periwinkle

I stare up at the looming rift, my skin prickling with the weird energy it gives off—that quavery push-pull as if it can't make up its mind whether to hurl me away or drag me in.

How can this one feel so similar to the other two odd ones I've encountered even though the landscape around us looks different?

There's no forest nearby and no city buildings either. We're standing in a small cove on a rocky beach, low craggy rocks surrounding us in a semi-circle and ocean waves hissing rhythmically behind us. The air tingles against my cheeks with the dampness of the salty spray.

Jonah looks a little weary after the unexpected plane ride Rollick summoned us onto last night. Unlike the rest of us, his body requires sleep. But he shakes himself to sharper alertness and glances at our headmaster.

I catch a twinge of apprehension before he speaks. "This is three of these rifts now. And it's been less than a week since you discovered the second one."

Rollick's mouth twists. "There are four, actually. My contacts in Algeria have encountered one there—I heard about it in the early hours of the morning when you were already on your way here. That one is even more out of the way than this one or the one in northern Canada, though, so there's no telling how long it's been around. It could be even older than the first."

"Four," Raze repeats with a solemn expression.

Mirage pipes up in a teasing tone. "Three's a crowd, four's a horde!"

The basilisk shifter shoots our companion a chiding look before focusing on Rollick. "There could be even more that we haven't noticed, then, couldn't there?"

"Warped rifts and demented creatures all over the world," Hail mutters, shifting restlessly on his feet. "Wonderful."

The demon inclines his head. "It's possible. Although they seem to have appeared somewhat at random, and three of them are shifting position close enough to human settlements that we heard reports relatively early on. I've had my associates seeking out stories of 'monster' attacks much more avidly, so if there are others we haven't identified yet, we should find them soon."

I open my mouth to ask a question of my own, but at the same moment, the rift's surface ripples. A furry frog-shaped creature with a rat-like tail hops out of the shadow realm and drops onto the rocks with a thump.

It peers around the cove, blinking blearily as if it tumbled out of bed into another world. Who could blame it for being confused?

All of us back up a few steps to give the creature space. It appears to be content with simply gazing around and stretching its legs one by one. Not much of a sprinter.

I dart a glance at Rollick. "Are you still catching them?"

His crooked smile slants even more. "I already have quite a collection at this point. I'm in the process of deciding the best way to handle their continued arrival. A few colleagues of mine who've been helping create a barricade around the city-side rift should be arriving soon to stem the tide here as well."

The creature rolls its eyes toward the sky, and a sharp kick of pain races from it into me. The sensation is followed by a dribble of discomfort that's sour as vinegar.

"The sun hurts its eyes," I say. "I'm not sure this one likes it here in the mortal world all that much. Maybe we could convince it to go back to the shadow realm?"

Rollick raises his eyebrows. "If that's true, it might decide to stay on the other side now that it knows what's waiting for it here. Let's give it a try. Just give it a little nudge, Jonah, so the effect will wear off quickly and we'll know whether it's inclined to return."

Jonah squares his shoulders and focuses his attention on the furry frog. His conflicted emotions about using his sorcery—strawberry-sweet pride that the powerful demon can count on him, cabbage-bitter shame that his magic depends on bending another being's free will—waft through our connection.

The indecipherable sorcerous words that slip from his mouth make me shiver even though they're not directed at me. I'm not sure the sound will ever not remind me of the years I spent tormented by a sorcerer who's the exact opposite of Jonah's kind, respectful self.

If David Blaver really were a bowl of rancid broth, I'd like to flip it over and stomp all over it.

The shadowkind creature twitches but otherwise doesn't

move. Jonah frowns. "I'll try again with more oomph. The other creatures like this have seemed a little resistant to sorcery."

He tried pitching his magic at the first rift we found too, but it didn't affect the portal at all. But then, Rollick said sorcery doesn't usually affect regular rifts either.

Jonah repeats the unnerving syllables in a more forceful tone, and the creature finally spins around. It hops over and heaves itself up toward the rift, vanishing into the shadows at the same time.

Jonah's posture relaxes. "Even with the extra push I added, considering the way it resisted, I don't think the effect should last more than a few minutes. We'll see if it comes back."

Mirage has swiveled toward the water. He walks to the ocean's edge, not seeming to care when the waves wash over his sneakers. Of course, if he wants he can simply duck into the shadows and pop out again with them perfectly dry.

He cocks his head. "I saw something jump in the water."

Hail ambles over to join him, careful to stay out of range of the waves. He studies the ocean with a typical casual stance, but I taste a tang of worry from him. "There are some fish that'll leap out into the air now and then. If it was farther out, it could have been a dolphin or a porpoise."

"Yes, they like to have their fun. This was different—I caught a bit of scent in the spray. I think it was shadowkind."

Could another of the warped beings have emerged without Rollick realizing and slipped into the ocean?

I squint at the rippling water, dark gray under the cloudy sky. It's hard to search for currents of emotion out there when there are so many sensations flowing into me so strongly from nearby.

"I'll go take a look," I announce, and spring into the patches of darkness that undulate across the water.

Raze lets out a disconcerted noise. "Peri!"

When I don't answer, he ripples after me into the shadows, traveling behind me.

He must be worried that any shadowkind out here might attack me. I'm not going to argue about the company. It's a little reassuring to drink in the hot-cocoa warmth of his protectiveness.

No one should have to work without refreshments.

I slip over and through the shadowy depths alongside the sway of the water, searching for any unusual flavors. Fish flit by beneath me without giving off any strong impressions. The curiosity—and a bit of consternation—from the companions we've left behind on the beach fades with the distance.

Then I catch it: a brief punch of exhilaration like salted caramel. It's coming from a presence that races past us through the water below.

The surge of emotion contains an eerie quaver that makes me suspect it *is* one of the strange shadowkind, not some regular mortal or shadow being. I push myself deeper into the thicker shadows below the water's surface, following its giddy trail.

All at once, the emotions shift, excitement chilling into a slash of panic. The creature dives, hurtling away from me so swiftly that I lose track of its presence in a matter of seconds.

"I only wanted to talk to you!" I call after it, but it's clearly not in a friend-making mood.

I wait a little longer, aware of Raze hovering nearby, before traveling back to the beach. When I pop out of the shadows with a crunch of the pebbles beneath my feet, three newcomers are standing with Rollick and the others.

I freeze. "Oh. Hello."

As Raze materializes just behind me, Rollick motions to me and then to the new arrivals: a woman as short as I am but much slimmer, with braided hair that gleams silver and darker gray; a big brawny guy with ruddy brown skin and a black buzzcut; and a leaner guy with an auburn ponytail and a couple of lumps stretching his light jacket just beneath his shoulders.

The demon's expression has warmed with a broader grin. "Shadowbloods, this is another associate of ours, Periwinkle. We're not sure exactly what label she should go by yet, but she consumes emotions and can also blast them out. Peri, meet Riva, Zian, and Dominic. Since they're hybrids, they're much better than we are at handling the kinds of materials that'll repel more beings from coming through the rift."

Zian hefts a sack he must have carried with him from whatever vehicle they arrived in. "And we brought lots of it. Where do you want us to lay the stuff out?"

The demon turns to consider the rift. "Let's lace the ground with silver and iron pellets all along this stretch of beach… Bury them under the pebbles so they're not obvious. And also scatter them through the nooks in the outcroppings around the cove and beyond. We can hope this rift won't wander *too* much."

The three shadowbloods move closer to the rift, the other two carrying bags of their own. Seeing the gleam of noxious metals in their hands, I step back, my skin creeping.

After they're done laying the materials down, we won't want to hang around the rift either. The portal might be indecisive, but those metals are all "push" when it comes to shadowkind. And very pushy about it.

If anything, the rift feels even more dithery now. The dissonant energy vibrates into my skin at a higher pitch.

Mirage cocks his head. "Is it excited to see them?"

Hail snorts, but Rollick's forehead furrows. "The rift does seem to be reacting to our new arrivals. Or possibly to the metals. I'll have to check with the shadowbloods at the city-side rift to see if a similar effect happened there."

Jonah turns to me. "Did you find another creature out in the water?"

I duck my head apologetically. "I think so. It felt strange like the others do—it was definitely shadowkind. But it got scared and rushed away. I don't think it'll bother anyone unless it morphs a lot. It mostly wanted to enjoy zooming around and to avoid anyone coming close to it."

Rollick gives a rough chuckle. "One less thing to worry about, if it stays that way. You know, I'm thinking I should have you pay a visit to the collection I've amassed. I can observe what's going on with their appearance and behavior, but not how they're changing internally. If anything stays consistent that could help us manage their behavior—and keep both them and the other beings they might encounter safe—it'd be good to know."

I draw myself up straighter. "Of course! Anything I can do to help."

The demon casts his gaze toward the men around me. "Any objections to a detour on our way back to the academy?"

Amid the shaking heads, Hail lets out a scoff. "It isn't as if we have much choice, is it?"

Guilt pricks at my gut, but Rollick simply gives the winter fae a narrow look and aims a smile at me. "Before we go, I think you might want to have a chat with Riva. She's ended up marking a handful of gentlemen of her own by supernatural means. It's possible she'll be able to advise you on your unexpected situation."

My spirits rise, but it's hard not to wince at the eagerness I sense from all four of my men at his suggestion.

They *all* want to break this bond between us. Even Raze.

Why wouldn't they? They didn't ask for it. I didn't even ask them. It wasn't fair to any of us.

Zian gives a low shout, and our heads snap around.

The furry frog creature is just tumbling out of the rift again. Jonah stiffens.

"That didn't last long," Hail drawls. "It must really want to be on this side after all. Makes you wonder how awful the shadow side is."

A chill races down my back. "I don't think I'd want to find out."

"That's something else I'd like to know," Rollick admits. "I'm not going to ask any of my associates to enter one of these questionable rifts, but I have sent some to try to locate them from the shadow-realm side. Unfortunately these portals seem to be rather… slippery. My assistants have reported some areas with strange 'vibes' but they always seem to end up turned around before they can delve very deeply into them."

Raze grunts. "Then the rifts probably aren't messing with normal shadowkind. They're producing creatures that are already weird in their own pockets of strangeness?"

"That's the conclusion I'd have to draw so far." Rollick sighs and waves to Jonah. "Send this creature back again. Once the protections are down, that should keep it away for as long as the rift is here."

After Jonah places another sorcerous command on the creature, the six of us draw farther and farther back along the shoreline, watching the shadowbloods do their work and avoiding the uncomfortable aura of the metals.

Riva and Zian move with impressive speed, which must be one of their supernatural talents. By the time they've laid out a swath of silver and iron across about half a mile of territory, Dominic is swiping at the sweat on his forehead, but the other two look unaffected.

Riva glances toward the dark ocean and wrinkles her nose. "Next time I'll take the one in the desert."

Not much of a sand-and-surf fan, then.

As her companions chuckle, Rollick nudges her toward me. "Why don't you and Peri have your little… girl talk, let's say. See if you can work out why our glowing emotion-eater might have tossed her version of bond marks onto her teammates—and what could be done about it."

A jitter of nerves runs through my gut, but Riva looks at me with only curiosity. The impressions I get from her are mild but friendly enough.

Rollick shoos us off to the scruffy fields beyond the jutting rocks while he and the other men head to the waiting vehicles. Riva waits until they're out of easy hearing range before picking up the conversation. "Tell me about these marks—what they look like, what they do, how it happened. I'm not exactly an expert, but there could be some overlap with ours."

I drag in a breath. "Sometimes when I get very emotional, the energy of the feelings kind of… explodes out of me. This time it hit the four of them and left glowing spots on their chests. I have one too."

I tug down the neckline of my T-shirt to show her and then explain about the two-way tap of emotions and the way I fainted when Raze roamed too far away.

"I've tried to shut down the connection, but nothing's worked," I finish. "None of the other energies that've surged out of me before lasted more than a minute or two. This one seems very stubborn."

I'm usually proud of my persistence, but in this one case, I'd welcome a little slack.

Riva's forehead furrows. "How long have you known these guys? From what Rollick said, you haven't spent all that much time in the mortal world?"

"I only met all of them about a month ago when I was brought to Rollick's academy."

She rubs her mouth. "And how involved had you gotten with them—like, emotionally *and* physically—before the bonds? If that's not too private a question."

My cheeks warm, but it feels easiest to answer plainly. "I've had sex with two of them. With the other two, it's just been feelings. Some attraction, but they had reasons for not wanting to pursue it."

Riva doesn't show any sign of judging me. A hint of a blush colors her own face. "With my guys, we'd known each other our whole lives. We were created—genetically engineered by scientists as human-shadowkind hybrids—using the same process at the same time and then raised together. And our bond…"

She pulls at her tee to reveal a row of five thumbprint-like bruises along her collarbone. "They formed separately, the first time I got completely intimate with each of them. It felt like something we were creating together, not something I imposed on them."

My heart sinks. "I didn't mean to impose on anyone."

"That's obvious!" Riva says quickly. "I wasn't trying to criticize, just explaining how it seems different. We've never tried to get rid of the connection between us either. But we could resist the urge to form it by doing the opposite of what it wanted—by keeping our distance, refusing to give in to the feelings… If yours formed out of joy, maybe stirring up a bunch of negative feelings would crack through it?"

The idea makes my stomach churn, but her suggestion makes sense. "We haven't tried that."

"It might be worth a shot. I'm sorry I couldn't be more helpful." She twists the tip of her braid. "I don't really understand how most of this supernatural stuff works myself."

"That's okay," I reassure her. "It was good to talk to someone who's been in a bit of a similar situation."

Now I just need to figure out how to generate the most intense of bad feelings between me and the men I like the most in this world. How fun.

I square my shoulders and prepare to summon a little more stubbornness.

8

Mirage

The place Rollick calls his "desert estate" reminds me of the academy, only smaller. And with different possibilities for amusement.

The single-story house wraps around a courtyard just like the school's reform building does, but this courtyard has not just a garden and patio but a whole swimming pool. Even though the saltwater makes my nose itch, I'm tempted to dive right in to escape the dry heat in the air.

Maybe later, when we're finished with our Serious Business.

The extra-cozy lounge chairs look perfect for curling up on, and more comfy sofas and chairs fill the expansive living room beyond the glass sliding doors. I slink around them, considering the possibilities.

Hail opted to wait in the house's front yard, saying he felt like soaking up some sun. I think he just wanted to show that he isn't interested in being any nearer to the rest of us than he has to be. It's very important to the chilly fae to keep his cool distance.

Raze prowled off on a quick hunt, and Jonah went down into the house's basement with Rollick to check that everything's secure before we visit the demon's collection of shadowkind beasts.

Picturing what that room might look like makes my skin go all creepy-crawly. I shake off the unnerving sensation and turn my attention toward the most unavoidable member of our team.

Peri must like the look of the pool too. She's vanished her sneakers and swapped her ripped jeans and T-shirt for a gold-to-blue ombre sundress. Now she's sitting with her pale legs over the edge of the pool, lifting her bare feet in and out of the water while she leans back on her hands.

The little smile playing with her lips and her casual stance should mean she's relaxed. But I'm starkly aware of the uneasiness winding through her and spilling out into the connection that joins us through the glowing spot on my chest.

The idea of all those caged creatures bothers her, just like it does me. We're both too familiar with the shape of cages from the opposite side.

We both did things we're ashamed of while captured that way.

Rollick isn't the same as the humans who imprisoned us, of course. He's keeping these shadowkind imprisoned for their own good, not to manipulate them. That doesn't make the creepy-crawly feeling any better.

If he can't figure out what's causing their impulses to warp so they go on the attack, what will he do with them?

I don't think Jonah can convince them all to travel back to the shadow realm and stay there. He barely managed to keep one away for ten minutes. That's less than a lunch break.

Are other things bothering Peri? I haven't talked to her much since she blasted her light into us in the woods. Even thinking about her sends a similarly uneasy sensation through me from throat to gut.

I want to go to her, and I want to get away from her. But I can't do the second thing. I'm chained to her, even more constrained than I was in the experimenters' cell.

At least the cell had a door I could hope to escape through. Peri's trapped me right down to the essence of my being.

It shouldn't bother me. I wanted to be close to her. My Rainbow has shone so much colorful light into my life, in ways I never imagined were possible.

I had the choice then. She didn't mean to take it away, but she did.

As much as that fact gnaws at me, I'm still drawn to her. Maybe even more than before. The desire to go over and wrap my arms around her, bury my face in her hair and then kiss her lips, is a dull ache that never quite goes away.

She's always pretty, but when I can get her to light up, she's absolutely breathtaking.

I don't have to get very close to her to brighten her up a little. Why shouldn't I distract her from the discomfort of this situation the way only I would think to?

Yes, that's what I'm meant to be doing. Playing tricks, bringing laughs, changing perceptions. Shaking her up a little might make us both feel better.

I duck behind a shed that holds various pieces of pool equipment and slip into the shadows. Shrinking my presence as small as I can, I wriggle through the patches of darkness along the patio stones.

Nothing to see here. Just a little shadow-worm.

As I ease closer, taking a winding route behind Peri, a spark of amusement lifts my spirits. The contrasting tension coiled in my gut resists the sensation, but I tune it out.

I'll get a little closer, and then—

Just as the trick is forming in my head, Peri glances around. A pang of her concern reverberates through our connection. "Mirage? Are you all right?"

Who, me? No one's here but the shadows.

She's looking straight at the sliver of darkness where I'm lurking. I hesitate, disappointment washing through me.

Of course she sensed me coming. She's even more aware of my mental state than I am of hers.

I'll never be able to surprise her again. Never be able to play with her or delight her with an unexpected jolt of joy.

Her smile disappears completely with a knitting of her brow. "Mirage?"

The worried quaver of her voice and the guilt I can sense winding through her concern snap me out of my downcast spiral.

I jerk myself back into physical form and dip into a foxy bow with a swish of three of my tails. "I'm fine. Just playing around. This seems like a good place for it."

"Oh. Okay." Peri's smile comes back, though it's tentative. "You can play as much as you want around me. Especially if you're enjoying it. I just thought—it seemed like —I'm sure you don't have to go downstairs if you don't want to. Rollick would understand."

I grimace. *She* doesn't have that choice. Rollick specifically wanted her to use her emotion-sensing power on the creatures.

Doesn't he care how the setting might rattle her? She's more than a feelings-omometer.

Someone has to be on her side.

I lift my head high with a flick of my fox ears into and out of existence. "Of course I'll come. We're a team."

Peri's stance softens. I got a bit of what I wanted.

It just doesn't feel like anywhere near enough.

"You know—" she starts, but at the same moment, footsteps rap on the other side of the patio doors.

Rollick slides one open and peers out at us. "I think you'll all be safe from the marauding beasties. Come down, and let's see if we can determine anything new about these creatures."

He's mainly talking to Peri, not me, but as promised I amble behind her into the artificial cool of the house. Raze hasn't returned, but Hail stands stiffly near the basement stairs.

"I don't even have to go down there to sense that they're upset," he tells Rollick. "Wild creatures aren't meant to be shut away."

Rollick gives the winter fae a mild look. "And shadowkind aren't meant to go showing off their strangeness in front of the mortals who'll want to do a lot worse than shut them away. We need to solve that problem before anything else. You can go back outside if you'd prefer."

Hail glowers at him. "I'm coming."

As we descend the stairs and wait for Rollick to open the secure door at the bottom, Peri's posture tenses too. This place must bring up even more awful memories for her than it does for me.

The sorcerer who caged her kept her in his basement.

I'd like to batter him with all five of my tails and shred him with my claws and fangs. If he wasn't dead already.

Jonah casts a pained glance Peri's way. "If it gets to be too much for you, you can take a break. I can tell Rollick's keeping the creatures as comfortable as possible, but still…"

Our lovely Rainbow squares her shoulders with

determination. "It's okay. I want to help them, and that'll be easier if I can see them."

The room we enter isn't as blazingly bright as the sorcerer's basement or the lab where I was imprisoned. A desk stands against one wall, stacked with papers and notebooks including some I recognize from the notes the sorcerer had tacked to the wall in his workspace. A tall steel cabinet stands next to it.

The only other furnishings in the room, if you can really call them that, are a stack of solid metal boxes along the far wall.

A prickle runs through my nerves with the impression of the unpleasant materials embedded within the cages' steel shells. The enclosures are all quite big, enough to contain a large dog.

Rollick motions to them. "Lesser shadowkind are simpler to contain. I don't turn on the lights inside once they're caught, so they can stay more comfortable in the darkness. There's only enough silver and iron embedded to ensure they don't go slipping out." He grimaces. "I know it isn't ideal, but I have tried to give them as much room as possible. It's difficult to cater to them properly when they keep changing."

Peri steps closer to the wall of cages, her gaze fixed on their doors. "How do you know they keep changing when you can't even see them?"

"I have devices monitoring the inside of the cages that keep track of certain types of energy and the physical space they take up if they materialize. They're all pretty erratic, similar to the readings we've gotten from the rifts, but they adjust their composition on somewhat regular schedules. Some change once or twice an hour, others no more than once a day, most somewhere in between. That variation matches what I've been able to decipher from that sorcerer's notes."

The demon walks up to one of the cages. "I'm going to let out one of the fastest-morphing ones now, after Jonah compels it to stay in the room. Peri, I'd like you to monitor its internal state, especially when and after it's adjusted its outer appearance. The rest of you can keep watch for anything you happen to observe in your own ways."

As he presses a couple of buttons on the outside of one of the higher cages, Hail leans against the wall and folds his arms over his chest. His expression looks stony as a statue, but he doesn't grumble anymore.

When Rollick opens the cage, Jonah speaks a few of those magical sounds that wobble through my nerves, louder and more emphatic than usual to get the sorcery to stick.

A creature currently the size and shape of a hamster—but covered in slick slimy skin that reminds me of a newt—hops out onto the ground. It trundles one way and then another on its stubby legs, its pin-like claws tapping against the tiles.

We all watch as the newt-ster keeps scurrying around without any clear sense of direction. Peri's gaze stays trained on it. "Right now, it feels curious and a little nervous. It's confused about where it is and how it got here."

"Understandable," Hail mutters.

It only takes a few minutes before the creature's small body shudders and expands. It balloons to several times its previous size, puffing out like a blowfish but sprouting feathers rather than scales.

Only its legs stay the same size, leaving it to sway and rock across the floor rather than really walking, as if the hamster has become the exercise ball rather than just running inside it.

It whirls around and snaps its teeth at me. I jerk back, not sure what I did to offend it.

"As soon as it transformed, it had a surge of unhappier

emotions," Peri says. "I think that's happened a lot of the times we've seen them morph."

Jonah makes a face. "It can't be fun constantly adjusting to a different form."

There's an odd urgency to the creature's movements around the room now, though. It might have snapped, but I have the unexplainable impression that it simply wanted to latch on to something.

Maybe I can distract *it* from its discomforts. Even a hamster-ballfish should get to have some fun.

I release my ears and all five of my tails and crouch down close to the creature's level. With a squeaky gurgle, it sways toward me.

Yes, it wants to join me. We can make that a joyful collision rather than a toothy one.

As it scuttles forward, I hop to the side with a swirl of my tails. When it changes direction, I make another leap. "Let's play, little guy! Seize the day, not my nose."

The creature lets out a snuffly-sounding snort and shoves itself toward me. Peri's voice comes out in a yelp. "Mirage, watch out!"

It's easy enough to dodge the little thing. It careens into the space I just left with a furious chittering.

My head droops. My invitation appears to have been soundly rejected. "I guess it's not feeling very playful."

Peri shoots me one of her sweet smiles. "It's just kind of jumbled up inside. I don't think it's in the right mood."

Her attention darts back to the creature. "Its temper is starting to simmer down, though. Just a little bit."

Can I say that's any thanks to me? I might have been keeping it stirred up rather than simmered down. That's what I always seem to do.

I wanted to be here with Peri so I can help, but what help

can I really offer? I'm not good at anything *other* than being ridiculous.

The knowledge niggles at me through two more of the creature's shifts. Each time, it snarls and snaps right after the change and then gradually calms, no matter what we try.

A few minutes after the third change, Peri's face has gone unusually solemn. The stream of emotion coursing into me from her feels even more unsettled than before.

Neither of the other men she's marked seem willing to ask the important question, so I will. "What's wrong, Rainbow?"

She shakes herself, but the impression of gloom doesn't lift. She turns to Rollick rather than to me.

"It's only a bit, and the changes are far enough apart that it's hard for me to be sure. But... I think every time they morph, they get a little angrier."

9

Periwinkle

In our shared dorm bedroom, Raze has usually preferred to stick to the shadows—although my most delightful memories are of the times we've spent together in physical form.

We haven't had that kind of intimate fun since we got back from our first mission. During the few days we've spent at the school, Raze has hardly seemed to be in the dorms at all. I was starting to worry that he'd asked for a new room.

So when I walk in after lunch and sense his presence coiled in the shadows beneath his bed, I want to break out the streamers and confetti.

As I turn toward him, he materializes so he's standing by the side of the bed. His dark gaze, the eyes that can kill tempered by his contact lenses, rakes over me with an intensity that leaves my skin tingling.

"No one hassled you in the cafeteria?" he asks.

I shake my head and step toward him with a smile. "People keep whispering and gossiping, but they seem to have decided it's mostly better to leave me alone. Other than Fen and Brine, of course. I ate with them, and everything was fine."

"That's good. No one should be picking on you, especially after everything you've done for other shadowkind."

There are lots of things I'd like to do with this other shadowkind right now. Simply snuggling would be scrumptious.

But when I take another step toward him, Raze's posture tenses just enough that I notice. He hasn't moved toward *me* at all, I realize.

Apprehension wafts off him, vodka-sour. He's purposefully keeping his distance—as far away from me as he can get in the small room.

I stop, my throat constricting. "I'm glad I can count on you to look out for me."

Raze's voice comes out gruff. "Always. If you need anyone put in their place, I'll be happy to teach them the lesson they deserve."

His teeth flash against his tan skin in a brief motion that's almost a grin, but it fades just as quickly as it formed.

I want to walk right up to him and wrap my arms around him, to thank him with the gesture as well as my words. But if something about being near me is making him uncomfortable, I won't push.

The depressing reminder that even he is bothered by the accidental connections I created reminds me of my resolve to do whatever I can to sever them. I offer him another smile and return to the door. "I've got a little more work to take care of. You can have the room to yourself."

"Peri!"

When I glance back at him, Raze looks pained. A twisted, bittersweet current flows from him to me. "It's your room too. I never *want* you to leave."

He doesn't exactly want me here either, though. Lies can't travel through the tap between us.

"I know!" I say brightly. "I really do need to get something done."

I step into the hall and go off in search of a certain wintery fae.

Hail doesn't respond to my knock on his bedroom door. When I push my awareness toward his ice-tinged part of our connection, I can tell he's not in there. I venture out of the dorms and on to the cafeteria I just left, the last place I saw him.

The room is set up like a casual restaurant today, with checkered tablecloths and a few students walking around refilling glasses now that everyone has ordered. Hail is leaning back in his chair where he's sitting with several other students, including Gloss, who's trailing her fingers along his arm in a gesture that makes me bristle for reasons I can't explain.

I've always tried to be friendly or at least peaceful with the disdainful shadowkind woman… but suddenly I'd like to blast that hand right off her.

Somehow I don't think the administration would accept "she was petting my teammate" as reasonable justification.

I don't get any sense that Hail is all that affected by her touch anyway. His poise shows only his usual disaffection. The emotions I taste through our heightened connection are all bland-toast boredom and a little over-salted egg uneasiness.

A pretty poor breakfast, let alone lunch.

Am I really going to walk up to him with Gloss and her

fawning friends right there? They cut people apart with just their words.

I hesitate in the doorway. Maybe I can use our connection to my benefit for once.

Concentrating on Hail, I summon a surge of urgency, an anxiety about something undone that needs to be addressed.

I've only been stewing in that feeling for a few seconds when Hail's head ticks toward me. Our gazes lock.

A shiver that isn't exactly unpleasant passes over my skin, but I ignore it and jerk my head toward the doorway.

The winter fae's mouth twists with reluctance, but he says something to his companions and gets up from his chair. I slip out the doorway before they can see me waiting for him.

Hail ambles into the hall after me with his hands slung in the pockets of his dark jeans and his gaze even more searing than it was at a distance. "What do you want now, Cream Puff?"

He's still not back to calling me pipsqueak. That's some kind of victory, isn't it?

But the fact that Hail is the most annoyed by the bond I've forced on him is the exact reason why I picked him for my proposition. "I have another way we can try to get rid of the mark and break the connection."

A jolt of exhilaration, sweet but tangy like lemon soda, passes into me, although Hail's eyes narrow. "I'm not going to say no to that. Is it something we can do here in the hall?"

A few other beings meander out of the cafeteria. An itch of self-consciousness wriggles through my nerves. "Um, let's find an empty classroom. It might take a while and look a little strange."

Hail's expression stays skeptical as he follows me down the hall. "What exactly are you thinking we're going to do?"

I peek through a doorway and determine the room

beyond it is unoccupied. As I motion Hail inside, my stomach knots.

Looking at him right next to me, tense as his gorgeous face is, I'm struck by a pang of loss. Which makes no sense at all, because this is the closest he's been to me in days.

I can't ignore the niggling question that rises up. What if this bond isn't a mistake?

I tip forward with a swift inhalation. Hail's crisp, foresty scent that fits him so perfectly fills my nose.

He blinks at me. "What the fuck are you doing?"

"I— Checking for tingles."

"*What?*"

I don't think he wants to hear a full accounting of my internet research into fated mates. "Don't worry about it. I'm just making sure."

I tap my fingers against his arm, but there's definitely no zap. Smelling him didn't make me any tinglier than I already was with him so close, which is quite a bit. And unfair, since if he's at all tingly about me, he's suppressing that feeling very well.

Maybe because I've completely bewildered him. "Look, Cream Puff, either tell me how we're supposed to break this bond or—"

I guess there's nothing else to do but lay it out.

I lift my chin. "When I was talking to Riva—you know, the woman shadowblood?—we came up with an idea. Since the marks formed when I was feeling really happy, maybe if we provoke enough negative emotions between us, that'll sort of… burn it away. Make it fade. Or something."

"Or something," Hail repeats, but his tone has gone distant rather than cutting. He studies me for a few seconds that feel horribly long. "Why did you decide to try this experiment with me? Don't you think that lug of a basilisk shifter would jump at the chance to help you?"

I open my mouth and close it again. I don't have any gentle way of answering that question either. "I figured that you're the one who has the most negative feelings toward me already, so it'd be easiest for you."

Something shutters behind Hail's dark eyes. He looks down at himself, toward the glowing spot I know is hidden behind his shirt, and then back at me.

I hurtle onward before he needs to reply. "So if you can just dwell on all the things about this situation that annoy you, and I'll do the same as well as I can, we'll see if it has any effect on the connection between us."

Hail releases his breath in a rush. "All right. Fine. That should be simple enough."

Of course it will be, for him. I start to push away the ache his words prompt in my chest and stop myself.

No, that's exactly the sort of emotion I need to focus on. All the ways his remarks have stung me over the past few weeks. All the cold shoulders he's given me. All the times he's acted like I couldn't possibly do anything important.

Don't think about how his attitude softened in the last couple of days before I threw my supernatural energy at him and left him marked. Don't remember the flutter his kindness could send through my pulse.

I set my jaw and think back to the most painful memories I can summon. Hail has always shunned me more than he's outright attacked me, but there's still plenty of discomfort and frustration in those recollections.

Hail must be able to sense at least some of the anguish I'm dredging up through our connection. As his expression tightens, the trickle of sensations coursing off him widens into a flood.

There's so much of it, cloyingly bitter like cough syrup and as searingly sour as a rotten grapefruit.

My lungs squeeze; a shudder runs through my bones. Tears I try to blink away spring to my eyes.

He hates me so much. How could he have treated me like I really matter when I disgust him?

I brace myself against the deluge and delve deeper into my own sorrows. The noxious emotions Hail is pummeling me with amplify my own distress.

I've been such an idiot. Of course he never really liked being around me. Was he outright agonized all this time—

All at once, the surge of emotion dwindles to a dribble. Hail's voice breaks through my concentration, a little choked. "That's enough."

I stare at him and realize my cheeks are chilled—with dampness. A whole torrent of tears has streaked down my face without my even noticing it.

With a rough sound, the fae man propels himself toward me. He slides his thumbs across my cheeks to wipe away the last of the tears, and I really tingle then.

His jaw clenches alongside another swell of sensation, bitter and sweet churning together. "I know you didn't mean to do it. It's not really *you* I'm angry with. Just... that it happened... what it means... You did a lot of good things too."

I don't know how to answer his sudden shift in attitude or the waft of concern mixed in with his conflicted feelings. It isn't as if he can separate me from what happened or the consequences.

I'm better off focusing on the concrete details. "Did it work at all? Is the mark any fainter?"

Hail grimaces. "I don't think so. It doesn't feel any different."

He lets go of me to tug out his shirt and peer down at his chest. The shake of his head confirms his comment.

Despair wells up inside me, so heavy it's hard to breathe. That was the only new idea I had, and it got us nowhere.

"Hey." Hail touches my face again, a gentle graze of his fingers. "It means something that you gave it a shot. I'll try—I'll try not to beat you up so much with the shit I'm feeling."

I smile stiffy. "You can't help what you feel. You should be able to feel it without worrying about me or anyone else."

He sputters a laugh. "Lots of beings should have lots of things they don't get."

His hand lingers against my cheek. An unexpected warmth blooms beneath his cool fingers and winds down through my chest.

I want to ease closer. I want him to touch me more.

I want to drink in every spark of heat he can offer—like the flame that's flickered inside him just now with a tang of lust.

Hail jerks himself back from me. He swipes his hand over his face. "It'll be easiest if I stay as far away as I safely can until we get this figured out."

He strides off without another word.

I stay in the empty classroom for a few minutes longer, giving Hail the chance to create that distance and sorting through my own muddled emotions.

I'm an expert on feelings. I've consumed heaps of them.

So why are my own like a plate of spaghetti dumped on my head?

I'm about to give up and head out to check my schedule for my afternoon classes when Gloss appears in the doorway.

With a toss of her sleek black hair, she sets her hands on her slim hips. Her sharp eyes pierce into me. "You still think you can steal him away from me when he doesn't even *want* you. I've supported him for months; he's going to be by *my* side. Why would you even deserve a shadowkind like him?"

"I—"

Her voice drops to a silky hiss. "Your supernatural tricks won't mean anything if you're not around to work them. Too bad your powers are *so* out of control."

"What—"

She doesn't give me a chance to speak. In a blur of frigid air, she hurtles into me.

Icy shards rake through my flesh, dispelling smoky blood. Pain erupts all through my limbs and torso.

I cry out, and another glacial blade plunges straight into my throat. My voice cuts off with a thicker gush of essence.

Footsteps thunder in the hall. Someone's yelling. There's plenty to yell about.

But all I can do is crumple to the floor under Gloss's onslaught, my mind blanking out with agony.

IO

Periwinkle

I wake up already blinking to clear the haze from my eyes.

Everything stays hazy white. My first glimpse of my surroundings is so blank my pulse hiccups with the fear that I'm back in an isolation room.

Then I notice that I'm lying down on a flat, softly padded surface. The isolation rooms I've been sent to before were one-hundred-percent bed-free zones.

I turn my head to take in the other simple beds and the cabinets beyond them. Oh, it's just the infirmary in all its antiseptic paleness.

Raze's gruff voice reaches me from somewhere near my feet. "She woke up!"

I twist to push my body upright, and a sharp tremor runs through my arm and down my chest. Okay, being upright is not on the menu today.

I flop onto my back again instead, peering toward the end of the bed.

Raze hustles over beside me, gazing down with his mouth twisted into a grimace. Jonah, Mirage, and Hail step into view too. Worry shows on all their faces and courses through our connections into me, a mix of sweet and sour like a tart apple.

"I told you it was only a matter of time." The horned female shadowkind who doted on me here before pushes past Raze to touch my forehead and examine my eyes. "You just needed to recover your essence. You should be right as rain in another few hours."

Raze shifts his weight as if it's taking all his self-control to stay in one place. He can't smooth the snarl from his voice. "What happened, Peri? Why did she hurt you?"

Mirage shudders. "You were all dismal misery, and then everything was *pain*. I was already coming to see what was wrong when the worst part hit." He flashes his fangs. "Now we hit back."

I open my mouth and close it again. The memories return in wavering images like a disjointed TV flashback.

Was it really— Did all that awfulness actually *happen*? It feels like it should be a bad dream.

But I'm here in the school's infirmary, recovering. Obviously I suffered from something.

With a rap of his loafers, Rollick appears by my shoulder, his expression tense. Ominous energy roils around the demon. "I'd like to know the answer to that question too."

How exactly is *he* going to hit back once he hears my report?

They seem to already know it was Gloss. Raze said "she." It won't help anyone to keep quiet about the rest and let them speculate.

Of course, the "dismal misery" Mirage mentioned must

have been my attempt to break my connection to Hail. I catch the winter fae's gaze, and his posture stiffens.

Does he think I'm going to accuse him? He was playing along with my idea.

It wasn't him who sent me here, though.

The pain from the slashes of ice echoes through me, stirring fresh aches. "Gloss was… She was so mad at me. She marched into the room, and I didn't even have a chance to say anything to her before she threw her power at me. From what she said, it's mostly because I marked Hail. She thinks I marked him on purpose—but I didn't even mean to. I've tried to fix it."

Hail's dark blue eyes flash like the start of a thunderstorm. "That's ridiculous."

My stomach lurches with the thought that he's accusing me of lying, but he goes on in a cutting tone. "I never made any promises to Gloss. We're just friends. She doesn't *own* me or get to decide who I associate with. And dealing out her idea of punishment…" His jaw clenches. "I'll talk to her."

Raze draws his brawny frame up even taller, his sinewy muscles rippling. "I'll come with you—and I'll do more than talk."

Rollick holds up his hands to stop them. "The staff will deal with this attack in our own way—and with all due consequences. Don't leave me having to punish the rest of you for vigilante justice as well." He returns his gaze to me. "You hadn't had any outbursts beforehand?"

I hug myself. "No. I was talking to Hail, and he left. A few minutes later, Gloss came in, accused me of stealing him, and started throwing her magic at me. She did say something about my magic acting up… Maybe she was hoping everyone would think my own powers turned on me?"

If she'd succeeded in crushing me, there'd have been no one to say what really happened.

Hail sucks a breath through his teeth in a sharp hiss. He catches my gaze. "I might not be happy about this thing tying us together, but I swear I didn't ask her to hurt you—I *wouldn't* do that."

Mirage hums an off-key tune. "Monkey sees, monkey does."

Hail scowls at the fox shifter. "What's that supposed to mean?"

Raze's eyes have narrowed. "You *have* been acting like you'd rather Peri would just go away. Maybe Gloss noticed that and was giving you what she thought you'd want."

The winter fae sputters. "I've never harmed the cream puff. I'm allowed to be unhappy about a shitty situation."

He snaps his mouth shut after the last two words, maybe picking up on the jab of pain they sent through me.

Raze steps toward Hail with a growl. "You're the one making it—"

"Hey, hey." Jonah pushes between them, his voice as calm and even as always but his expression taut. "Fighting amongst ourselves isn't going to help Peri. The administrators will deal with Gloss. The best thing you two can do is stop sniping at each other."

Raze glowers at the fae man but stands down. Hail's scowl only deepens, but he hunches his shoulders slightly as if he's trying to disappear into himself.

Another tremor passes through my body. I make him so unhappy.

I make all of them unhappy in different ways. I wish I could go to sleep and wake up to how things were right after we defeated my former captor, before I got us into this mess.

Rollick has watched Jonah handle the other men without comment. Apparently satisfied with his underling's approach, he brushes his hands together. "Very good. Now, there's something I'd like to discuss with Peri alone..."

"Is it urgent?" Jonah asks before the demon can go on.

Rollick blinks at him. "Not incredibly. Why?"

Jonah tips his head toward me without meeting my eyes. "Peri's energy is flagging. She needs more recovery time. If the conversation can wait, it might be better to give her a few more hours so she's completely back to herself."

Raze's forehead furrows with consternation as if he's annoyed he didn't notice my dwindling spirits first. I'm surprised Jonah spoke up out of concern for me at all. I guess he's in the best position to challenge Rollick, considering he's staff rather than a student, but his stance has tensed as he waits for his boss's response. He's afraid he's misstepped.

But he intervened anyway. For me.

After a moment, Rollick simply chuckles. "It can wait a few hours. It isn't the sort of discussion we should be having while she's still out of sorts anyway." He pats my arm a little awkwardly. "You're safe in here. Get some rest."

He waves to my men. "All of you, get out so she can do that. The horde of you skulking around is hardly relaxing."

In a matter of seconds, I'm alone except for the shadowkind nurse.

A breath rushes out of me, seeming to take my remaining vigor with it. My eyelids slide shut, and my mind drifts away like a cloud in a brisk breeze.

BY THE TIME ROLLICK RETURNS, I've been awake for nearly an hour. I'm sitting on the edge of my bed, flipping through a book of landscape photography that the nurse allowed Fen to hand over to me, though she wouldn't let the naiad stay and properly visit.

I don't see how friendly chatter would slow my recovery, but I'm not really in a position to argue.

The nurse won't let me leave either, even though I can stand and walk around without any lingering weakness. I'm starting to think this is a confinement room after all, just with more beds so it's a little comfier. Very sneaky.

Rollick tips his head to the nurse, who vanishes into the shadows. I set down the book and swivel on the bed to face him. "Can I go back to classes now? I promise my emotions are all settled down. I won't explode or anything even if I see Gloss."

The demon gives me a crooked smile. "You don't need to worry about seeing Gloss for a long time if ever. A purposeful, premeditated assault of this level on a fellow student—rather than the accidental ones you've perpetrated —is undeniable cause for banishment. She won't be returning to the mortal realm for a decade or so."

I stare at him. "Because she attacked me? It was only one time—and she had reasons to be angry…"

"Pretty poor reasons, I'd say, over delusions and circumstances that aren't exactly your fault." Rollick considers me. "Would you have any hesitation about her fate if it'd been your friend Fen she'd attacked and left close to death?"

Was I really in that bad a state?

I picture Fen lying crumpled, bleeding essence in clouds, and shiver. "No, I guess I wouldn't."

"Then you should have the same devotion to your own well-being. We can't have someone who'd behave so spitefully representing shadowkind among mortals." Rollick pauses. "Which in a roundabout way is what I need to talk to you about."

Does he think I'm spiteful too? I thought he liked me.

Please tell me I haven't gotten on an uber-powerful demon's bad side.

I knit my brow, tamping down my instinctive anxiety. "I don't understand."

Rollick props himself against the end of the cot. "With the current state of affairs, I'm not sure it's safe for you to remain at the academy. Gloss isn't the only student who's unsettled by the reports they've heard about the marking. And she had a lot of friends among her peers, I gather. I don't want to risk you facing additional hostility from Hail's various paramours or whoever else."

My stomach sinks. "Then…"

"I'm not suggesting *you* leave the mortal realm," he says quickly. "I have a much better idea. You've proven useful in evaluating the strange shadowkind who've emerged from these unusual rifts. I'd like you to come work with me until we can determine how to remove the bonds you accidentally forged, or at least until tempers settle down."

I find myself staring at him again. "You want me to take an official job working for you? Like Jonah does? But I haven't even made it out of the reform building—"

Rollick waves off my concern. "I've seen with my own eyes how quickly your control has developed with the right guidance. At the moment, what's most important to me is ensuring these new rifts don't end up revealing shadowkind existence to the entire human population. I need all the assistance I can get."

And he wants me to help him. He thinks I'd contribute enough that my mess-ups don't matter.

A smile springs to my face. "Of course. I'll do whatever I can. I want all of us to stay as safe as possible—the mortals too."

Rollick smiles back. "That's exactly why I knew this would be a good decision one that works in everyone's favor. I'll see about making arrangements right away."

His mention of "everyone" makes my stomach dip. My happiness deflates. "Oh. If I go with you… then the men I marked have to come too, don't they?"

They won't get a choice. Just one more way I've disrupted their lives.

Rollick gazes at me evenly. "I'd imagine their skills will all come in handy one way or another. It'll simply be another team effort like the first one I sent you on."

I don't think any of the men, even Hail, will refuse a direct request from the school's headmaster. But he wouldn't be making the request if it wasn't for me.

What's the alternative? Should I camp out in the infirmary for the rest of my student career?

Maybe if we spend more time together, we'll finally work out how to turn off the tap between us. How to snuff out the glow.

Avoiding each other seems like a terrible way of finding answers.

There's one other question that's been niggling at me since Rollick mentioned the sorcerer's notes when we were inspecting his confined shadowkind. I hesitate and then ask, "When you looked through all those papers we got from the bunker… did you see anything that told you why and how David Blaver came up north?"

How did he end up so far from his home turf? I'm guessing it wasn't for the fresh air and delightful scenery.

And did he drag his daughter, the girl who saved me from his clutches, with him?

The demon cocks his head. "His ramblings are disjointed, but I gather that he caught wind of an odd occurrence or two in the area and came in the hopes of gathering a 'better army' for the petty destruction you've mentioned he was prone to. He talked about wanting more vicious shadowkind than before, studying them and figuring out how to best work with their warped nature. Not that he got any farther than using brute sorcerous force."

"Was there anything about someone named Gracie?"

"That name… no. I'm sure it would have stuck out to me. He didn't mention anyone other than himself and the targets of his irrational wrath."

Then I can still hope Gracie got away. And if the weird rifts pose a threat to mortalkind, I owe it to her to do whatever I can to solve the problem too.

Two missions at once. I can be ambitious.

One last twinge of guilt ripples through my chest, but I give Rollick a firm nod. "All right. Let's go unravel the mystery of those rifts."

I I

Raze

I'm annoyed the moment I sense Peri arriving outside our dorm bedroom door—and hear her thanking the staff member who escorted her.

If Rollick wanted to make sure no one hassled her on the way from the infirmary, he should have asked me. Who cares more about keeping her safe than I do?

I spent most of the past few hours prowling around outside the voluntary student building, hoping the spiteful snow wraith would show her wan face so I could flay her with my fury.

Except I'm not sure I actually would have no matter how much I wanted to, because then the staff might banish me, and who else might hurt my Glowbug without me here?

And then I found out they'd already banished Gloss, so all my pacing was pointless anyway.

I emerge from the shadows before the door has even

swung shut, leaping to Peri's side. "Are you all right? You're feeling totally better now?"

She steps into the room smoothly enough. I'm not picking up any twinges of pain through the glowing spot on my chest, but I'm not sure if I'd notice milder sensations.

Subtlety has never been my strong point.

At least I know she's not blaring with agony. I'd recognize that in an instant.

Like the jumbled froth of distress that brought me hustling her way. Like the more vicious spike of anguish that followed.

When I remember seeing Gloss poised over Peri in the hall, the essence streaming off Peri's body and the savage expression on her attacker's face, my stomach ties itself in knots.

I can't remember the last time I experienced anger like the rage that seared through me at that sight. My contacts cracked; I'm sure one brush of my fingers would have been fatal.

I might really have killed the icy woman, shadowkind or not, if Jonah hadn't dashed over a moment after me and locked me in place with a shout of sorcery.

He did also get Gloss off Peri, which I guess I can give him credit for. As much as part of me wishes I'd gotten in a fatal swipe before he showed up.

The staff wouldn't have blamed me for acting in my beloved's defense in the moment, would they?

The brutal longing only twists my gut up more. I ease back a step to give Peri space.

All those venomous emotions are coming even closer to brushing up against her now. How can I keep a careful wall up when she's got a direct line to my inner state?

Peri offers me one of her soft smiles, but it's not quite as vibrant as they often are. "I'm completely back to normal. It is nice that our physical bodies can heal so much faster than regular mortal ones."

I don't know about "fast." Does she realize our shadowkind nurse took her into the shadow realm for a few days before she was healed enough to finish the process in this plane?

I make myself smile back despite the conflicted emotions roiling inside me. "That's good. If I'd gotten there sooner—"

Peri shakes her head dismissively. "I didn't have any idea Gloss was that angry with me, so you definitely couldn't have. It's over now. It sounds like no one has to worry about her going full monster again."

She pauses for a moment, studying me, and then flops down on her bed on the other side of the room. The urge spreads through my arms to follow and cuddle her close, but the jab of uncertainty on its heels holds me in place.

Instead, I stand aimlessly in the middle of the room like the lug Hail would say I am.

Peri aims another smile at me, this one more hesitant. "I'm glad to be back in a regular bedroom instead of having to spend what might be my last night at the academy in the infirmary. I know no one can hurt me when you're right here."

A growl creeps up my throat automatically. "They wouldn't get past the door. But I'm sure Rollick will think it's okay for you to come back to the school once everything has… settled down."

"I guess we'll see." Peri looks at her hands and then at me again. "I'm sorry that I'm having to drag you along with me to keep working on the rifts. You shouldn't have to leave too. If it wasn't for the marks…"

I frown at the distress in her voice. "I'd rather go wherever you're going than stay here wondering what's happening to you. I'm not sure I was learning all that much from the classes I could take anyway."

To tell the truth, being around Peri gave me more confidence that I could eventually mingle with humans again than anything else has in the several months I've been stuck at the academy.

Peri's hands clasp on her lap, her fingers twisting together. A faint glow wavers through her hair, a paler blue than its natural turquoise. "I've just seen—you don't want to get very close to me anymore. I can understand why you'd be worried that some other strange power might jump out of me. I don't want you to *have* to worry about that."

What crazy ideas is she talking about? They're not even the good kind of crazy.

I knit my brow. "What do you mean? I never thought that might happen."

Peri blinks at me. "Then why— When we've talked before, you've kept your distance. Even right now, you've avoided touching me or getting close."

Maybe I'm the crazy one. Did I really think she wasn't going to notice?

I grapple with my words. "It's not about you. It's never about you. You know what kinds of impulses I have… How my powers can come out reflexively… This connection that's between us now—I don't want any of the poison in me to leak into you. It seems like the feelings that pass through the mark are stronger when we're physically closer. I thought it was safer this way."

When Peri brightens, it's so obvious that her natural light had dimmed before. A peachy glint shimmers over her hair, melting away the blue with a warmer sheen.

A pang shoots through my heart.

She is a rainbow, like Mirage always says. My Glowbug.

She's *meant* to be glowing, and all the confusion of the past couple of weeks has dwindled her light.

Peri gets up and walks over to me, her hair still shining. My stance tenses, but I force myself to stay still and in bodily form rather than shying away.

If I start running from the only being who's ever made *me* feel remotely safe, then I might as well throw in the towel.

She stops right in front of me and reaches to touch my chest over the mark, which with our different heights is level with the top of her head. The warmth of her hand courses through my shirt and sets off a flare of a deeper heat that streams down to my groin.

I love everything about Peri, but this strange connection heightens certain sensations to torturous intensity. Her affection and desire for me waft into my chest and set off a sizzle through my nerves.

And I know she can taste my reaction even more clearly than I can sense hers.

"I'm always safer when I'm close to you than when I'm not," she says, her voice so tender it sends the giddiest of shivers over my skin. "You've never hurt me. The impulses you have, they're just part of how you're made. You still decide whether to act on them."

When she talks like that, it's hard not to doubt all my good intentions. "It's never been exactly like this before. We don't even know everything the bond might mean."

"Then we'll figure it out together." She lifts her hand to stroke her fingers along my jaw, and that's all it takes for my dick to harden in my pants. "Do you still want me?"

Fuck, she must feel how much I do. My voice comes out hoarse. "Always."

She bobs up on her toes to tuck her hands around my neck, gazing up at me with that brilliant grin I've been missing. "Then take me. Show me all that strength and how good it can make me feel."

A groan reverberates from my chest, and I scoop her right off the floor. As our mouths collide, her brightly sweet scent filling my lungs, I whisk her to my bed.

Peri loops her arms around my shoulders and kisses me back so eagerly I couldn't possibly doubt that she wants me just as much as I want her. Her lips tease over mine, coaxing my mouth open and tempting my tongue to dart out to meet her.

My hand comes up to grasp her gorgeous hair. I drop onto the bed, and her legs slide around my waist.

She sinks into my lap, the pressure of her rounded ass and thighs setting off a pulse of need through my groin. My cock throbs, stiff as steel now.

She isn't afraid. She's never been afraid of me, so that shouldn't come as a surprise.

I only wanted to protect her—I wanted to make sure I didn't ruin her—

But maybe my caution almost ruined this wonderful thing we have. How can I tell her what risks she's allowed to take?

I haven't hurt her before. I *have* made her feel incredibly good.

I can do that again, make up for any accidental pain I've caused her with my fears.

As I kiss her again, I run my fingers over her back. She's gone without the leather jacket that she decided was part of her new "tough" persona and chosen a dress more like the pretty ones she always wore when she first arrived at the school. The fabric is so thin I can chart every slope of her curvy body.

Pleasure trickles through our connection, flaring when I cup one of her breasts. My hunger rears up in turn.

Desire floods my entire body with a scorching heat, mingling with the matching longing emanating from her, until I can hardly think about anything except closing the last tiny distance between our bodies.

Peri lets out a shaky giggle against my lips and lowers her head to trail kisses along my jaw. "It feels like we're supposed to do this, doesn't it? Like… Like we haven't quite fit together properly yet, but when we do, it'll be the best thing ever. I wonder if that's got something to do with the marks."

I can barely manage more than a rumble. "If so, I won't argue."

Then I yank her mouth back to mine.

She slips her hands between us to fumble with the fly of my jeans. The brush of her fingers over my groin provokes an even more urgent swell of desire.

I yank her dress up over her hips and wrench at her panties, knowing she can conjure replacements later with a simple dip into the shadows.

The rasp of tearing fabric earns me another breathless laugh. Peri's lips graze mine with her eager murmur. "That's right. I want all of your power. What can you do for me, my fierce mate?"

That last word sets off a bolt of heat and hunger unlike anything I've felt before. I tip her over and bury my face in her hair, branding her jaw and the side of her neck with my lips.

"Everything. I'll do everything."

That's what she wants. That's what I'll give her. She's strong too—so fucking strong.

I shouldn't have let myself forget that.

Peri yanks open my boxers so my rigid cock springs free. I adjust her hips to line her up, my breath stuttering at the impatient wriggle of her hips.

Then I'm plowing into her with the full force of my desire.

For just an instant as I complete that first brutal thrust, my pulse hitches with the fear that I've hurt her after all. But Peri lets out a heady moan as if she's been dying to feel me inside her.

Maybe she has. More torrents of need and delight rush from her body into mine, stoking my own pleasure.

Everything is her—the slick pressure of her channel closing around me, the tightening of her fingers in my hair, the pants of breath through our increasingly wild kisses.

The bliss that fills her with each pump of my cock washes over me in turn through the mark on my chest. With every slam of my cock home, more of my own body lights up with heat and joy.

I have to peek at myself between kisses to check that the mark hasn't actually spread over the rest of my skin.

The visible sign of it hasn't. But the hold Peri has on me? That ripples through every particle of my essence with a light so bright and heady I never want it to fade.

I drive into her harder, spurred on by every fresh flare of bliss. She rocks up to meet my violent thrusts, chasing her release, urging on my own.

As I buck into her, I do hold on to a few shreds of control. If I can plunge a little deeper, hit just the right spot inside—

Fuck, I'm aching to explode, but I'll be damned if I don't bring her with me.

Peri's whimper nearly ends me. She tucks her head against mine, her breath wavering over my neck, and clings to me like I'm a rock in the storm. But I can feel just how ecstatic a storm it is with every surge of emotion that passes between us.

I will be her rock. I'll stand between her and anything that dares to aim a single unkind glance her way.

I'll fill her like no one else ever will.

A strained sound escapes me. Pleasure tremors through my veins. I grip Peri's thigh, swivel my hand over her breast, pound into her again—

We shatter apart at the exact same time: my cock erupting inside her, her channel clamping around the shaft with a blissful shudder that shakes her entire body.

My mind blanks with the rush of the release. The crackling pleasure whirls between us—mine, hers, ours—utterly consuming me and yet melding me with her.

We collapse onto my bed in a sweaty heap. Peri snuggles close to me, her hair beaming warm pink now.

"It's even better like that. One good thing from this accident."

"Everything about you is good," I mutter against her skin.

And with her, in these moments when we're entwined, I feel like maybe I could be good too.

If only I could be sure my endless venom will never poison her light.

12

Periwinkle

Jonah's voice flows through the trailer's small interior, calm and steady. "Think of something that relaxes you. A particular setting or scenery, or maybe a specific smell or sort of music."

We all have our eyes closed, but I sense Mirage perking up with a hint of interest. "The gasps when I've startled someone just right!"

Our teacher's tone turns dry. "That isn't what I'd have thought of, but if it's what you find most soothing, go with it. But let's keep our personal imagery to ourselves so everyone can concentrate."

Another thin waft of the emotions he's been giving off since we arrived near the city-side rift trickles through me: lightly sour like watered down orange juice. Pale amusement drizzled with sharper frustration.

"Right, right," Mirage murmurs, abashed. There's a rustle

that I suspect is him jerking his finger past his lips in a zipping motion.

My own lips tick upward with a smile at his playfulness, but I yank my focus back to the task at hand. Time to figure out my own relaxing imagery.

I've gone through this sort of meditative exercise before with Shanty in our one-on-one tutoring sessions. I've tried thinking of parks full of laughing humans or snuggling under soft blankets on my bed, but no matter where my mind goes, memories of some trouble that turned up in that setting seep in too.

The last time I visited a park on my own, I accidentally blasted out a flare of happiness and blinded a bunch of mortals. I've enjoyed wonderful interludes with Raze in my dorm bedroom, but it's also the place Gloss splattered with her bloody, gristly prank.

I guess that's a long way of saying a lot of things in the past month have sucked.

I can't let that get me down. There has to be some sensation no blasts or bullies have left dirty fingerprints on.

What can I think of that's only cozy calmness?

I grope through idea after idea, but none of them give me the reassurance I know Jonah wants us to find. If anything, I'm getting more anxious at the thought that I'm failing even in my own head.

Maybe I can't go with anything all that personal. Something bland and innocuous should do fine.

I picture the vast blue sky dotted with a few fluffy white clouds, as if I'm gazing up at it while sprawled in a wide-open field. The clouds drift like dandelion fluffs in a gentle breeze. Everything is clear and bright.

Mmm, the clouds look almost like cotton candy. That spun sugar melting on my tongue…

The itch in my nerves dwindles. There, that worked well enough.

A deeper swell of relief reaches me from where Hail is sitting on the floor behind me, though it's tainted with a trace of melancholy that's tart as an unripe peach.

What does the winter fae take comfort in, and why does it make him a little sad too?

I don't think I can ask without him glaring at me. Anyway, as Jonah just pointed out, we're supposed to be minding our own business for this exercise.

The sorcerer's words wind around us again. "You look like you've all settled in reasonably well. I want you to remember the imagery you're picturing and how it feels. Sink into it and let go of anything that's bothering you. When you have the urge to release your powers in a situation when it wouldn't be wise or fair, reach for that place of calm. It'll take some practice, but it can help you diffuse harmful impulses before you act on them."

Raze exhales roughly. "What if it's too difficult to concentrate on anything except the thing that's provoking us?"

"The best action to take alongside a meditative retreat is to retreat physically," Jonah says. "Put as much distance as you can between yourself and the being or situation that's affecting you."

Hail's snort nips at my nerves even before he speaks. "Other than the times when we can't put much distance without setting off an even bigger problem."

His tone is more resigned than annoyed, but heat rises in my cheeks all the same.

He's obviously talking about the connection between us. The reason they're all here taking lessons in a trailer rather than at the academy.

Rollick managed to frame the displacement more like a

field trip than mandated service. He's the one who suggested that Jonah lead tutoring sessions in between our stints of helping at the rift.

"Think of this as a practicum in your studies," he said in a nonchalant tone that implied there was no possible reason for any of my men to complain.

Hail clearly objects to being dragged out here, even if he didn't dare say so directly to one of the most powerful demons in existence. He might have promised not to take his anger out on me anymore, but why should he pretend he's overjoyed about the situation?

We both know I can tell exactly how he really feels.

Jonah's voice stays even. "We adapt to the circumstances we find ourselves in. All right, I think that's enough practice for now. I want you to try slipping back into your relaxed state at random times throughout the rest of the day. Tomorrow we'll try tapping into that zone while there's more activity going on around you."

I let my eyes pop open and aim a smile at him. Someone should show appreciation for his work. "Thank you! It's good to have these strategies even now that I've gotten a better handle on my powers."

Hail's gaze flicks over to me with a twitch of his jaw. He strides out of the trailer without a backward glance.

Mirage gives himself a shake and bounds after the winter fae just as swiftly. The fox shifter might hate being tied to me even more than Hail does; he's just nice enough not to vent about it.

I suck my lower lip under my teeth, worrying at it. My supply of optimism is running low—could anyone put a positive spin on my teammates' discomfort?

"Hey." Jonah walks over to me with a vibe of concern I can read on his face as well as in his stream of emotions.

"We're doing useful work out here, and no one's getting behind on their schooling. Hail's just feeling prickly in general. It's not as if he was ever all that happy at the academy either."

"I don't know if that guy would take happiness if you handed it to him on a platter," Raze mutters, looming behind me protectively.

I offer Jonah another grateful smile. "I still don't like that you all have to follow me wherever I go. I'd never have wanted to *force* you to stick by me."

Jonah smiles back. "I think we all know that, even if not all of us are willing to admit it."

He touches my arm—presumably to offer a reassuring squeeze. But the moment his fingers graze my skin, a jolt of more enjoyable heat shoots through my nerves, amplified by the matching pulse of attraction that sparks in Jonah.

A blush flares in his cheeks. He yanks his hand back and dips his head. "We'll get it all sorted out. You don't need to worry."

He hustles to the door without waiting for me to respond. Any good spirits I summoned go swirling down the drain.

I've imposed on Jonah even more than the others— roping him into a relationship that conflicts with his job and his morals. He gets all the downsides and none of the delight of acting on his desire.

I open my mouth, hoping for a magical bolt of inspiration that'll bring the words to make everything all right. But before Jonah even reaches the door, there's a quick knock.

As he stops, one of Rollick's assistants pokes her head in. "Periwinkle? The creature that came through the rift today— based on our readings, it's going to morph soon."

"Oh! I'll come right away." I hurry over.

Rollick wanted me to see if I could discern any clues about why the warped shadowkind are getting wilder and more vicious when they shift.

We emerge onto the scruffy terrain not far from the borders of the city. My gaze veers to the skyscraper Rollick said is called the Diamond Victory Tower, shining in the warm late-afternoon sunlight, before I drag it back to our more immediate surroundings.

Since we're so close to human civilization, we can't just camp out here and hope no one notices us monitoring the rift. Rollick set up a few trailers for his equipment and for us to hole up in as needed, arranging them as if this is a film set.

Any mortal who spots us won't wonder what sneaky deeds we might be up to, only what movie we're making. Brilliant!

Most of our actual sneaky deeds have been focused on the latest creature to slip out of the rift, flying right over the makeshift silver and iron barrier.

It's amazing the duck-like being could fly at all with its undersized wings, which are much less impressive than its extra leg or the fringe of fur sticking up from its feathered head like a mohawk. After its sudden entrance, it seems to have given up on the whole idea of flight.

Instead, it's been trundling around the nearby terrain on its three feet for a couple of hours. Rollick's assistants have blocked it from roaming too far while monitoring it with his devices, but the demon decided we should observe the creatures in a more "natural" habitat.

I spot the punk-duck waddling through a patch of coarse grass several feet beyond the trailers. Rollick left earlier this afternoon to take care of other business, but a couple of his shadowkind assistants hover nearby, one of them holding a metal wand that detects the creature's energies somehow. One of the shadowbloods is observing the scene too: Zian, the big guy with the pinkish-brown skin and smooth black crewcut.

As I step closer to the creature, it ruffles its feathers with a spastic twitch. A twang of sweet-and-sour emotion drifts off it. Like most of the other strange shadowkind who've come through the equally strange rift, it mostly feels mixed up and confused.

Is it echoing the push-pull vibe of the rift? It veers this way and that, its webbed feet smacking the ground, its neck swaying from side to side as if it's reaching out to us and trying to get away at the same time.

It can't have both. Is there some way I can explain that before it gets peeved?

I crouch down a short distance away and cluck my tongue at the creature like it's a cat I'm trying to coax over. It ignores me.

Maybe I should try quacking?

Well, I don't need it to come toward me anyway. I'm only supposed to be following the shifts in its emotions.

Another ripple runs through the flavors coursing off the punk-duck. Its whole body shudders with a flap of its stunted wings.

It shakes its head—and its neck contracts closer to its body.

A fourth leg juts from its belly. A lashing tail shoots from its torso.

A surge of harsher emotion smacks me like I've tried to bite into an unpeeled cactus fruit.

It's angry—it's scared—it's hostile—it's panicking—

There's so much discomfort in the whirl of urgent feelings that I wince. The poor thing. *Someone* has to help it.

The only someone who knows what it's going through is me.

My mind leaps to the soothing calm that filled me when I pictured the peaceful, cotton-candy-laced sky. Without thinking, I grasp on to that sensation and push it toward the creature.

The morphed beast was just charging at one of Rollick's assistants as if it thinks it can bowl over her ten-times-bigger form. I'll give it credit for ambition.

At my shove of emotion, it swings its head away abruptly.

With a hiss that sounds vaguely disconcerted, it retreats, its raised hackles coming down. The aggressive and anxious impulses keep churning inside it, but not quite as frantically as before.

My jaw goes slack. Did I do that?

I've never changed what anyone else was feeling using my own emotions before.

Zian prowls closer, frowning. "What just happened? It backed off all of a sudden."

As I straighten up, my legs wobble. "I think—I think I might have managed to cool down its temper. I pushed some calm at it... and it ate the feeling up."

Should I be surprised? If agony and joy can blaze out of me, why wouldn't I be able to project smaller emotions in moderation?

I just never tried before. With other beings, a smile and a conversation made more sense than lobbing feelings like snowballs, hoping they'll stick.

Zian's eyebrows have shot up. "Rollick will definitely want to know about that."

I'm sure he will. The other possibilities send a thrill through my limbs.

If I could offer this weird shadowkind creature peace...

could I maybe help the men I've found myself connected to as well? Moderate their emotions when they're struggling to control their powers?

If only I could find out without tapping into the connection they'd rather shut off.

I3

Jonah

A thread of warm emotion tugs at my chest. I find myself drifting along the trailers toward its pull automatically, even though I've resolved to put as much space as I can between me and the shadowkind woman who's now so woven into my awareness.

It's been a while since I felt contentment from Peri. There was that one period while we were still at the school when the sensations seeping through our connection turned so heady I had to step away from class and duck into a bathroom to compose myself. Just remembering it sends a renewed tingle of heat over my skin that I try to will away.

But simply happy? Satisfied and assured, without a pile of worry mixed in?

I'm not sure I've gotten that impression from her in the entire time her feelings have been leaking into the four of us through the strange marks on our chests.

I spot her crouched near the shadowkind creature that now looks vaguely badger-like, other than the feathers it hasn't lost in any of its morphs. She coos at it, and it sprawls out on the grass like a cat stretching before it takes a nap.

Another flicker of delight passes from her into me. She's been working with this beast all afternoon, watching over it when it shows signs of another shift. Its form has changed two more times, but something about the pulses of calm she says she's sending at it have soothed any bad temperedness.

It's not as if she can hover over every one of the creatures that tumble through the odd rifts, moderating their impulses for all time. She won't even be able to keep the shadowkind emerging from *this* rift under control if it moves away from the increased protections the shadowbloods and I laid down.

But it's progress. She's done more to eliminate the threat the warped creatures pose than anything anyone else has accomplished so far.

I stop beside the trailer Rollick's claimed as his main base of operations, watching her from a careful distance. Even observing her like this feels dangerous in a very different way.

Watching the fading sunlight gleam off her vibrant teal hair, the soft smile that curves her lips and the glimmer of compassion in her eyes, I want even more than usual to walk right over to her and pull her close. To hear every sound I know I could encourage from those lips, from laughter to eager gasps.

I want to be the one stirring the flares of passion and delight inside her that I assume Raze did just days ago.

The twinge of desire shoots through both my heart and my groin. My foot eases forward another step before I catch it and yank myself back.

I nearly collide with a slightly taller form looming behind me.

Rollick chuckles and rests his hand on my shoulder to

steady me. "What are you running away from, Jonah? There's nothing to be afraid of here."

His gaze settles on Peri, and a satisfied grin of his own crosses his face. "Not since our glowing wonder figured out yet another dimension to her powers. She stumbled into our path at just the right time, didn't she?"

My gut twists. "Yeah, I guess she did."

In a lot of ways. To solve a lot of problems. But not for me and maintaining the standards of professionalism I've spent years cultivating.

I was already having trouble getting her out of my head, and now I can never tune her out completely. I can't stop myself from reacting to what I sense from her.

Rollick's gaze slides to me. He studies me, a knowing gleam coming into his eyes. "There's nothing wrong with appreciating her."

My voice comes out terser than I like. "There are a lot of ways it would be totally unethical for me to 'appreciate' her while I'm one of her teachers."

"I suppose. Humans do like to create their complicated moral dilemmas." Rollick pauses. "You know—"

To my relief, he's cut off from pursuing this awkward subject by the peal of his ringtone. He pulls out his phone, frowns at the display, and ambles away from me, his voice dipping low. "Rollick here. What? Are you sure? Where exactly…"

His words fade out as he passes behind the trailer.

Apprehension settles over me. He didn't sound pleased. Has something else gone wrong? Has there been trouble at the academy or at a different rift?

Before I can drag myself away to distract myself from those questions, the demon reappears. His mouth is set in a flat line.

When he catches my gaze, he motions vaguely to the

east. "Another one of these questionable rifts has appeared—off in Mongolia. I think I'd better take a look in person and direct the initial efforts to contain it firsthand."

My pulse stutters. "Another one?"

Hell, how many of the things are going to pop up? It's becoming a game of whack-a-mole—except nothing about this feels like playing.

What are we going to do if there ends up being dozens of these rifts—each hurling out beings that have no sense of caution when it comes to mortals?

Rollick's expression tightens into a frown. "I don't like it. But at the moment, there's nothing we can do except continue to observe and experiment."

He brushes his hands together and waves to one of his shadowkind assistants. "Make sure the jet's fueled up. I'll be out there in ten minutes."

As the being nods and darts into the shadows, Rollick turns back to me. He considers me for long enough that my skin starts to itch.

"I probably should have done this sooner," he remarks. "You've put so much of yourself into helping the academy grow and thrive, and it's meant a lot to me—and I know to Quinn too. But neither of us, or Sorsha and her partners, would have wanted your dedication to shadowkind to hold you back from having an actual *life*. I don't think you can serve me or yourself best right now as a member of my staff."

A surge of cold lurches through my gut. "What are you saying?"

The demon claps me on the shoulder again. "Consider yourself relieved of duty, Jonah. You are no longer employed by the Quinn Moody Academy for the Shadowkind. I assume you'll continue helping here at the rift out of the goodness of your heart, but it'll be as a volunteer consultant with no special authority."

The chill spreads through my entire body. I have to struggle to stop my voice from shaking. "But—I don't *want* to stop teaching—I've done a lot of good—"

"Of course you have. Now I'm repaying you for that good. I think you'll thank me once you've seen how you can go forward."

Rollick tips his head toward Peri. "You no longer have any authority over *her*. You can't decide whether she earns a higher level or faces sanctions. So appreciate her however you like."

He strides off, leaving me feeling as if a sinkhole has opened under my feet and at any second I'll be swallowed up entirely.

He doesn't think the comment I made was a hint that I wanted him to fire me, did he?

Fuck, what are the other administrators going to think when they find out? That I tossed aside all the responsibilities I've taken on just to pursue a fling?

Even as that thought passes through my head, part of me rejects it. Whatever I feel about Peri, it goes a lot deeper than fling territory.

But that doesn't make any of this okay. I devoted so much of myself to my job. I thought I was helping at least some of the shadowkind students who came through my classes.

Apparently not enough. Not so much that Rollick needed more than a few minutes to toss all my efforts aside.

I'm so lost in turmoil that I don't notice Peri approaching until her feet are whispering through the grass just a few paces away. At the jerk of my head toward her, she stops, twisting her hands in front of her.

"Are you all right?" she asks hesitantly. "What happened with Rollick? You seem really upset."

And she knows that for a fact, because no doubt every

anguished emotion that's wrenching at me is echoing into her. Fucking hell.

I open my mouth and close it again, afraid of what I might say to her if I don't think it through—afraid of how much frustration might spill out that she doesn't deserve.

You could let her comfort you, a little voice murmurs in the back of my head. *That's why Rollick made this call—so you can pursue* her *without feeling guilty.*

The demon may be wise and worldly when it comes to a lot of subjects, but he's miscalculated for once. The fact that my conflicted attraction was obvious enough for him to kick me off his staff only doubles my load of guilt.

Despite my best efforts, my voice sounds hollow to my ears. "He demoted me. Dismissed me. I'm not part of the academy staff anymore."

Peri bristles with a rush of outrage so potent it reverberates into me on the inside as well. "What? You're one of the best teachers there."

She spins on her heel, peering across the landscape. An orangey-red glow wavers over her hair like firelight. "Where is he? I'll talk to him. He'll see how wrong he was."

Seeing her so vehement on my behalf sends a pang of affection through me, but it's stifled by my horror at the image of her chasing down the demon and giving him a piece of her mind in her own Peri way.

"He's already headed out to his plane," I say quickly. "Another rift showed up halfway around the world that he's going to take a look at. Maybe he'll have rethought the situation by the time he gets back."

From the way Rollick talked, I don't believe that at all, but at least the suggestion seems to simmer Peri down.

She lets out her breath in a huff and focuses on me with an expression that's more worried than angry. "No wonder you're upset. I'm sure you didn't do anything wrong. He must be distracted by the problem with the rifts—maybe he thinks you'll be able to pay more attention to dealing with them if you're not feeling responsible for the school too."

I'd find that possibility easier to believe if I was doing anything more constructive than peering at the rifts and scratching my head in bewilderment.

I manage a small smile. "Maybe. For now, all we can do is wait and see."

I'm not telling her the real explanation he gave. I don't know whether Peri would feel more guilty for the part she played in it or excited to realize that the main barrier between us has been dissolved—or which reaction I'd find worse.

One of the shadowkind assistants has drawn closer to the creature we've been monitoring. She motions to Peri urgently. "I think it's about to morph again!"

Peri shoots me an apologetic smile and hustles off to work her powers.

With a rumble that resonates through the air, Rollick's private jet lifts into the sky from the airfield a short drive from our camp. The plane pierces the blue sky and dwindles into the distance.

The shadowkind creature lurches, shudders, and sprouts a shaggy mane like a lion, with massive, clawed paws to match.

Raze ambles over to join me. Peri's impact on him has been nothing but good—his loosened movements show his new confidence in his self-control.

"Is there anything for us to do right now?" he asks.

I glance toward the wavering patch of air I can only make out when I focus intensely. "I'm not sure. I guess it depends on whether the protections continue to hold, and what the creature we're monitoring—"

Before my eyes, the rift ripples and vanishes. My words snag in my throat.

Raze flinches at the same moment. Clearly I'm not imagining things.

A growl rumbles out of him. "What—where did it go?"

Peri has scrambled up from where she was soothing the shadowkind creature. Three assistants jog over with identical expressions of bewilderment. Zian hollers to Riva, who emerges from the trailer they've been sharing.

As disconcerting as this development is, I find I'm not exactly upset. Finally, I've got a concrete problem I actually have some hope of solving.

I motion to the terrain around us. "The other rifts have moved before. We knew this one probably would at some point too. Anyone who can move quickly, spread out and search. Report back if you locate it. They haven't usually traveled far from their previous position."

The assistants dart into the shadows. Zian and Riva dash off while still in physical form, relying on their supernaturally enhanced speed.

I scan the horizon, even though I have no hope of spotting the rift when I could barely make it out right in front of me.

Peri shifts her weight from one foot to the other. "Should I go too?" She glances down at the creature she was soothing.

Raze makes a dismissive grunt and steps toward her with his usual protective stance. "There are lots of beings already looking. Someone should stay and monitor the situation here too."

Hail materializes nearby, his face already set in a scowl. "What's the sudden fuss out—" His gaze jars to a halt where the rift used to be. "Oh. We're chasing the damn thing now."

"Catch it if we can!" Mirage declares, emerging after the winter fae with a short laugh. He hops into a handstand as if he thinks he might be able to spot the rift better upside down.

I glance at the trailers, narrowing my mind to the practicalities with my renewed sense of purpose. We're going to need to move these to the new location. We only have a couple of vehicles to haul them, so it'll take a few trips. And then…

Before I can finish working out the logistics, one of Rollick's assistants pops back into view. She speaks breathlessly. "It's jumped almost a whole mile. All the way over by the edge of the city."

My spine stiffens. "It's that close?"

She nods, her mouth twisting unhappily. "Right next to one of the factories just outside the city limits. There'll be all kinds of people passing by."

Fuck. Any satisfaction I'd gathered disintegrates.

We can't put the trailers right next to any buildings in human use, at least not close enough to easily monitor the rift.

How are we going to contain this unnerving portal when it's right on top of the people we're trying to protect?

14

Periwinkle

As Jonah drives toward the outskirts of the city, I squirm impatiently on my seat in the back of the van.

We shadowkind can examine the rift in its new location from the shadows without the human employees at the nearby factories noticing, but our vehicles and our mortal companions can't lurk the same way. What if one of those strange shadowkind creatures emerges while the workers are, well, working?

What if it's in a fighting mood?

Will we be able to drag it into the shadows with us before the mortals realize something odd is going on? Before it hurts any of them?

Raze materializes next to me so he can take my hand. The firm squeeze of his fingers settles my nerves a little.

"If any beings come through while people are around,

you can try using that new aspect of your powers," he suggests. "Why wouldn't it affect the creatures even from the shadows? It's not like emotions are at all corporeal."

"Thank fuck for that," Hail mutters from the opposite bench where he's sitting stiffly, but I can tell from the currents of emotion coursing into me that he's more uneasy than annoyed.

The rift's relocation has thrown us all for a loop. Why did Rollick have to leave right now?

Of course, the new rift that popped up is probably more urgent than this one that simply took a hike. Even before the protections were in place, only a few creatures emerged in the course of a day. We shouldn't need to worry about a deluge.

Jonah pulls the van into a parking lot outside a long, squat building that's down the road from the factories along the edges of the city. Half the letters have fallen off this business's dented sign like gaps in a mouthful of teeth. The rusted doorframe and grimy windows suggest no one's been doing any business in there for quite a while, unless they're selling dust bunnies.

As Jonah parks, the rest of us spill out into the shadows beneath the van. Mirage weaves through the darkness near me, as do Rollick's assistants who joined us.

The shadowbloods who were helping out haven't learned how to merge with the shadows the way we can—Zian told us that it's possible that they simply can't. I guess that's one downside of being a shadowkind-human smoothie.

He and Riva stayed at our old base of operations to send a message to Rollick and prepare the warding supplies. They might be able to leave some silver and iron around the rift after the factory closes for the night.

Any metal items we plant will have to blend into the environment so the mortals don't notice and move them.

Whether we can protect the area at all depends on exactly where the portal has reformed.

The unsettlingly dithery energy of the rift wavers through my being. It's still faint, but it push-pulls me from a definite direction.

One of Rollick's assistants takes charge, her voice warbled but understandable in our shadowy state. "We all go together. Stay close, avoid the mortals."

We slink across the open ground, leaping between the splotches of darkness in the cracks in the concrete, beneath the leaves of a weed, along the edge of a chain-link fence. The tremor of dissonant energy gets stronger.

We come up on a thicker fence made of wooden posts with swaths of rippled metal in between. It's easy enough to slip beneath it, but then I pause.

Several humans are walking across the cement yard on the other side. A couple are gabbing on their phones, one is getting into a truck, and a few others are shoving boxes into the back of that truck and another beside it.

The rift looms over all of them, hovering a few feet above the ground some ten feet away from us along the fence. It only distorts the air slightly, so vague none of the mortals appear to have noticed, but I can see that it stretches up three times the height of the fence.

I think it's gotten bigger with the move. All the better to toss creatures out at us?

Would it be too much to hope that the beasts stay small even if the portal didn't?

The assistant who directed us heads toward the rift first. We circle around it, checking the ground nearby.

The terrain is all plain concrete and asphalt, a few small cracks here and there but nothing we could drop more than some tiny silver and iron beads into. That won't ward off more than a shadowkind flea.

One of the other assistants speaks up in a doubtful voice. "There's a strip of bare earth on the far side of the fence. We could bury some metals there."

I tip my ephemeral head. "They'll only help if we can stop the creatures from wandering in every other direction instead. Could we surround the entire fence?"

Raze speaks up gruffly. "Then we'd be shutting the beasts in with the mortals. It might be better to let them roam and then collect them after they've moved farther away."

Mirage darts past me with a shimmer of his upbeat energy. "The mixed-up beings are usually in a good mood when they first come through. We have a little time."

Anywhere from hours to days, true. We just have to make sure the warped shadowkind move away from the city rather than deeper into it, and that they don't appear too blatantly in front of the humans working here before that.

Our problems have expanded even more than the rift has.

Whatever the problem, we can figure it out. I lift my spirits through sheer force of will. "Maybe if we—"

One of the assistants flinches with a jolt of nervous shock that smacks me like a splash of lime juice. "What's happening to it?"

The words have barely left her mouth when I see what she means. The rift is moving again—right now, before our eyes.

A wave of darkness courses out of the portal like it's vomiting up a surge of shadow. Chunks of the spew flicker with a thicker blackness. A flurry of chaotic sensations rushes over me.

As I shudder, wondering if this might be the first time in my existence I entirely lose my appetite, the wave of shadow puke ripples through the yard.

The first human to see it yelps and scrambles away. The

others turn to look and back up, swearing under their breaths.

Their fear smacks into me like the chilliest of unsweetened iced tea. Another shudder runs through my essence. "What do we do? How do we stop it?"

Raze lets out a growl. "I don't know."

Another assistant sputters. "We have to— Maybe the shadowbloods will know—"

He flits away from us toward Jonah's van, I guess to reach out to our base camp for backup.

Which I suspect we're going to need. The rift is still heaving out more condensed shadow, retching it all across the factory's yard. The flood surges forward faster.

One of the workers isn't able to dodge it fast enough. He yelps as the mass of darkness sweeps over him.

Through the warped shadows, his form twitches and flails. Pain lances from him through me.

A cry breaks from my throat. "It's hurting them! We have to help him—help all of them."

Hail's voice sounds strained. "We don't know what'll happen to *us* if we touch that stuff."

I leap forward. "I don't care. We're supposed to protect them from the rift. We can't stand here while it suffocates them. I'm getting them out!"

Whatever's happening in the shadows, it's definitely not a carnival for the mortals. The man who got trapped in the wave seems to have deflated, his movements sluggish, but I know he's alive. Discomfort still wafts off his form.

I plunge into the spewed shadow after him. The darkness prickles at my essence in a way I've never felt before, as if it's nipping at the edges of my being, digging in and jerking out. I gird myself against the disturbing sensation and hurtle on toward the trapped man.

As I reach him, I focus on my physical form just enough

to turn me slightly corporeal. My presence takes on enough heft to shove the man through the shadow vomit.

He stumbles and staggers. I ram into him again, as carefully as I can while still using enough force to move him.

My three shadowkind men dive in to join me.

"Keep pushing!" Raze hollers through the shadows. He propels the man toward the edge of the flood with a heave of his own.

"Sink or swim!" Mirage crows, his voice garbled, and appears to heft the man up and onward as if giving him a brief piggyback ride.

I make out Hail grumbling indistinctly, but he throws himself into the rescue effort too. The smack of his shoulder sends the man finally tumbling out the side of the growing torrent.

It's still expanding. I leap out of the unnerving darkness, solidifying into physical form at the same time so I can grasp the man's arm. "Come on! We have to get as far away from it as possible."

The man gapes at me, probably wondering where the heck some turquoise-haired chick in a sundress came from and why I'm jumping to his rescue, but he keeps his wits enough to listen. As I yank at his elbow, he scrambles with me across the yard toward the factory building.

Footsteps thump against the pavement as my shadowkind men materialize around us. Yells reverberate from the other side of the building. My head snaps around to see a couple of Rollick's assistants herding other workers farther away from the spilled shadow.

It's still coming, surging forward like an endless gush of filmy toxic sludge. Before my eyes, the dark current collides with the back of the factory.

My breath stops in my throat. As far as I can tell, the

strange shadows slide straight through the brick wall as if it's not there.

But the bricks feel it. The mortar between them starts to crumble away. Little pock marks form in their surface like dimples—but not the cute kind.

"What the fuck is going on?" Hail says, staring alongside me.

The man we've been guiding sways on his feet and crumples over in a faint.

I don't know if he blacked out because of the effects of the shadows or simply from shock. My pulse stutters. "We can't leave him here."

Raze is already springing forward to scoop the limp man into his muscular arms. He jerks his chin at us to motion us to keep running with him.

We skirt the building and dash out onto the street beyond just as the spreading spew of shadow churns straight through and across the road.

Cars honk and swerve. Gasps and shrieks reverberate from the other industrial buildings around us.

One SUV skids straight into the current and whirls around as if the tires have hit ice. I get a glimpse of the driver's blanched face through the windshield.

As I whip around to help her, a familiar white van careens into view on the other side of the flood.

Rollick's assistant made it to Jonah quickly. Our sorcerer brings the vehicle to a screeching halt. The doors have flown open before it's even finished moving.

The two shadowbloods jump out and charge into the dark flood. I spot Zian wrenching open the SUV's door so Riva can drag the woman out.

More shouts and tire screeches carry from beyond the next building. How far is the rift's shadowy vomit going to spread?

"Let's go pick up the pieces we can," Mirage calls to us, and bounds toward the nearest side street.

Raze sets the unconscious man down a few buildings away from the current, and we all dash after the fox shifter. Mirage's ears flash amid his red hair, but he manages to tuck them away as quickly as they emerged.

As we sprint around the hulking buildings, other sorts of unnerving noises reach my ears. There's a metallic crashing sound, over and over as if someone is repeatedly driving their car into a wall. Then a hollow groan that sounds like something mechanical being torn in two.

Are the shadows from the rift throwing a temper tantrum now? How much worse is it going to get?

My feet and ankles sting with the pounding of my shoes against the ground. The pain must be echoing into my marked men, because Raze glances back at me with a concerned expression that seems to make Hail's jaw clench.

"I'm fine!" I gasp out past the dryness in my mouth.

We hurtle out onto the next road over—and discover that the flood hasn't made it this far after all.

It appears the wave of shadow brought at least a few shadowkind with it. A couple of creatures are weaving between the parked cars, lunging at any mortals who venture out of the nearby buildings. One that looks like a leopard with quills poking from its spots snarls and gnashes its teeth at the figures behind a first-floor window.

And in the middle of the street, jumping up and down on the roof of a truck that's had its door ripped off, is a higher shadowkind who looks almost human.

Her corporeal form is a tall, gangly woman with a sharp jaw and sharper elbows. Her roughly chopped hair rustles with each hop.

She must have more strength than her normal human-like size would suggest, because her weight is denting the roof farther down with every jump, provoking that awful crashing sound. Or maybe that's the effect of some supernatural power, I realize at a flash of cracking energy beneath her feet.

Out the back of her baggy jeans, a ridged crocodile-like tail lashes back and forth in time with her hopping, as if she's using a very thick skipping rope.

She doesn't seem to care that the mortals might see her monstrous feature or her powers. Maybe she's the kind of troublemaker Rollick would have ordered to the academy if he found out about her. With no one around to ground her, she's taking advantage of the sudden chaos.

Then, as I watch, the edges of her body quiver.

All at once, her hair shoots out twice as long, halfway down her back. Her pointed chin widens into a square-ish shape. Her eyes sink deeper, and her ribcage juts broader.

My heart stops.

She isn't an ordinary shadowkind being, higher or not. She's morphing like all the weird lesser creatures who've tumbled out of the strange rifts.

15

Periwinkle

"What the fuck," Hail mutters, which I'm guessing means he noticed the shadowkind woman's sudden makeover too.

A chill ripples over my skin. "She must have come through the rift. Maybe there were a bunch of beings in the flood."

The crocodile-tailed woman leaps from the smashed truck to the roof of a car parked nearby. She slams her fist into the windshield with a flicker of supernatural energy and then yanks at the driver's-side door.

It tears off its hinges with a squeal like a dying animal.

Yikes. "She's strong."

Mirage has frozen next to me, his ruddy hair even more rumpled than usual. "And cruel."

The woman hurls the car door as if to punctuate his

124

point. It slams into a nearby store window, smashing through the glass.

I extend my senses toward the higher being, but the only emotion I pick up from her is a dull sense of satisfaction, like a thin layer of peanut butter. She's pleased with the havoc she's wreaking. I can't taste any anger or fear that could tell me why she's treating the street like a buffet of destruction.

"What should we do about her?" I murmur, a little nervous that she'll hear us and aim her aggression our way.

It's hard to imagine I could defend myself against a being that powerful. I'm not sure a full blast of the emotional energy I can gather would make her even wince.

Rollick wanted me out by the rift because he thought I could help… but he didn't expect that problem to start stomping around and flinging doors. I don't see how I'm equipped to handle this.

But we can't let her keep bashing up people's belongings in full view of who knows how many mortals, can we?

Raze flexes his shoulders. "I'll subdue her. We'll capture her and wait until Rollick can come decide how to deal with her."

He strides forward, merging into the shadows as he does. I watch him vanish with a hitch of my heart.

Is even Raze strong enough to overcome this being? The basilisk shifter has plenty of power of his own, but from what he's said, his searing eyes and poison skin harm mortals much more than they do fellow shadowkind.

Against the lesser creatures we've encountered, he's mostly relied on brute force. This woman is showing off her own like she's competing in a demolition talent show.

I drag in a breath, focusing on the churning emotions inside me. Trying to compress them into a blast I could aim at the woman if she lashes out at Raze.

I don't want to really hurt her anyway, just make sure she doesn't hurt *him*.

My anxiety jitters through my concentration. How could any power in my pudgy body be enough to shake her?

How can I make sure I only hit her and not Raze if they're fighting?

I'm not ready to take on a city-wide catastrophe in the form of a higher shadowkind.

Mirage shifts his weight next to me with a tremor of his own uneasiness. More discomfort pulses off Hail in tandem with my own.

"I could try to encase her in ice—just enough to stop her from moving, not to kill her." Uncertainty winds through the winter fae's voice.

I don't think he's convinced he has enough power to restrain her either.

"Maybe…" Mirage lifts one hand, and an illusion wavers along the street.

He's obviously been inspired by the woman's reptilian tail. Bullrushes and reeds appear to sprout up from the sidewalks and storefronts. The road transforms into a flowing stream.

The imagery expands toward the car the woman is jumping on—

But before she even notices it, Raze leaps out of the shadows straight at her.

His sinewy body collides with her only slightly smaller frame. They crash onto the road.

I flinch, and Mirage's growing illusion fractures apart.

The fox shifter cringes with a trickle of curdled-milk shame. "Not really needed, no harm done," he says in his singsong voice as if to cover up the fumble.

Raze and the woman tumble over each other on the

asphalt. In the first few seconds, I think the basilisk shifter might pin her down and end the fight just like that.

Then her tail whips out and batters his head with its jutting scales. A cry quavers up my throat.

Raze loses his grip. He scrambles to catch the woman's limbs, but she's already wrenched both of her legs up. She shoves him away with a kick hard enough to send him soaring into the crushed truck.

And basilisks aren't meant to fly.

A louder yelp bursts from my lips. Pain jolts from Raze into me, sending my panic spiraling sharper.

The woman cackles hoarsely and bounds down the street. She rams her fist into every window she passes, shattering them so glass rains down on the street in her wake. It crunches under her feet like the sharpest of snow.

For the first few seconds, my legs stay locked in place. Then Raze groans as he pushes himself off the truck, and my concern for him overwhelms my terror.

I sprint down the road to join him, the other men following behind me. The being who attacked him is just hurtling around a bend in the road up ahead. Another metallic screech follows moments later.

I tune out her concerto of destruction as well as I can and grasp Raze's arm. "Are you okay? How much did she hurt you?"

Before I've even finished speaking, I spot the smoky essence wafting from a few gouges in his back.

Raze shakes himself, emanating a mix of consternation and pain. "It's not that bad. We can't let her keep going. She's bashing up the whole city."

She is, out in the open for anyone to see. She's that confident no one will stop her.

I have no idea what the mortals watching from their high windows over the road must think is going on. Are they really going to convince themselves that a regular human put on a fake crocodile tail to rampage through their streets?

As Raze spins toward the new series of smashing sounds, Riva and Zian dash into view.

Riva is already talking. "The rift sucked all those weird shadows back in, so that's okay for—"

She halts to stare at the broken cars and shattered windows. As she catches her breath, she sets her hands on her hips. "What the hell happened here? It looks like a herd of pissed-off elephants stampeded through."

I point toward the road ahead. "There's a higher shadowkind who must have come through the rift—she's warping like the lesser creatures we've seen. And she doesn't seem to care about much except wrecking everything she can. She… she's part crocodile, not part elephant."

"Not much better." The shadowblood woman lets out a huff and glances at Zian. "Come on. We might need you in wolfman form for this."

The big man grimaces, but then he rubs his hands together.

With a tensing of his form, his muscular body expands even bigger. More dark hair sprouts from his pinkish-brown skin—down his neck and across his shoulders under the collar of his stretching T-shirt. His nose and jaw protrude into a canine muzzle.

I knew the shadowbloods had their own supernatural abilities, but I haven't seen them reveal anything so visibly inhuman before. Maybe a wolf-man will be enough to tackle a crocodile-woman.

A little relief trickles through me at the sight of them marching toward her, but it doesn't wash away all my fear.

I motion to my marked men. "We should go with them, see if there's any way we can help."

Even if the possibility of pitching in feels increasingly absurd, at least for me.

We all set off, Raze pushing into the lead. When I look at him, I can't help flashing back to the moment the being flung him into the truck.

My heart skips a beat, and Raze's muscles twitch. The determination I sensed from him dwindles with a tang of his own nerves. "Maybe we'll only get in the way. We shouldn't press too close while the shadowbloods are dealing with her."

Why is he saying that now? A moment ago, he seemed totally prepared to go at the hostile shadowkind alongside Riva and Zian.

Until I turned chicken about it.

My stomach sinks more than it already had, which means it's about to hit my heels.

Of course. Our emotions are all intertwined through the bond I forced on these men.

When I get nervous or outright afraid, the feelings seep into my companions as well. It might even be my fault that Mirage's illusion faltered, that Hail didn't believe he could work his icy powers effectively.

I've spent my whole existence tasting the difference between the emotions that hit me from the outside and the ones that form within me. My teammates aren't used to making the separation.

The turmoil inside them must be even more muddled than what I experience.

None of us will get anything done if I let my nerves and doubts get the better of me… and so overwhelm all of my marked men as well.

Recognizing my latest mistake doesn't erase my doubts. If anything, the realization makes me want to shrink into one of the cracks in the road where I can't screw up anything else.

No. I need my men to feel better, not worse.

Even if I'm worried that *I* can't contribute to solving this disaster, I believe that *they* can.

Maybe the only way I *can* contribute is by making sure they believe in themselves too.

I raise my chin, summoning every scrap of confidence in me. Let's just pretend it's real.

"This is a difficult opponent, but we've defeated dangerous villains in the past!" I declare. "She's a shadowkind like us—she's probably confused after coming through the rift. She might think the mortals are the enemy. We need to restrain her so we can talk things through and make sure no one else gets hurt."

A slight smile returns to Mirage's lips. "Reason with her until she's reasonable."

Raze lets out a grunt, but there's a hint of amusement to the sound now. "After we shut her away from all these things she wants to demolish."

My spirits lift for the time it takes us to hustle around the corner. At the sight of the battle waging on the street before us, I stall in my tracks.

Riva and Zian are racing to and fro at incredible speeds, their shoes squeaking on the asphalt. At times, they pick up such speed their limbs blur.

But no matter how they close in on the shadowkind woman with her scaly tail, she manages to dodge. As I watch, she dives into the shadows, emerges beyond their reach with a ragged laugh and a smash of an innocent postal box, then slips away again as they lunge at her.

The shadowbloods can't follow her into the patches of darkness.

Riva's face has tightened with frustration. Zian's lips draw back from his wolfish fangs in a silent snarl.

Hail narrows his eyes. "She's toying with them. Mocking them."

The being reappears to slash claws she's shot from her fingertips through a van's tire. A lance of burnt-caramel defiance pierces my chest.

I shiver. "She doesn't want to let anyone tell her what she can do or where she should go."

Raze's expression turns hesitant. "I could try to ambush her in the shadows where they can't…"

Crap. My wobbly emotions are setting him off-balance again.

But what if he rushes in there and she hurts him much worse than the first time?

I'm about as much use here as a fork in a bowl of broth. I could retreat like I wanted to before, let Rollick see that I can't fix this problem after all, have him send us back to the academy where the men would probably rather be.

The longing to give up sweeps through me—and Raze takes a step back as if I've compelled him.

My heart squeezes with a spurt of my own defiance. A being that fierce shouldn't be forced to crumple.

We've kicked butt together before, and we can again.

I don't think any of us really wants to disappoint Rollick or see what destruction this warped woman will cause if we don't step in.

I need to bring more happiness to the world, and right now I have the chance to stop a whole lot of unhappiness. It's basically the same thing.

Spinning toward Raze, I grasp his hand with a quick squeeze. "Go do what you can. You could help tire her out. She can't keep moving like that forever, right?"

His stance straightens. "Exactly."

With a flash of a smile, he springs into the shadows.

I can't leave it all to him. If we're fighting together, I need to hold up my end.

So I'll tackle this being with the one skill that's never failed me.

I train all my attention on my awareness of her presence in the shadows, tracking her as she pops in and out along the street. Taking in every splash of flavor that leaps from her to me.

She's determined and rebellious, yes. She enjoys the sensation of breaking all these objects around her. A shot of lemonade-sweet exhilaration rushes through her when she evades the shadowbloods yet again.

Then she materializes next to a lamppost halfway down the street. As she slams her fist into its side hard enough to crack the cement and send the pole teetering over, a brisk gust of wind sweeps across the road.

It blows through her hair and the baggy clothes she's wearing—and she goes rigid for an instant with a smack of icy terror.

It's the first hint of weakness I've sensed from her. Urgency grips me.

"She's afraid of the wind!" I shout out. Maybe that's not surprising—it's an invisible but potent force that doesn't exist in the shadow realm, not like the mortal version anyway. "Can we trap her with that?"

Hail's eyes light up. He steps forward, extending his arms. "I'll take care of it."

As a frigid breeze laced with snowflakes whirls from his hands, Mirage perks up too. "We can make it a real blast!"

A warbling roar fills the street, amplifying the natural whoosh of Hail's wind. The fox shifter must be creating an illusionary impression of fast-moving air to enhance Hail's efforts.

Riva aims a thumbs up our way. The errant shadowkind ducks into the shadows again, but she squirms into view just seconds later with a hiss that makes me think Raze must have pounced on her.

Hail's wind blasts her from all sides and swirls around her. A sharper shriek bursts from her lips.

Riva and Zian dash in. Riva produces a chain of silver and iron from the bag slung across her back.

Just as she moves to throw it around the rogue shadowkind, the crocodile-tailed woman hurls herself through the whirlwind and into the shadows.

Riva and Zian pivot, searching for our target. Hail keeps his wind coursing through the streets, ready for her to reappear.

She doesn't. After a minute, Raze materializes at the far end of the block.

He sighs. "She ran off—too fast for me to keep up."

Riva shakes herself as if dispelling the tension of the battle. "Fine. At least we stopped her from trashing this street. Now we patrol and see if she shows herself again."

16

Mirage

Rollick sprawls in his seat in his private jet, but he's only giving an illusion of relaxation. His fingers flex against the leather arm. There's a tightness to his shoulders like he's on the verge of jumping out of his skin.

I know that feeling. It comes over me often enough.

Right now, after everything we've seen, part of me wants to burrow way down in the dirt away from all of it.

Of course, that's impossible while I'm tied to Peri by the glowing spot on my chest. And also when we're thousands of feet in the air.

The man who's awfully kind for a demon rubs one hand across his brow. "So there haven't been any further incidents since the initial flood? No more shadowy material spilling out of the rift and no more destruction from any of the beings who might have spewed out with it?"

Jonah shakes his head. "We think the higher being who

was causing the most obvious destruction is lying low after we got close to capturing her. Or maybe she's left the city for someplace that feels less overwhelming."

"Or maybe she went back into the rift and will stay there," Raze mutters without much hope in his tone.

Peri pipes up, her voice as bright as ever even though her expression looks serious. "Now that it's sucked everything back in, the rift feels the same as it did before—unnerving but not more than usual."

I nod, remembering the chaotic vibrations the portal gave off right before we left it. "All wibbly-wobbly but not spewy-stewy."

What *was* the mess that flooded the streets around the rift for a short time? Nothing about it felt like the shadow realm I've dipped back into now and then, where it theoretically came from.

I like surprises and curiosities, but not the kind that try to drown people and crumble buildings.

Rollick sighs. "The shadowbloods will keep monitoring the situation, and Sorsha should be on the scene soon. She's just wrapping up another matter she was called away to."

Peri hesitates. "Are you taking us off duty? We did our best."

The worried note in her voice tugs at my heart. My teeth itch to sprout into a full set of foxy fangs, as if there's anything here I can defend her from.

Rollick is already waving off her concern. "No, no. You handled the situation as well as could be expected. The way you read that being's emotions to figure out her weakness was a particularly impressive move. Your talent should also come in handy for quelling continuing fears among the humans who witnessed the strange events and can't quite ignore them."

I cock my head. "*Should* they ignore them? If that being

comes back, she might bash them up as much as their cars and windows."

Rollick's mouth twists. "I know it's in your nature to want to 'play' with humans, but they're the biggest threat to our existence in this world. Every type of shadowkind they've encountered, they've turned into a new monster to build a mythology around. If more of them realized those 'monsters' and dozens more kinds are real…"

"How can you be sure it'd be so bad when we haven't had a chance to find out?" Peri asks.

The demon arches his eyebrows. "Just in the past few decades, we've had to contend with an organization that experimented on shadowkind with the intent of wiping us out, another that created the shadowbloods and then tried to use them to expose and destroy us, cabals of sorcerers slaughtering beings to enhance their powers and enslaving masses of others… Even if some are accepting, it doesn't take many mortals to create a potential disaster."

His words have set off a prickling chill that claws into my chest. Experiments on shadowkind—does he mean the same ones who caged me?

I don't ask. I don't want to stir up the memories even more.

No one knows except Peri, whose gaze I refuse to meet.

Rollick pauses and then shakes his head with an air of bemusement. "When humans and shadowkind collide, it almost always ends in catastrophe, going back as far as the devastation of the wingéd wars. But there's been even more disruption between our realms than usual recently. So much they'll be ready to blame us for, so many people on the verge of realizing. I'd hate to see what happens if we tip the balance too far to swing it back."

Peri's bright blue eyes have widened. "Shouldn't we all be in the city doing damage control, then?"

The demon offers her a wry smile. "Some of your companions' temperaments aren't ideally suited for comforting rather than clashing. And I have something else I thought we should apply your talent to that might prove even more urgent."

All of Rollick's words have been ominous as rumbling thunder, but that last remark hooks me with a tug of curiosity. "What's that? Did the other new rift do something extra strange?"

From the sounds of things, this surprise wasn't a good one either.

Rollick chuckles, but without the humor the sound deserves. "That rift looks the same as all the others to me. I'm not taking you that far. I got a report from my assistants who are studying the warped beings at my estate. There's been an... unusual development there. I suppose it could bode well for our current problems, but I find it unsettling all the same."

Jonah frowns. "What kind of development?"

"It'll be easier for you to see for yourselves." Rollick's gaze returns to Peri. "But I'll be especially interested in hearing what feelings you pick up from the creatures now."

And the rest of us are crammed into this narrow hunk of flying metal because getting too far apart from her would tear all five of us apart—worse than if we were tossed through the turbines.

I suppress the urge to squirm.

There's no one around but my fellow shadowkind. I should be able to switch into fox form—why should any of them care?

Except that Rollick is the head of the school that's taught us to hold human form whenever possible.

I don't want him changing his mind about my ability to

control my impulses and send me back to even the dreary, not-horribly-surprising part of the shadow realm.

Is that what would happen anyway if the humans took up a mass hunt? A deeper shudder runs through me. Let's get back to the city quick and prove how very okay everything is —even if it isn't.

Thankfully, it's a short flight to Rollick's estate. We land before I've literally crawled out of my skin, and the airfield is close enough that we can simply flit through the shadows to reach the house, with Jonah following on his mortal legs.

As we weave through the expansive home to the stairs that lead to the basement, my skin starts creeping with a different sort of restlessness. Despite my best efforts, flickers of images pass through my head—metal walls, searing lights, harsh voices alongside the prick and jab of blades and needles.

The room down below isn't like the lab where the humans who captured me poked and prodded me and all those other shadowkind, I remind myself. Rollick is one of us. He's trying to stop these beings from getting into trouble, not looking to torment them.

But his mention of the humans who did revel in torment is still pinging around my head. My nerves stay on edge all the way down into the white-walled research room.

One of Rollick's assistants is waiting there, tapping on a computer keyboard. At our entrance, she stiffens. "Sir, the subject that was farthest advanced… is gone."

Rollick grimaces. "I'm sorry to hear that. Let's see the one that's next worst off."

Gone? Does she mean *dead*?

What could be killing shadowkind down here? Rollick wouldn't let anyone hurt the creatures.

The woman goes to the stack of cages and opens one near

the top. She coaxes out a creature that currently looks like a huge dragonfly with feathered wings.

In the first moment as it glides down the floor, I have no idea what Rollick could have meant about it being "worst off." Then, as it lands, the impact sets its wings fluttering—and tendrils of smoky essence drift off them. A couple of feathers outright disintegrate into the air.

Peri gasps. "What's wrong with it? It doesn't look injured. It doesn't *feel* injured."

"That's what I'm trying to determine," Rollick says. "The creatures that came out of those odd rifts the longest ago… Their bodies appear to be breaking down. Maybe it's the overall instability from all the morphing they're doing, and they simply can't hold their essence together after too many transformations. We've attempted various approaches that work on actual wounds, and nothing—"

The words burst from my throat before I know I'm going to say them. "You have to let them go!"

Everyone's head swivels toward me. Hail's lip curls disdainfully. "What are you going on about now, fur-brain?"

As if he wasn't grumbling about the cages when he first heard about them. He just likes to sneer at whatever he can.

I can't stop a tremor from rippling through my limbs. My fox ears flick in and out of being through my hair. "Let the creatures go back to the rift. Back to the shadow realm. They can't die there. They shouldn't be *here*."

They shouldn't be trapped in cages while they fall apart. They shouldn't dissolve into nothing surrounded by an alien world of iron and light.

Rollick steps toward me with his hands held up in appeal. "We've tried sending them back. They don't want to go. Any way we send them, they come right back. Not even supernatural compulsion will stick."

No. It isn't right.

I shake my head, and my whole body moves with it. "Maybe now that they're breaking—maybe they'll go now. You have to try!"

"It isn't that easy to transport these beings to the nearest rift. By the time we get them there, it could already be too late for some. I'm trying to save them right here."

My ears protrude again to lie flat back on my skull. "What if you can't find a way to make them better? Will you let them go then? Leaving them trapped here for the last small bit of their lives—it's horrible."

How many beings did I consign to that horrific fate because of the experimenters' tricks and traps? I never wanted to be part of that kind of awfulness again.

I want to make everyone jump and laugh, maybe scare them a little but only enough so they enjoy the relief afterward. These strange beings have been nothing but confused since they came through their weird rifts.

And with all my foxy powers, there's nothing I can do to solve that problem.

Rollick meets my gaze solemnly. "I don't want them to live out their last few hours in misery either, my friend. We'll do what we can for them, and if it doesn't seem there's anything *to* be done, we can let them roam at least a little."

Raze's voice comes out raw in its gruffness. "We'd still need to make sure they don't hurt anyone before they go."

What about the creatures? They don't deserve to be hurt either.

I shake again as if I can dispel the collision of twisted thoughts and memories inside me. They squeeze tight as silver chains around my body.

Rollick isn't budging. Maybe there really isn't anything more he could offer.

Maybe this really is the best *he* can do.

With a growl of frustration, I spin and sprint back up the stairs.

By the time I reach the ground floor, I'm scampering across the hardwood in full fox form. My claws scrabble against the polished surface.

I skid toward the nearest door, blink into the shadows to dip through the sliver of darkness beneath it, and burst out into the patio around the small pool.

I stop there for a moment, panting, braced for Rollick to come charging after me.

But that's not his way. He isn't a tyrant like the humans who captured me. He'll give me my space.

What am I supposed to do with it?

Groaning, I flop onto one of the lounge chairs and stretch into humanesque form.

The shade of a nearby umbrella drapes over me, diluting the sun's piercing rays. I close my eyes and press the side of my face against the plasticky fabric of the cushion.

All those weeks confined in the brilliance. Walls everywhere I looked. Suffocating…

"Mirage?"

I should have felt Peri coming, but I was too lost in my inner turmoil. Her tentative voice makes me flinch—and provokes a pang of guilt that shoots from her into me and then resonates with my regret at prompting it.

I push upright to face her. She's standing on the pool deck a few feet away, alone.

A grin pushes up the corners of my lips automatically. "Shouldn't you still be downstairs? Head-shrinking the shadow creatures?"

My softly beautiful woman lets out a faint snort. "I'm not doing therapy on them like on TV. It's just sometimes easier to tell how to help someone if you can pick up on what exactly they're feeling."

Has she figured out how to help me?

I swallow that question behind my smile and swish one of my fox tails behind me. "You can go help the weird ones then."

Never mind how many beings would say I'm pretty weird too.

Peri comes over and sits on the end of the lounge chair—beside me but leaving half a foot between us so we're not touching. The compassionate warmth that emanates from her body turns the tug I often feel when she's around into a yank.

It takes all my self-control not to scoot over right next to her and lift her into my lap. I'd love to bury my face in her vivid hair and drink in her sweet smell...

Those memories burn straight to my groin. I adjust my position before she can tell that I've gone half-hard.

How does she have an even stronger effect on me now than she did before? Something about this connection stokes the attraction I already felt into a hotter flame.

Why does it have to come with so many chains too?

"I did taste their emotions," Peri says. "It doesn't seem as if the disintegrating effect is causing them any pain. They're disoriented and frustrated, but they've been that way since they tumbled out of the rifts. I... I couldn't sense anything that gave an answer about why it's happening or how to stop it."

Her head droops, but then she looks at me with unusual firmness. "So it's not your fault that you don't know how to help them either. We're all doing everything we can. That's what matters, right?"

I can't tell her it doesn't and make her feel she's to blame. But I don't want to lie to her either.

She'll probably be able to tell if I do.

"It's not *their* fault," I point out. "I don't like seeing them having to live this way."

Or not live, as the case seems to be.

Peri's hand twitches toward mine as if she's considered taking it but then stopped herself. She can tell I'm still on edge.

On the edge of what, I couldn't say anymore. I don't know what I'd do if she touched me now.

"I don't like it either," she says. "Rollick is going to let them wander near the house a bit and see what happens. Maybe getting more freedom will heal them up!"

My smile relaxes at the optimism in her voice. Peri is always hoping for the best, for all of us.

That's why she's here with me now.

A swell of affection sweeps through me so forcefully I'm leaning toward her before I realize it. With a hitch of breath, I spring to my feet instead.

"Mirage?" Peri says, blinking.

"I'll be okay," I tell her. "I just… I feel like I need to keep moving. It'll be good to see the creatures get a little freedom. Thank you for coming to talk to me."

Then I bound toward the front of the house before the glow she's attached to me can drag me any further into its bright but inescapable cage.

17

Periwinkle

I've always had mixed feelings about cities.

Oh, I love the currents of human emotions ebbing and flowing all around me. I love the energy that thrums through the air, connecting people and mingling their joys and struggles into a vibrant smorgasbord. I love how easy it is to slip from one place to another in a blink and find a totally different atmosphere.

The thought of how many people I could end up hurting if my powers got away from me… That was the factor that made me hesitate.

Now, it's the harm a different being caused that's left my stomach hollowed out. It doesn't help that slinking through the downtown streets in the wee hours of the morning, too late for any of the businesses to still be open and too early for most early birds to have risen with the sun, makes for a pretty spooky setting.

The sides of all the buildings are painted with shadows. The only light comes from the streetlamps poised over the sidewalks, some of which are dimmed or flickering.

Everything is still and quiet with the hush of sleep. Only every now and then do I hear the distant growl of a single vehicle heading to some unknown destination.

I suspect this city is especially quiet right now because a lot of the people are afraid to come out of their homes at all.

The destruction we're looking at is definitely the most disturbing part of this walk. Every new sight makes me want to dart away into some cozy patch of darkness and think happy thoughts instead.

A sidewalk bench has been folded over on itself almost in half. One car has been tossed onto another, smashing the first so it sags on its tires.

Cracks and scorch marks ripple through the asphalt of the road. Several streetlamps farther down have toppled over like chopped-down trees.

Glass crackles under our feet from the car windshields and the shattered windows on the nearby buildings. I spot a glimmer of reddish liquid in the hazy light, splattered across one frame of jagged shards.

Did the strange crocodile-tailed woman start hurting people as well as their belongings?

The six shadowbloods who've been monitoring the city wander through the wreckage alongside me and my four men. Riva's mouth is set in a tight frown.

"We didn't manage to get here in time. It's hard when there's a whole city to keep track of..." She balls her hands into fists. "This shadowkind seems to have figured out that she can get away with more chaos if she only pops out for ten or fifteen minutes, does as much damage as possible, and vanishes before we can make it to the scene."

The warped higher being is a fast learner. All the more

reason she'd be better off at Rollick's school than terrorizing mortalkind.

I shiver. "Is there any way to protect the whole city against her? If we scattered silver and iron on every street…"

One of the shadowbloods who arrived while I was away, a lanky guy with dark curly hair who Riva called "Drey," snorts with amusement. His tone comes out dry. "It'd take a lot of metal, but at this rate, I think Rollick might ask us to try. It could work better than anything we've accomplished so far. Paint the whole city in silver! It'll look pretty, at least."

Despite his lighthearted words, I can taste the sour-apple apprehension drifting off him. He's just as worried as the rest of us.

My gaze travels to the most silvery building already standing in the city. The peak of the Diamond Victory Tower protrudes over the shops and low rises around us, glimmering in the moonlight like a beam of hope.

We won't let the humans here down.

Even if that means we have to lie to them to keep the peace. A man in a hoodie ducks out of the steps leading from a second-floor apartment, and I spring into damage-control mode.

"Gosh, I can't believe the police still haven't caught this terrorist gang," I say, just loud enough for my voice to carry. "Our fellow humans can be so mean. Hopefully the cops will track the bad guys down soon!"

Mirage beams in a way that doesn't fit our topic of conversation at all, joining in my charade. "Catch them and send them all to jail. That's what they deserve! Vicious vandals—gotta see them handled."

One of the other shadowblood men, a guy with pale hair and a permanent scowl, gives a slightly choked sound. His voice comes out in a low mutter. "We're not supposed to compose poetry about the 'terrorists.'"

The hoodie man has already disappeared down the street. I don't think he looked at us too oddly.

A flicker of embarrassment passes over my hair all the same. I tug my own hood lower.

Riva bumps her shoulder against mine and catches Mirage's eye. "Maybe we just sound a little less cheerful about it next time? You'll get better with practice."

Her blond partner kicks at a broken headlight lying on the ground. "All we need is to get our hands on this psycho shadowkind *once*, and then there won't be any more craziness to explain. We know how to tackle beings that are fucking around."

Riva shoots him a look that's as fond as it is exasperated. "We've mostly faced off with other shadowbloods, Jake. It's always harder with shadowkind when they can slip away so quickly."

"We have a better idea of what we're doing now. It shouldn't be that hard. As soon as we can get to the same place she is."

Hail aims a glower at Jonah. "Can't you summon her to do your bidding the way you did when you dragged us off to the school?"

From the tang of uncomfortable emotion that passes from him to me, Jonah has just suppressed a wince. "I'll try again. When I can't focus on her exact location to aim my sorcery directly at her, all I can do is put out a general call. So far that's only brought in a bunch of beings who had nothing to do with her. Either she's heading far enough away in between outbursts that she isn't in range… or like the other beings from these new rifts, my sorcery doesn't work as well on her as it usually would."

I think back to our encounters with the lesser beings who've come through the odd rifts. "Have you seen any reason why they're less affected?"

Our sorcerer spreads his hands. "Nothing definite. It could be the morphing—that sets every part of them off-kilter, so however my magic would normally affect them, it can't quite grip on the same way it would with a normal shadowkind. Or maybe there's something different enough to make them not quite a shadowkind. I can't use sorcery on a human being or a mortal animal at all. At least it does work with these ones some, just not as easily."

That makes sense. There's got to be another strategy.

I reach out to Raze, tucking my hand around his elbow. "Does she leave enough of a scent for you to track her? You've been so good at that in the past."

The basilisk shifter aims a grateful smile at me for the recognition, but the shake of his head is all resigned disappointment. "She moves too fast. The trail fades in the shadows."

Mirage gives me a tentative poke on the arm. "You can sense emotions even in the shadows, can't you? And the strange beings have different kinds of feelings from regular ones."

I pause. "They do. I don't know… I guess I could hurry through the streets in the shadows and see if I can pick up on any feelings that seem to be coming from her. I think I could recognize her. But what would I do then?"

"That's perfect!" Riva digs into her pocket and tosses me a phone. "If you keep that in your clothes, it should travel with you into the shadows. All my guys' numbers are programmed in. If you can figure out where she's hiding, just switch to physical form and text us the nearest address. We'll catch up and follow her from there, maybe even force her out of the shadows before she's on the attack."

Raze's forehead furrows. "We should go with her. This being is dangerous."

My nerves are jittering, but I know the right answer to

that question. "I'll have an easier time avoiding notice if I'm by myself. If she senses a being who gives off an aura of power, she'll probably leave before we can get close. You can roam around so you stay close enough that we won't end up in pain, but I think you should give me as much room as possible."

Jonah's mouth has tightened, but he nods. "So far this rogue shadowkind has only attacked parts of the mortal world. We haven't seen any reason to believe she'd harm a fellow shadowkind who isn't posing a threat."

That's me—totally not at all threatening. I can put my cream-puff exterior to good use.

I suck in a breath and slide the phone into the pocket of my leather jacket. "All right. I'll travel through the whole city checking for her presence and let you know as soon as I stumble on her."

I leap into the shadows before anyone can say anything else, because if one more doubt is raised, I might lose my nerve.

I still don't understand why any shadowkind would act so horribly.

Maybe I'll get the chance to find out, if I can find *her*.

As I flit through the darkened streets, I think back to our first encounter with the crocodile-tailed being. To the sickly sense of satisfaction that accompanied the shadowkind woman's feats of destruction.

It reminds me a little of the sorcerer who held me captive —who tortured me to aim my own destructive powers at people he wanted to hurt.

I haven't met many beings, mortal or shadowkind, who take pure enjoyment out of doing harm. Even the students who've been cruel to me at the academy always had tender spots underneath, fear or anger they were covering with their hostility.

Wafts of more peaceful emotions reach me as I navigate around a series of apartment buildings and through a sprawling residential neighborhood. The sensations of sleep taste like warm custard, other than a few spikes of spicy arousal or the metallic panic of a nightmare.

Fainter tendrils of feeling touch my awareness in the midst of that blend. A couple of cats spar over their territory, hissing and arching their backs to claim an alley that doesn't seem worth the fight. A man behind a lit window emanates a trickle of stress as he types on his computer.

Maybe he should turn off its artificial glow and go to sleep like his neighbors.

Then, as I veer back into streets of storefronts and office buildings, a surge of something sharp and hot as roasted jalapeños brushes against my awareness.

I pause and turn toward the impression.

As I venture closer, my sense of the being grows. Along with the sharp flavor comes more of that sadistic satisfaction shot through with a speckling of impatience like bits of orange rind.

It has to be her—the crocodile-tailed woman. She's somewhere nearby.

But I can't tell exactly where yet.

I slink onward more cautiously. The jumble of emotions gradually comes into clearer focus.

She's drifting through the shadows at the end of an alley across the street, between a dry cleaner and a pho restaurant. Her restlessness wriggles through my essence.

I don't know how long she's going to stay there.

I pull into the thicker shadow in a shoe-shop doorway on the other side of the road. If I move far enough away to materialize out of view and send the text, she might leave without me realizing.

But what's the point in having found her if I don't let the others know?

Apparently my talent for stealth is a little lacking. I haven't made up my mind about how to handle the situation when the strange being steps out of the shadows, taking on her physical form at the mouth of the alley.

"Hey," she calls in a crackly voice that brings to mind all that glass she's smashed. "I can tell someone's there. Don't just hang around staring. Let's see you."

I could flee, but I don't see how that'll help anything. The emotions she's giving off now taste more of curiosity and a hope of escaping boredom than aggression.

If I run off, she'll definitely never trust me when I get close again.

I ease forward and into the physical realm, my leather jacket and sundress forming around my curvy body with a ripple of fabric that's vaguely comforting. I've decided I like this combination of tough and soft more than an outfit that's all one or the other.

Lifting one hand, I offer the shadowkind woman my sunniest smile. "Hi! I'm Periwinkle. I haven't seen you around the city before. Are you new here?"

It seems smartest to pretend I have no idea who she is. Her impassive expression suggests she didn't notice me during her first rampage.

She lets out a scoffing sound and swishes her tail across the pavement with a rasp of scales. "You could say that. But when I'm done with this place, there won't be much of a 'here' left."

I knit my brow in confusion I don't have to feign. "Are you going to wreck the city? Why would you do that?"

As I speak, I exude calm and warmth as well as I can. If I could settle down the lesser beings from the rift, maybe I can get this one to chill out too.

She gives another swish of her tail. "Why not? These mortal beings stacking up their bricks and bolts, trying to shut us out—it looks much better when it all comes crashing down."

Her body twitches, and all at once her arms jut a little longer from her shoulders. Her hair shrinks into her head until it's only a spiky bob.

The curiosity I sensed from her morphs too, with a jolt of brussel-sprout-bitter agitation. I can't tell if my attempt at soothing her affected her at all before her emotions jerked around.

"I actually like the buildings and everything," I say brightly. "They make lots of shadowy spots to move through. And the people can be pretty entertaining when they're going about their business. Seeing them scared all the time gets boring fast."

The woman's eyes narrow. "I don't think so. It should all be the same. When this place gives off so much shaky shuddery energy, everything feels like *me*."

She stomps her foot with that last word. With a spark of supernatural energy, a broad crack opens all the way through the road between us. The hairs on the back of my neck stand on end.

I grope for another approach. "Maybe you could feel other ways too. I know lots of shadowkind who'd be happy to have someone else to hang out with. I could take you to them and we could all get to know each—"

The strange being cuts me off with a mocking laugh and another bitter jab of frustration. "Oh, no. I'm only for me."

She rams her fist into the wall of the pho restaurant, and bricks crumble around her knuckles. "Tell your friends that this city belongs to Viscera now. It wanted to stomp me, so I'm stomping it to the ground."

As if to make good on that promise right now, she hurtles

forward, slamming into a nearby parked sedan. For just an instant, it's a rare flying car, careening through the air.

Then it crashes through the shoe shop window just a few feet from where I'm standing.

Even as I leap to the side with a yelp, the shadowkind woman—Viscera?—vanishes into the darkness.

"Wait!" I cry out, snatching after her, but the flares of her emotions fade away so fast that I'm not sure which way she's gone.

I stand in the middle of the street, the crack quivering wider beneath my sneakers. A car alarm blares where the sedan sticks halfway through the shop window.

A wave of despair washes over me.

I learned a lot tonight. But I don't see how any of it will solve our problems rather than making more.

18

Hail

Mortals mill around the latest scene of the rogue shadowkind's reign of devastation, talking in nervous voices about the car protruding from the storefront. The pale faces and twitchy hands tell me they're having trouble processing what sort of mortal being could possibly have caused this damage—or why.

Because it wasn't mortals at all, even if Rollick insists that we trick them.

Humans keep themselves so ignorant about the world they call their own. The wild animals they don't consider more than hunting prey and scenery have been aware of the shadow creatures that've lurked alongside them for ages.

To avoid causing suspicion now, we're watching from the shadows rather than interacting with those humans in our physical forms.

Peri, Mirage, and Raze made a few stabs at selling the "terrorist gang" story. After I chilled their overly enthusiastic account with a remark about the horror of the situation that apparently sounded "too sarcastic," we were shooed to the sidelines.

Jonah—the determiner of excessive sarcasm—and a few of the shadowbloods have been circulating through the crowd, spreading the story as they prefer, checking for additional information, and encouraging people to stay off the streets if they can.

We have to pretend we don't even exist.

Because if these people got one hint of what we really are, they'd declare us just as much monsters as the being who tossed their cars around. They'd shower us with bullets and slit our throats if that didn't do the trick.

Who exactly are the terrorists here?

Peri's nearby presence radiates uneasy impatience through the persistent mark on my chest.

She's still grousing about her encounter with the warped being. "I tried to tell Viscera it doesn't have to be this way. That there are shadowkind who'll welcome her into the community. But she wasn't interested in making friends."

I have the impression of Raze drawing closer to her, which sends a jab of ridiculous jealousy right through the glowing spot I can feel even in the shadows. A quiver runs over my skin at the memory of the emotions I caught from her days ago, that stirred my blood and had my cock straining at my pants until I summoned frigid air all around me.

I'm pretty sure the carnivorous lug was responsible for her heated reactions. But why should I care?

"You did your best," he says to her. "There's just something wrong with the beings who stumble through those rifts. We've seen it with the lesser creatures too. They come out messed up."

"And mean!" Mirage pitches in.

I can't help it—I let a scoffing sound slip.

Peri turns toward me. "You think we're being absurd. What's wrong with what any of us said?"

I know from the twinge of emotion that tickles my essence that she's genuinely curious, not accusing. Somehow that brings my hackles up more than if she was pushing for an argument.

I back away through the patches of darkness, putting the humans' ugly, panic-blotched faces out of my sight. "Don't worry about it."

My "team" follows me around the corner and down a quieter street. Peri waits until I come to a halt in the patch of shadows by our van before piping up again. "You can't tell someone not to worry. Feelings don't work that way. We need to know what everyone's thinking about this problem if we're going to have the best chance of solving it."

She sounds so cheerfully determined that whatever nerves I have in this shadowy state set on edge. I spin toward her, as much as I can face her while we're ephemeral. "Did it ever occur to you that maybe it's not really a problem?"

Her frown carries through her voice. "What are you talking about? Viscera is running around destroying parts of the city. She said she wants to crush the whole place. How can that not be a problem?"

Of course the cream puff would never see things my way. Her tender heart aches for every being, mortal or otherwise, in the whole world.

Even me, even after I've been cruel to her.

That thought stokes the sparks of my irritation. "Look at what she's actually wrecking. Cars. Buildings. Lamp posts.

Mailboxes. It's all human-made crap. She isn't tearing up trees or smashing squirrels."

"There's a lot more human stuff in the city than anything else," Mirage points out, which I'll grudgingly admit is a pretty logical comment from the fox shifter. "Even if she's smashing at random, she's more likely to hit buildings and cars than trees."

"But she's here. She doesn't want to leave the city and go somewhere with fewer people. She wants to ruin what they have."

If Peri were standing in front of me, I think she'd stick her hands on her hips right now, but her expression would be pained rather than defiant. "How is that not a problem? The people who own those buildings and use those cars and everything else still need them in one piece. There must be hundreds of thousands of humans living here who are terrified."

"You only care about that because you can feel them being terrified. Do you think they give a shit about *you*?"

"They don't know me," Peri says. "I'm sure a lot of them—"

I break in before she can make an absurd claim. "They wouldn't care. Most of them would like to see beings like us as battered and broken as that store window, if they knew we were here. You remember that they call us monsters, right? Even though hardly any shadowkind actually hurt them? Some of them go all out with delusions of power like that asshole sorcerer who kept you in a cage, but almost every human would stamp us out if they knew how."

Peri's voice quiets with a pulse of sadness through our connection. "I don't think that's true. Humans haven't had a chance to really understand us, and we haven't given them one because it'd be too complicated. That doesn't make them *bad*."

Something in me snaps. "It does! Even Rollick thinks so. They don't want to understand us—they want to hate us and cut us down and destroy *us*. So maybe it's time they got a little payback. Maybe this Viscera being is giving the humans exactly what they deserve. Why shouldn't they have to watch the things they care about get turned into rubble?"

Raze speaks with a hint of a growl. "None of the people here did anything—"

"You don't know that," I retort before he can finish. "You have no idea how awful most of these people probably are to the parts of this world that are actually good—to all the other life that they don't think is worthy."

Peri's distress pulses on, too intense for me to ignore it. "Most of them don't think that way. Just because they like living in the cities—"

"And how do they treat the other life in these cities? How many of them carve up the trees, take potshots at pigeons, and chain up their dogs like slaves?"

"Lots of them don't do anything awful. They're just adjusting the world so it does what they need it to. Shadowkind do the same thing."

A dark laugh tumbles out of me, propelled by an ache that's searing through me like it hasn't in years. "Not like humans do. Not going around ruining life for their own satisfaction. If this new shadowkind has decided to ruin their crap right back at them, then I say good for her."

A deeper pang of pain hits me from Peri, along with a brief shudder. "You don't really mean that." She pauses for a second and then takes a firmer tone. "Something else is bothering you. If there were humans who hurt you, you have to know that doesn't mean—"

I whirl around, denial screaming through every particle of my ephemeral body. "I don't have to know anything. *You* don't know anything. Some things are awful, and that's the way they'll always be. Thinking happy thoughts isn't going to help."

As the last words spill out, I shoot off through the shadows as fast as my essence can carry me. Away from Peri and her boundless optimism and compassion. Away from goofy Mirage and glowering Raze.

What do any of them know? They want to close their eyes and pretend human beings aren't a stain on this world…

I haven't gone all that far before the first prickling discomfort through the bond draws me to a halt.

If I race off much farther, Peri will collapse. And our connection will rip into me too.

With a gnash of my teeth, I whip around in the shadows. But my fury is already fading, leaving only a dull simmer of anguish in its wake.

Not all of that agony is mine. Even at this distance, Peri's dismay wafts into me, full of guilt and regret that even I know it isn't fair for her to feel.

She *doesn't* know what I've been through or why I can't see good in human beings. I've never given her the chance to know.

How is it fair for me to beat her up over her ignorance when I shut her out in the first place?

For fuck's sake, why should *I* even care? I didn't pick her. I—well, maybe I did want her a little—but I didn't ask to be tied to her for what might be forever.

I do care, though. A significant part of the pain inside me comes from recognizing how much pain I've put Peri through with my arguing. How I've disappointed her with my caustic remarks.

How I've treated her like she's pathetic when I know she isn't at all.

I curl up in a corner of an alley, condensing my presence

around the ache inside. None of it's fair—not to me, not to her.

Maybe not to all the humans out there either, if I let myself think beyond my knee-jerk anger.

Now the rest of my team is going to want me around even less. And I can't say they'd be wrong to turn their backs on me.

19

Periwinkle

As I walk up to the school in the stark desert sunlight, I can't help thinking that the smooth tan structure looks smaller than I remember. Maybe because I've been surrounded by city high rises for the past few days.

But though both the reform building and the neighboring one for voluntary students are teeny in comparison, a quiver of apprehension runs through my nerves.

Even if Gloss is banished, her friends are still attending classes in there. Who knows how much they'd like to chop me into kibble or punt me through the nearest rift now that I'm responsible for her expulsion? If you look at the situation in the least generous way, which I suspect they will.

And then there are all the other students I've managed to rub the wrong way somehow or other.

I've never tried to make enemies, only friends. Why do I keep stumbling into opposite world?

Raze strides along beside me, his mouth set in a scowl. "No one's even getting close to you. I'm not leaving your side for one second."

He cuts his gaze toward Hail, who's sauntering across the dry packed earth just behind us. "Maybe you should find somewhere else to be. We don't want any more of your fan girls to get ideas about 'protecting' you."

Hail raises his hands in a casually defensive gesture. "I didn't incite anyone to begin with, and I can continue keeping any provocative thoughts to myself. Aren't we supposed to be a *team*?"

He sounds as if he tried to turn that last word into a sneer, but his voice falters instead. In the aftermath of yesterday's searing anger, the current of emotion passing from him into me is tinged with sour, smoky gloom like barbequed ribs left on the grill too long.

I think he meant all those things he said, though. He really believes that Viscera might be right, that the humans in the city deserve her demolition spree.

I don't see how that's possible… but I haven't seen that much of life in the mortal realm. I did spend most of my time on this side of the divide in a sorcerer's cage, after all. My captivity didn't exactly provide a buffet of experiences.

My former captor deserved the destruction that came down on him. What has Hail experienced that made him feel so many other humans do too?

There's a tang of pain deep down inside him that he normally manages to hold back. I tasted it through his anger, and it laces his melancholy now.

Maybe that's why he puts on such a cool, uncaring front —like a wall to stop anyone from picking up on the tender spot he's protecting underneath.

If Mirage has surrounded himself with a barricade of jokes, why couldn't the winter fae be shielding himself with snark?

For now, I have to let it go. I can't do anything about his pain if he thinks I'm too much of a pipsqueak to bother talking to me about it.

Mirage bounds across the terrain beside us, staying in human form but still managing to pull off a couple of forward flips and a twist in midair. He lands gracefully on his feet and spins around. Then he shoots a cautious glance toward Jonah. "There's no one around to complain. The monsters can run a little wild."

Jonah lets out a stiff laugh. "Yes, you don't have to be as careful here as we were in the city. It's probably good to burn off some of that restless energy. But don't worry about me. I don't have the authority to place sanctions on your behavior anyway."

A smack of bitterness flows from him with those words. He's ashamed and frustrated that Rollick took away his title as teacher.

I don't understand the demon's reasoning. While he was away from the academy, Jonah was only teaching the four of us. It isn't as if he was handling full classes to distract him.

But Rollick must have had his reasons, and Jonah hasn't been willing to talk to me about his troubles either. No one wants to take the ear I'd love to lend.

As we reach the door, our sorcerer catches my gaze. "You shouldn't have to worry about your safety, Peri. You won't be attending classes, and Rollick arranged for you to stay in one of the outbuildings rather than the dorms for the one night we're here, if you want to rest. You need a break after everything you've been through. Try to enjoy that and the promotion—that's why he arranged for us to come."

Another decision that confused me, not that I'd tell the

demon that to his face. Once Rollick heard all our reports, he shipped us back to the academy for the day even though Viscera is still on the loose.

Then again, I've already shown I couldn't rein her in when it mattered. How much good was I doing in the city? Rollick has the shadowbloods to pitch in, and Sorsha and her crew are on their way.

The demon seems to appreciate the little bits I have contributed, though. He's sent word ahead, even faster than his jet.

When we step into the air-conditioned chill of the school hallway, Shanty is waiting for us. Well, mostly for me. She offers a warmer smile than I'm used to and motions for me to follow her.

The men trail behind me into the administration meeting room. The other shadowkind who run the school—other than Rollick—stand behind the curved table.

Jonah starts to step toward the curving desk and catches himself with a hitch of his stride. A sharper jab of bitterness careens from him into me.

He doesn't belong beside the others now. Will Rollick take him back as part of the administrative staff when this mess is over?

I guess that's hard to say when we don't even know if the mess *will* be over… ever.

The unnerving thought knots my stomach, but the figures behind the table all look pleased—or at least only mildly disinterested. They stand up to greet us with nods of their heads, Pearl bobbing eagerly on her feet. Albumin's expression is bored, but Gnash's typically fierce expression has softened. Toni is smiling.

Shanty pulls a container the size and shape of a ring box from her pocket.

This had better not be a surprise marriage proposal. I'm already bonded enough for four lifetimes.

"We're not going to get into a lot of fanfare about this, but we hope you'll still consider it an honor," she says. "Periwinkle, you're the first student to receive a promotion to the next level of the academy while *not* attending classes. We judge that your control of your powers and determination to help in the field make you worthy of graduating to level 2. Keep it up, and you'll ascend to the upper levels in no time."

She opens the box to reveal a new badge, marked with a two.

I expected that. I wasn't prepared to see that the circle indicating I'm a danger to my fellow students is gone.

My heart skips a beat. All at once, I feel like crying and also laughing, which would probably result in a lot of sprayed snot, so I contain both impulses.

"Thank you." My voice comes out too quiet. I look around at the other administrators and pitch it louder in the most grateful tone I can summon. "Thank you! I'll keep trying my best."

They offer a round of applause—polite from some, wildly enthusiastic with a couple of whoops thrown in from Pearl— while Shanty pins the badge just below the neckline of my dress. I look down at it, still caught in the same contradictory whirl of emotions.

"What about the rest of the team?" I have to ask. "They've all been working hard too."

Shanty sets her hand on my shoulder. "They have, but Rollick feels you've gone above and beyond what anyone would have expected. I'm sure the others will be receiving new badges before much longer. For now, celebrate the progress you've made!"

It is hard to believe that just a couple of months ago, I

was on the verge of being banished. A smile touches my lips as the full realization hits me.

I'm moving up in the school. I'm proving that I can fit in with regular society, that I won't hurt people anymore.

I'm even helping stop the beings that *are* still hurting people, however little I'm accomplishing there. Every tiny sprinkle makes a cake more delicious.

Raze grabs me in an emphatic embrace, but to my surprise, it's Hail who speaks up first. "Don't let anyone tell you that you don't deserve it, Cream Puff. I know *I* don't."

Mirage jumps in as if to join the hug but instead only coils a strand of my hair around his finger with a teasing tug. "Our Rainbow lights up every place she goes."

"All right," Al says in a bland tone, sinking back in his chair. "We have other work to take care of. You can go off to enjoy… whatever pastimes you're inclined to indulge in."

Jonah tilts his head toward the door. "Come on, team."

For just that moment, his voice sounds more spirited. But when we're in the hall, his expression has darkened again.

"You have the rest of the day and night as free time. We'll head back to the city in the morning. You're welcome to grab some food in the cafeteria—although Peri, I think you should let someone else bring you a meal, just to be safe."

Raze draws himself up to an even more imposing height. "I can do that. I'll get you everything that looks good and come right back to wherever you are."

Jonah watches the basilisk shifter leap into the shadows with an odd slant to his mouth before he goes on. "You can also make use of the gym if there's no class going on, watch a movie in the media room, just take a walk—it's all—"

"Peri!"

A slim, wide-eyed figure sprints down the hallway to meet me. Fen pushes past the guys and grasps my hands, her gaze darting to my new badge and back to my face.

She beams at me, not an anxious droplet in sight. "They told me I could come hang out with you as long as I didn't spread the word that you're stopping by. It's been such a long time. Is everything okay out there? What do you want to do while you're here?"

I have to laugh at her breathless torrent of words. "I'll tell you what I can. Things are… confusing. For now, I think I'd like to get off my feet." Little twinges are starting to radiate up through my ankles. "Wasn't there a movie you said you wanted to show me the last time I was here?"

"Right, right!"

She tugs me toward the rest of the school, but Jonah steps in front of us. "Actually—we'd better make sure the way is clear. I'll see that you get exclusive access to the media room for the next couple of hours. Why don't you travel there through the shadows so you're less noticeable—it'll be easier on your feet too."

He puts that considerate spin on the request, but my momentary exhilaration fades.

I slink through the shadows after him. Fen darts along beside me, chattering about the latest school gossip.

The media room is totally vacant by the time we arrive, which gives the space with its cozy sofa and armchairs an oddly lonely vibe. I guess Raze will come join us soon.

But as I tuck my legs up on my chair while Fen searches for the movie, the sense that I don't really know this place creeps over me.

I just gained a new level in my schooling, but I can barely participate at the school. Will I ever belong even here?

Viscera's crackling voice rises up from my memory. *All these mortal beings stacking up their bricks and bolts, trying to shut us out.*

It twines with Hail's harsh words just a few hours later. *Almost every human would stamp us out if they knew how.*

Even Rollick seemed to think we don't really belong anywhere in the mortal world—not out in the open, at least. *When humans and shadowkind collide, it almost always ends in disaster.*

Is that really true? Is *everything* this school is working toward pointless in the end, because we'll always be hiding, risking lighting the fuse of a full-out war?

That can't be right, can it? Jonah's human, and he doesn't hate us. Toni works with shadowkind all day.

Gracie, my former captor's daughter, freed us all from our cages even though she knew her father would turn his rage on her.

But the question swells at the base of my throat until I can hardly breathe. I need to know just how big a blunder we could be risking.

My gaze slides toward the door. "Actually, Fen... Would you mind if we watched the movie another time? There's something I'd like to look up while I'm here."

Fen tips her head, brightening with curiosity. "More mate bonds stuff?"

I have to laugh. "No, I think that was a dead end. But this is a shadowkind academy... There have to be records about things shadowkind have done here somewhere, right?"

"Oh, yes, there's a whole section in the library. But what are you looking for?"

I swallow hard. "I want to find out everything I can about the battles between humans and shadowkind."

Jonah

I pause outside my office door, asking myself why the hell I walked down this hallway in the first place. Kicking myself for letting instinct take over.

This room isn't mine anymore. I doubt Rollick has ordered all my student files and classroom notes be confiscated, but I'm not supposed to be accessing them.

I have no more classes to lead. None of the shadowkind I taught are technically my students now.

I'm just a random human wandering around a school that was never meant for me.

Is Rollick even going to continue calling on me for my sorcerer powers outside of my limited help at the rifts, or have I been taken off that duty too? It didn't occur to me to ask him, I was so startled to be demoted in the first place.

I waver in the hallway, unsure where I'd want to go

instead. The cafeteria is currently bustling with students getting their dinner. After classes, the gym and other workout areas are often occupied.

I can't even wander into the staff lounge area as if I belong there. The only part of the school I have a stake in now is my own small apartment.

If Rollick's going to keep me off-duty, I suppose eventually I'll lose that too. There won't be any reason for me to return to the Quinn Moody Academy.

As the gloomy thoughts settle over me, a familiar figure creeps down the hall in my direction. At the sight of the shadowkind man's bristly hair that seems to echo the spikes that jut from his neck, I automatically draw myself straighter.

Larch has been at the school—and in my classes—for nearly a year. In the past, I've offered him one-on-one advice in the office I haven't dared enter today, trying to guide him through his discomfort with his humanesque appearance and the monstrous features he can't hide. We've spent hours talking about various locations where he could more easily keep the spikes covered or, alternately, present them as a fashion statement.

There are more options for the former than the latter, naturally, but I like to cover all the bases.

I felt like we'd made progress. Now I'm not sure I'll get to see where that progress takes him.

"Hey, Teach," Larch says in his usual tentatively familiar way. He likes putting on the airs of human slang and other playful references but never seems confident that he's nailing it. "You haven't been around in a while."

The nickname sends a fresh jab of shame through the center of me, but I can't pretend nothing's changed. It'd be a betrayal of trust to act as if I still have authority over him.

I dip my head, managing a crooked smile. "I'm not a

'teach' anymore. Our headmaster has taken me out of that role, at least for now."

Larch's eyebrows leap up, but he doesn't look entirely surprised. "Right! I heard…"

He hesitates. "It's something to do with that weird being, the chirpy one with the shiny hair, right? Some kind of mark?"

I restrain my hand from rising to the glowing spot that's become a constant presence under my shirt. Whatever Peri's up to now, my awareness of her comes with contrasting tickles of contentment, sadness, and determination.

Of course she'll have found some cause to champion even while she's supposed to be taking a break.

"It's not entirely because of that situation," I say. "I'm part of a team that's been working on some new developments outside the school. All my focus needs to be there."

That's the polite way of looking at my demotion, anyway.

Larch shifts his weight from one foot to the other. "So… are you going to be back at the front of class later, after the special project is done?"

I open my mouth and close it again to gather myself before I can answer. "I don't know. For now, it's easiest to assume I won't. You definitely don't have to worry about me grading you or anything like that."

I summon a little wryness into my tone. The shadowkind man's shoulders ease down.

He offers me a warmer smile than usual. "I'm really sorry. I could tell you liked teaching us a lot—and you helped me so many times. It's too bad one being throwing her powers at you could mess things up that—"

The words leap from my mouth before I've thought them through. "It isn't because of Peri. She's made important contributions to the school—and to shadowkind in general. I'd like to see everyone here be more welcoming."

Larch blinks at me. Is that skepticism in his gaze?

Maybe he thinks I'm only defending Peri because of our supernatural bond.

Then he shakes his head with an apologetic grimace. "Sorry again. I was just trying to say—it's too bad in general. It seemed like you had a good thing going here."

I did, but it makes my throat ache to consider acknowledging as much.

All the same, I soften my tone. "The new work I'm doing is a good thing too. I want to pitch in wherever I can be the most useful."

"Yeah. Okay. That makes sense." Larch dips his head, looking abruptly more awkward again. "Does that mean I shouldn't be talking to you at all? Like, if I wanted to check about a disguise or ask about a specific city and see what you think…"

It finally occurs to me that my former student might be more bothered about how my being demoted affects *him* than how it affects me. A little of the shame pricking at me melts away.

Even if I'm not an authority figure, he still values my guidance—because of what I've done for him, not the job I held.

"Of course you can still talk with me," I reassure him. "I mean, that's one of the most human-like things you can do —getting advice from a friend. You were assigned a phone, weren't you? I can give you my number, and if there's anything you want to chat about where you'd rather get the perspective of someone who isn't on staff, feel free to reach out."

Larch's face brightens. "All right!"

He fishes his phone out of his pocket, and we exchange

numbers. Then he pulls up a few pictures he found on the internet of high-collared coats he's hoping look "rad"—his slang isn't entirely up to date.

I grin. "Nice style! I think this one would work best. Although if you paired a scarf with that one, it could look pretty cool."

"Cool," the shadowkind man repeats. He flashes me a grin in return and starts chattering about a fashion website he discovered that he thinks will help him fit in even better. When he asks me whether I've ever had to worry about what I wear all that much, I find myself admitting to studying fellow teenagers at the mall a decade ago, when I realized my shadowkind guardians weren't exactly up to date on the norms of human teens either.

Larch heads off with a jauntier stride and a wave good-bye. I return it, caught up in a clashing jumble of emotions.

The jumble breaks with a flicker of panic when Rollick emerges from the shadows just a few steps away.

The demon chuckles and tips his head toward the shadowkind man who just vanished around the corner. "I see you're still contributing where you can."

"I—I didn't realize you'd made it back to the school. I told him right away that I'm not teaching anymore," I say hastily. "I didn't even mean to come to my office… Old habits."

Rollick claps me on the shoulder. "It's fine. I liked seeing you get friendlier with the beings we're trying to help. Do you really think you need an official title for them to respect you? I've never had one except the titles I've given myself."

I'd point out that he's also an incredibly powerful demon that all other shadowkind can sense could pulverize them in an instant, which tends to generate a lot of respect all on its own, but I know that's not the point he's getting at. And even if not every student I've taught would care about my opinions now, I'd already come to the same conclusion about Larch.

I can't help balking at his assessment anyway. "I won't be able to guide him the same way as before."

"Is the current way necessarily worse? It sounded as if he still shared and listened plenty." Rollick gives my shoulder a quick squeeze and steps away. "I have a few things to go over with Shanty and Pearl—I just happened to be passing through the hallway. You've really become immersed in this place, haven't you? I wouldn't take it away from you, you know. No matter what capacity you're coming here in, you'll always be welcome."

"Oh." I fumble for my words, my chest constricting. "Well, thank you."

The demon vanishes into the shadows again, leaving me standing there with a new mix of confusing but gentler emotions churning inside me.

He didn't sound like he intended to knock me down a peg. He was *glad* that I'm still talking to the students.

And he's right that Larch didn't seem to appreciate our conversation any less. Actually, once the shadowkind student relaxed knowing that we're on more equal footing, he opened up more than he ever has before.

I might have helped him more in that ten-minute conversation than I did in any of our hour-long office discussions in the past.

My gaze travels along the direction I think Rollick went, a tingle of unexpected exhilaration passing through my veins.

Is it possible that Rollick didn't relieve me of duty to punish me for my conflicted desires… but to give me *bigger* opportunities to make a difference?

That's what the whole mission started as, didn't it? Putting myself out there against a problem much more urgent than any we've been tackling at the academy.

And if I can tackle that problem better when my team sees me as someone working alongside them rather than someone calling the shots, that's better for all of us.

All I've ever wanted is to help shadowkind live alongside humans. Maybe it's time I paid a little more attention to how *I* can best coexist with them.

21

Periwinkle

I slip out of the car through the shadows and materialize by our current base near the city rift, only to find Riva and a couple of the shadowbloods waiting for me.

Riva's voice comes out wry. "The famous Periwinkle is finally back."

Famous? Finally?

I've only been gone for a day and a half, and I don't see how I could be anything like famous.

A chilling thought occurs to me. My gaze veers to the city skyline, the streaks of clouds turning ruddy in the late afternoon sunlight around the Diamond Victory Tower and its shorter companions. "Did I end up getting video-recorded while we were trying to stop Viscera—did someone put me on the news or—"

Riva holds up her hand to stop me before I can spiral into panic. The vibe I'm getting off her isn't irritation or fear but mostly caramel-corn amusement. Well, layered across some frustration she's suppressing beneath the tastier emotions.

"Nothing like that," she says. "Sorry, bad joke. It's just—we're still trying to hunt Viscera down. So far we haven't managed to do more than shout at her from a distance a few times, she's so slippery. But the times we *did* shout at her, she asked us where you are. It seems like she found you… interesting."

Based on the way the crocodile-tailed woman spoke to me, I wouldn't have thought she considered me interesting so much as pathetic or naïve.

Based on how she bashes up whatever she's paying attention to, I'm not sure I *want* her finding me interesting.

"She ran away from me," I point out. "She laughed at me. It didn't seem like she wanted to talk to me at all."

Drey shrugs where he's standing next to Riva, his mouth slanting into a crooked grin. "Maybe she likes you now that she's gotten to compare you to the other supernatural people who're trying to talk to her. She definitely doesn't want us anywhere nearby."

"She can tell you'd have a much better chance of catching her."

"And that might be true," Riva says. "But the fact that she's asking about you might give us a different sort of edge. Now that you're back, maybe she'll stick around a little longer in one spot if it means you two can have a chat. That gives us opportunities."

The men I marked have materialized around me, other than Jonah who had to step out of the car the human way. Raze lets out a soft growl. "You're talking about using Peri as bait."

Riva raises her hands. "Only if she's up for it! And we'd

be very careful. It just seems like a strategy that might work… and we're in pretty short supply at this point."

Jonah's expression darkens. "You haven't made *any* progress toward containing Viscera since we left?"

At Riva's other side, Zian shakes his head. "She's fast, and she never hits the same area twice. We haven't seen any pattern to where she pops up and starts smashing things. No matter how thoroughly we patrol, there are always some places none of us can get to fast."

Drey grimaces. "She jumps out of the shadows, does as much damage as possible in ten minutes or less, and vanishes before any of us can reach her. Rollick's shadowkind employees have been patrolling too, trying to keep tabs on her, but she moves faster than any of them can."

Nausea pools in the base of my stomach. "How much has she destroyed since we've been gone?"

Riva sighs. "A bunch of storefronts, one whole row of houses, several dozen cars, and more telephone poles than I can count. We've been able to keep the humans talking about marauding gangs and electric blitzes for now, but I don't know how much longer we can avoid them drawing the conclusion that there's a monster rampaging through their city."

"Just the tail, not the whole Godzilla," Mirage pipes up. He offers a tight smile. "It could be worse?"

Hail looks abruptly concerned. "Those monster movies—Godzilla and King Kong and all—aren't based on real shadowkind, are they?"

Jonah manages a rough laugh. "Not as far as any of us know. I suppose the fact that this Viscera being isn't as bad as a skyscraper-tall lizard is a small comfort."

"She's still wrecking too much stuff," I say. "The people must be so scared." Little eddies of uneasiness drift from the city like trickles of pickle juice. How much stronger must the flavor be up close?

It took a lot of digging in the academy library to find out much about the incidents Rollick mentioned between shadowkind and humans. What Fen and I did scrounge up showed a whole lot of bad behavior on both sides—sorcerers using shadowkind and shadowkind eating sorcerers to compel each other, researchers experimenting on us while one of our own toyed with them for malicious ends.

But even in the most horrifying accounts, there were sprinkles of hope I couldn't miss. Mentions of humans who pitched in and risked their lives alongside the shadowkind.

Maybe a super-powerful demon wouldn't think much of them, but I know better than to dismiss how much impact even a trace of sweetness can make. No matter what Hail thinks, humans aren't all bad. Whatever happens here, we have to give them a chance.

And they won't get much of one if Viscera buries them in rubble.

I square my shoulders. "If she'll come out for me, we have to use that. Maybe she's getting bored, and she's thinking about what I said. She might start to settle down if she realizes we really will help her!"

Hail snorts. "Always so optimistic, Cream Puff."

There isn't much rancor in his voice, though. I catch a strange twinge of uncomfortable affection, like chocolate laced with the bitterest of ground coffee.

Raze shoots me a sharp look. "You shouldn't do anything that'd give Viscera a chance to hurt *you*."

"The shadowbloods and Rollick's assistants are putting themselves in danger every time they go out to track her down. I've got to do *something*. If she attacks me, I'll bounce back easier than any mortal being would. I'll be fine."

A pang of distress hits me through my connection with Mirage. "We can't let her break our Rainbow."

I can't remember the last time the fox shifter has called me *theirs*. The fondness woven into the nickname only solidifies my resolve. "She won't. Maybe I'll break through all her messed-up thinking instead! And we can use our bond. You can find me through it if you try, and I'll intensify what I'm feeling so you know when I've run into her."

Riva rubs her mouth. "If this works the way we were thinking, we'd stick close by so we'll be right there to jump in."

I turn to her. "But Viscera's been able to sense you before. She might not come talk to me if she knows you're around."

The shadowblood woman folds her arms over her chest. "I'm not saying we'll be right on your ass, but we'll make sure we're not miles away. If even that's a problem, we'll cross that bridge when we come to it. We're not tossing you into the deep end immediately."

To my surprise, Jonah touches my arm. A tingling jolt races through my nerves that I know he can feel too, but he doesn't jerk his fingers away like he has before.

"Before we left the academy, I talked with Rollick about your reports," he says to the shadowbloods. "He has some ideas about how I might factor into a trap. For now, why don't we give Peri a moment to think through what's being asked of her and how far she's willing to go?"

Raze nods reluctantly, and the shadowbloods follow suit.

I glance up at Jonah, the mix of assurance and protectiveness in his stance making my pulse wobble like Jello. And who doesn't like Jello? "Should you fill me in on your part of the plan while I'm doing my thinking?"

"I'm happy to if it'll help you decide."

Despite his agreement, a waft of reluctance and

discomfort passes from him into me. There's something he and Rollick talked about that he doesn't actually like.

Mirage steps forward. "We can all get a lecture from our former teacher." He grins to show he's being playful rather than criticizing.

Another twinge of tension reaches me from Jonah. He likes the idea of discussing Rollick's ideas in front of a larger group even less.

I give Mirage an apologetic smile that I turn toward Raze as well. "It'll be easier for me to sort out what I'm okay with when I don't have a bunch of other opinions to distract me. When I have a clearer idea of what danger I'll be dashing off into, I'll give you all a chance to argue about it."

Raze's expression turns grim and Hail's eyes narrow as if he doesn't totally like the idea of me rushing into danger either, but Mirage beams at me. "As long as we all get the chance to dash in too."

I have to laugh. "I guess we'll see about that."

"Here." Jonah leads me toward one of the trailers set up along the side of the road. Rollick's assistants have ramped up the film-set details for extra authenticity, with folding chairs and camera equipment strewn around. We dodge those pieces in silence and step into the portable room that's like a miniature house.

I flop down on the tiny sofa and look at Jonah. "What did Rollick say and why does it bother you?"

Jonah winces, but I don't taste any real surprise from him. He must be getting used to me picking up on his emotions that quickly.

"You don't need to worry about that part," he says.

Because Jonah always protects all of us as much as he can.

I study the angles of his light brown face, the pensive features that draw a flutter into my pulse so easily even if he'd rather I didn't admit it out loud.

I want him to feel the swell of friendly affection that rises up inside me alongside the glaze of attraction.

"I do worry, because it's worrying you. Maybe you didn't really want this bond, but I think… I think it's a good thing I can tell how you're feeling if it means I can stop you from trying to handle everything alone."

Jonah gazes back at me for long enough that my pulse outright stutters and then rakes his fingers back through his dark hair.

His mouth twists. "Fine. That's basically the problem. You know my sorcery hasn't been very effective at controlling these strange shadowkind. I'd like to put my full strength into bending Viscera's will and see if that's enough, but Rollick's concerned we won't get more than one chance. He wants to bring in another sorcerer to add their power to mine."

That last sentence is punctuated with a jab of resistance.

I cock my head. "Does he know other sorcerers?"

"Well, there was one, but she had to give up the talent… I'm sure he could find another that's not outright awful to shadowkind and convince them to do this one task. He's Rollick." Jonah spreads his hands helplessly. "Which also makes it very difficult to argue with him."

I'm still sorting through the contrasting emotions flowing out of him. "Why would it be a bad thing to work with another sorcerer if it means it's easier to catch Viscera?"

Jonah sighs and sinks down at the other end of the sofa. "It might not be bad. I just—most sorcerers *are* pretty awful to shadowkind. You've experienced that firsthand. I've done my best my whole life to play a constructive role despite the talent I inherited from my parents… A lot of the time it doesn't feel like enough even without me joining forces with someone who might have manipulated and killed beings for the hell of it."

The melancholy of that statement hangs in the air.

I peer at him. "Do you really think any of the shadowkind at the school see you as that kind of sorcerer? You're nothing at all like the one who captured me."

You might as well compare a golden retriever to a rabid wolf. Absurd as a cauliflower pie.

"I've still had to force a lot of them to act against their will." Jonah shakes his head. "But we're not supposed to be talking about my hang-ups. You need to decide how you want to handle your part of the containment mission."

"I can already decide. If Rollick brings another sorcerer on board, I know you'll make sure anyone helping you sticks to the rules. They'll just be backing *you* up, and you'll be trying to stop more harm from being done, like you always do."

It's Jonah's turn to stare at me. Disbelief courses out of him, but it's tinged with a relieved sort of contentment. "You trust me that much."

I shrug, a smile crossing my lips. "Even when we'd only spent a little time together, I could tell you were trying to make things better for all the beings around you. Having this bond with you has meant I've seen even more how much you care. What's there to distrust?"

He opens his mouth and closes it again while he gathers his answer. "I'm not a shadowkind. I'll never really understand what it's like to be one. I'll always have this power that can steal your free will."

"So? I'll always have powers that you don't, that've hurt you in the past. You might not be like us, but none of us are all like each other either. I bet I've got more in common with you than I do with Hail."

Jonah can't restrain a chuckle. "All right, I'll give you that."

As he holds my gaze again, the familiar butterscotch

sweetness of desire passes between us—both ways, mine flaring at the first taste of his. But Jonah stays where he is, a couple of feet away from me, his shoulders tensing.

I don't want to push him. I don't want to bring back the surge of guilt that's jolted out of him before.

There is one thing I feel needs to be said. "You know, I was never afraid that you'd use your authority against me, even when you were part of the teaching staff. I can't see you giving me a better report because I kissed you or taking away marks because I didn't."

A flush creeps up Jonah's neck, but for once, he doesn't pull even farther away. "I don't think it's that simple. If your head gets clouded with emotions, it's hard to judge anything objectively."

"But you're not judging me officially anymore, right? We're equal teammates now. I'm not trying to convince you that you should act on how you feel. I only want to understand why it still makes you worried."

Jonah hesitates again before he answers. "I guess… I can't help thinking that if I act on it now, it means I always would have, no matter what happened. That I must have encouraged you in that direction when I shouldn't have, set the groundwork when you should have been able to count on me not to."

Oh. How can he have himself so mixed up?

I blink and then laugh. "But *I* know that's not true. I always picked up on your emotions when we were together. There's no way you'd have encouraged any kind of closeness like that when you were my teacher. As soon as you recognized what you were feeling, you backed off. I might not have marked you on purpose, but it wouldn't have happened at all if I hadn't been sure you were a person who'd always look out for me."

A deeper surge of happiness tingles through my senses.

Jonah relaxes enough for his tone to turn dry. "You marked Hail too. It doesn't seem to be that exclusive a club."

I wrinkle my nose at him in mock-offense. "Hail means well underneath. He just has too many prickly pieces overtop that I haven't figured out yet. He would never really hurt me either."

"I guess you might know us better than we know ourselves."

"It's easier to understand emotions when you're not the one stuck in them," I say brightly. "At least one good thing came out of these connections, even if you all didn't really want them."

Something softens in Jonah's expression. "You know, if I had to be tied to anyone, I'm happy it's you. There's something about you…"

He looks down at his hands and then back at me. "I always think of the first time I called you in to bring you to the academy. Seeing your true form, all glowing. Maybe sometimes your light gets too harsh, and sometimes it's overwhelmed with darkness, but mostly a perfect glow shines through. And it lights up everything you touch."

There's so much fondness in his voice that my heart skips a beat. "Maybe that's why I lit the four of you up. You're the ones who've made me glow the most."

Jonah's throat works. He eases over on the sofa and trails his fingers across my cheek.

The gentle caress wakes up every nerve in my body with the giddiest of shivers. I want to touch him in return so badly, but he's been so unsure. Doubt drizzles across his desire.

This decision needs to be his. He needs to be sure it was a conscious decision, not a mindless giving in to temptation.

So I hold still and simply let the bond between us shine with all the admiration and longing he stirs up in me. It feels so much more right pouring myself into the connection than trying to shut it off and resist it. Like a matching shine is reverberating back into me.

"Fuck," Jonah mutters, and then he's lowering his mouth to mine.

The kiss sends sparks through my veins. I slide my arm around his shoulders and kiss him back with a tenderness to match his own. His breath stutters against my lips.

A needy sound I can't hold back slips out, and then he's kissing me again, even more thoroughly than before. As if he never plans on stopping.

He does though, with his breath coming roughly and his arms tucking me close against his well-muscled frame. Glittering joy passes between us, airy as champagne fizz.

Jonah brushes one more kiss to my temple. "I think if I keep going, it'll be very hard to stop."

"Who says you have to stop?"

He chuckles and tightens his embrace around me. "We do have a rampaging rogue shadowkind to bring in. I'm supposed to be helping you work out your plans. Whatever else we have between us... There'll be time for it once the catastrophe is over, won't there?"

Is there a tiny thread of fear in his voice—the anxiety that I might reject him? I have to melt it away.

I set my hand on his chest and peer into his eyes. "You make me so happy that I tapped you right to my soul. I'm not going anywhere."

Jonah grins back at me, so genuinely pleased the sensation radiates through every part of my body.

I'm still reveling in the joy when a shout of alarm rings through the trailer wall.

"It's happening again!"

22

Periwinkle

I burst out of the trailer with a blink through the shadows. Jonah's right behind me, throwing open the door I skipped beneath.

"What's going on?" I ask, my heart in my throat. Has Viscera made another attack already?

One of Rollick's assistants is standing at the edge of our pretend movie set, wringing her hands in the growing dimness of the falling evening. As my other men materialize nearby and the six shadowbloods lope over to join us, she gulps for air.

"The rift. It's spewing out that shadowy substance again, all over the factory yard."

My pulse stutters. I don't know if that's better or worse than Viscera lashing out.

At least with her, we have some idea what's driving her

and what she'll do. The bizarre rift vomit is still a total mystery.

Jonah takes charge with the confident air that served him so well when he was a teacher. "Let's get over there and see what we can do to mitigate the damage. Anyone who can carry silver and iron, there are chains in the storage trailer. Grab them fast and get in the vans!"

He hustles off to follow his own orders with the shadowbloods darting alongside him. I dive into the nearest van and reform my physical body on the bench.

Raze, Hail, and Mirage follow me. Another of Rollick's assistants leaps into the driver's seat.

As the assistant starts the engine, his voice wobbles. "I don't know what's going on with the rifts. We got a report that the one up in Canada did the same thing a couple of days ago—just upchucked a mass of shadow material over about an acre of forest."

I shiver. "Did anyone get hurt?"

He shakes his head and yanks at the steering wheel to guide us toward the road. "No one was around except the shadowkind keeping an eye on it. The other odd rifts are all pretty far away from humans. But it warped the bark on the trees and frightened the animals. It doesn't make sense. I've never seen rifts act like this—any of it. And we still haven't been able to get at the rifts from the shadow-realm side."

His words tie my stomach into a knot. I've never seen anything like this either, but I'm relatively young as shadowkind go. A lot of Rollick's people have been working with him for centuries.

This is a brand-new flavor of strangeness. Which means no one has any idea how to deal with it, not really.

We just have to do our best to whip it into something palatable.

The van's headlights streak through the thickening

darkness. Dusk fell quickly while I was talking—and doing other things—with Jonah.

Do the other men I marked realize how close I was getting with the sorcerer? I can't imagine my joy was all that subdued.

None of them mention anything. Raze slides his arm around me to tuck me close with his usual protective fierceness, and Mirage flicks out his ears with a mischievous twitching when he catches me looking at him, maybe in an attempt to make me smile.

It works.

Hail peers out the window morosely as if the rest of us aren't here at all. At least the impressions I'm picking up from him don't feel outright upset, only tense and uneasy.

Another van rumbles behind us. We careen toward the city together and grind to a halt just outside the factory's fence.

No vehicles remain in the adjoining parking lot. A tiny waft of relief runs through my body.

The workers must have gone home for the night. There isn't anyone in the building who could be hurt by the rift.

In *this* building, at least. Last time, the shadowy deluge spilled all the way past the brick walls.

The current flood is lurching out of the rift's mouth as if it's vomiting pure darkness. The filmy sludge courses across the yard and into the factory building. The bricks that had already deteriorated with the first onslaught are crumbling further, little chunks disintegrating into the flow of shadows.

If that mess *does* swallow any mortal beings for long… I hate to think what will happen to them.

Riva looks at the shadowy muck with a shudder. "Last time it just… stopped and pulled back into the rift. What are the chances that'll happen again?"

Jonah has hopped out of the other van too. "I don't think we should count on our problems being solved for us."

Movement in the deluge catches my eye. My skin crawls as if I've been splattered with the ephemeral goop. "It's not acting exactly the same way. It's… bulging and dipping."

As I make the observation, the whole flood heaves more. Its upper surface undulates like a lake in an increasingly forceful storm. The sort-of waves smack into the factory wall, passing through the solid surface but dragging more crumbs out of the brick and mortar at the same time.

Hail grimaces. "That doesn't look good. I don't think we can hold back an entire ocean of shadow."

"Let's hope it doesn't come to that," Jonah mutters, and gestures to Riva and Zian. "Come on, quickly. We'll get out the silver-and-iron chains and see if they have any effect."

We didn't have those metals on hand when the rift took us by surprise last time. As Jonah and the shadowbloods haul the sacks of noxious metals out of the back of their van, I head around the building to check how far the flood extends.

Along the side wall, some of the dark substance sloshes out to puddle in on the concrete walkway, which dents beneath the unnerving substance. Little cracks open up in the cement.

As I dodge the puddles in a manic game of hopscotch, Mirage bounds after me. "Back and forth, back and forth. Rock-a-bye shadows. No one's going to sleep here."

It takes a second for me to realize he's talking about more than our jumping when he says, "Back and forth." The puddles contract into the walls, giving me a jolt of hope that the rift is already sucking the deluge back in, but then they dribble out again.

They're acting like waves—up and down, in and out.

Why is the shadowy substance so volatile today? Last time, as far as I remember, it just flowed straight out.

Has the rift caught a more exotic disease than indigestion, with some crazy new version of vomit?

I don't suppose chucking a few buckets of antacid down its gullet would cure the problem.

Raze frowns and hurries onward. "This doesn't seem like a *good* development."

At the front of the building, the dark flood has spread as far as the road beyond—shallower but still knee-deep, like a drift of snow in the opposite color.

A couple of cars have jarred to a halt on either side. One driver has gotten out to stare; another peers from the side window with an incredulous expression.

I wave my arms at them, reaching for an appropriate human-ish explanation. "Get away! The terrorist gangsters made a toxic spill!"

They remain frozen like deer in headlights.

Do I need to make the situation sound even more ominous? My mind scrambles. "It was terrorist gangsters *from space*!"

If anything, the humans only look more stunned. Not the effect I was going for.

With a roll of his eyes, Hail steps in.

"This stuff will damage your cars," he says, without even sounding all that concerned, but the news spurs the humans into action. They throw their vehicles into reverse and zoom away.

The edge of the still-expanding pool spasms, and a separate body pops out—a creature about the size of a pigeon, though it has four wings instead of two and four scaly legs to coordinate. As its head jerks around, a waft of fear hits me.

I scoot closer. "Hey, there. Everything's all right."

I mean, other than the fact that it's at the edge of a strange shadowy spew, it might morph into an even more awkward shape at any moment, and if it changes shape enough, it could completely disintegrate. But I'd like my words to be true.

And nothing about this situation will get better if the creature freaks out.

Raze makes a rough sound. "There are more."

With a couple of pops like bubbles in simmering sauce, a second creature and then a third spill out of the deluge.

The new ones aren't much bigger than the first, none of them higher beings, but my nerves jitter all the same. "We've never seen more than one come out at once, have we?"

Mirage shakes his head. "The more the merrier?" he says, but he can't quite make the question sound hopeful.

As we circle the three creatures, which all look more dazed than anything else, Zian comes jogging over. "The metals aren't having any effect on the stuff from the rift, but the flow seems to be slowing down. Oh, hell, what are those?"

"New shadowkind creatures that tumbled out with the flood." I crouch down so I'm closer to their level. The stream of sensations I'm picking up from each twitches and quivers, and I tense up. "I think they're going to morph already. I'll try to keep them calm."

"Peri," Raze says in a worried tone. He positions himself at my flank, ready to leap in should he need to.

Zian takes in the scene and then rushes off. "Maybe the chains will help with them."

I focus on the three beings, summoning all the peace and happiness I can inside me. The way I felt when Jonah admitted he wants to be with me. The comfort of Raze watching over me. The delight of Mirage's jokes, keeping our spirits up even when it's hard. Hail's cool nonchalance that nonetheless ensured the humans got out of harm's way.

Like I did before, I push the sense of contentment out of me toward the creatures.

I've never attempted this with more than one being at the same time. I've barely experimented with what I'm capable of at all.

But if we can't settle them down… I don't know what we'll have to do to them.

Sparks of anger and flares of frustration hit me with a caustic tang. I keep aiming my calming emotions at them, not shoving too hard, simply sending out a steady glow of warmth.

The creatures stumble and spasm—and two of them collide into each other.

One second, there's the quadruple-winged pigeon and a being with scruffy fur and three oversized paws like a lopsided bunny. The next, there's just one beast—wings protruding on one side, fat paws groping at the asphalt on the other, two heads merged at the cheeks, mouths opening in a joint squawk-squeal.

I jerk backward in surprise. As the merged creature squirms, it morphs further: one paw lengthening, one wing taking on a ridge of spines.

But it can't seem to propel itself in any direction with its mishmashed limbs. And…

Pain washes through me with a sharp edge of panic that turns the mixture as bitter as raw mustard. I flinch.

"It hurts. Something about the way the bodies combined —it isn't right. So much of them is in pain."

Mirage shifts his weight from one foot to the other. "Can we pull them apart?"

"I don't think so. They look—and feel—like they're totally fused. I don't know how that happened." My own horror merges with the anguish still streaming into me.

It doesn't matter if Zian brings metals to restrain the combined creatures. They'll still be in agony.

My own distress must be reverberating into my men. Raze eases past me. With a blink, he erases the contacts that cover his stark black eyes. "I'll put it—them—out of their misery. They shouldn't have to live like that."

Hail grunts. I half expect him to argue, but instead he strides in front of Raze, holding out his arm. "I can do it. A sudden freeze will be totally painless."

The basilisk shifter stares at the winter fae, but he backs up to give Hail room.

Hail's discomfort mingles with my own. I swallow hard. "Hail, you don't have to—"

"*Someone* has to," he interrupts. "I can do it best. So it should be me."

With a soft crackle in the air, a sheen of frost whips over the merged creature. The pain emanating from it vanishes.

It rocks over on its side, frozen solid.

I offer Hail a strained smile. "It isn't feeling anything anymore."

He ducks his head. "Good. As long as they don't all start mashing together like that."

We look up at the sound of pounding feet. During our distraction, the flood contracted all the way back into the building. The rift must be collecting it again.

Zian rejoins us, his face flushed. "That rogue higher shadowkind—she's just popped up on the other side of town."

23

Hail

Raze glances down the city block and pulls back his lips from his teeth in a silent snarl. "Too late again."

The street looks like a war zone. The rogue shadowkind has been stepping up her game.

One row of neighboring buildings has been reduced to rubble amid the broken skeletons of their frames. A stack of crushed cars at least ten high stands next to them, like some bizarre modern art piece.

Humans would happily do shit like that to each other. They *do* when they can find the means.

Why is it suddenly such a problem when the perpetrator is a shadowkind?

Oh, right, because if they realize shadowkind exist, they'll rain down all kinds of hell on us too.

A pang of distress resonates into me from where Peri is studying the ruins nearby. Her mix of grief and guilt makes me want to go over to her—to hug her? To shake some sense into her?

She shouldn't get this upset over these people who'd murder her if they knew what she is. Why can't she see that?

I keep my mouth shut, because I know enough by now to realize snarking at her would only make her more upset, and I'd have to feel that too, along with my own guilt.

Mirage cocks his head with a more deflated air than I'm used to from the fox shifter. "Knock 'em down and build 'em back up? Can we help fix this?"

One of the shadowbloods who's joined us, a guy nearly as pale as I am whose demeanor is awfully icy too, shakes his head. "I could use my telekinetic power to lift up the blocks, but I don't have a clue about the engineering that goes into making a whole building stable."

Riva pats his shoulder. Her touch seems to melt a little of the tension from his stance as if by magic. "No one expects you to handle it all yourself, Jake."

She glances at the rest of us. "Rollick is arranging for some workers to volunteer in the rebuilding under the guise of one of his corporations… But that doesn't help unless the buildings *stop* being knocked down."

My self-control wavers, and my mouth pops open despite my intentions. "Maybe the humans should move someplace else. They have lots of other cities. Let the shadowkind have this one."

Raze glowers at me. "You know that's not a good idea, even if there was any chance of them agreeing to it. They shouldn't have to leave just because one higher being has gone insane."

Insane or committed to dealing out reasonable justice?

I manage to hold in that question, through considerable effort. "Fine, fine. When you have a better idea, let me know about it."

Raze, Mirage, and Peri start murmuring to each other, maybe about the actually insane plan to trot her out as bait. Do they really want to offer up our cream puff to a shadowkind they see as a maniac?

I might not blame this weird being for the havoc she's wreaked on the mortal city, but she knows we've been trying to stop her. Attacking Peri would also be justified from her perspective.

And based on past experience, none of us would be able to dash in there fast enough to stop her. Even Peri's startling power might not do much good against this being, if she could manage to blast her energy out despite the fact that she wants to help the vigilante, not harm her.

As that unnerving thought shudders through my mind, a twinge of a different sort of discomfort touches my fae senses. Like a forest creature caught in a trap… except there's no forest here, not really.

My head swivels toward the impression instinctively. With a few steps, the tug gets stronger.

Some part of the natural world has been disrupted. I can feel it the same way I picked up on the mindless aggression of the shadowkind Peri's sorcerer sent to attack us weeks ago.

I don't like the idea of explaining my fae awareness to the others or looping them in on my private quest. Without glancing back, I call over a vague remark. "I'm going to check something out. I won't go far."

Raze lets out a huff. "I don't think that's a good—"

There's a rustle that I think is the shifting of Peri's leather jacket over her dress as she grasps his arm. "It's fine. Maybe Hail will notice something the rest of us wouldn't. There's no reason we have to do *everything* together."

"Thanks, Cream Puff!" I toss out.

The words come out more mocking than I meant them. I

do appreciate her offering me my space—but it also gnaws at me that she thinks she needs to defend me.

My resentment isn't really her fault, though.

I stalk out of my teammates' view as quickly as I can, shedding the sense of their curious—and probably wary—gazes following me. The faint pulsing of Peri's concern clings on through the glowing spot on my chest that I can't tune out.

I ignore it as well as I can and focus on the prickle of distress I caught. There's a creature in trouble somewhere nearby… Maybe more than one creature?

I veer down an alley that runs between the backs of the buildings to allow deliveries and other vehicle access. As I come up on the wrecked stores, my steps slow.

A small, furry figure squirms beneath the rubble. Plumes of smoky essence streak up toward the darkening sky.

My heart lurches. It's not just a creature but a shadowkind being—a lesser one, but that doesn't mean it deserves to be in pain. And it must be in a lot if it can't concentrate well enough to escape into the shadows.

A recent memory twists my gut. Am I going to have to freeze it out of its misery—and its entire life—like I did those strange creatures that jumbled together?

Fuck, I hope not.

As I hurry over with a lump in my throat, a plaintive mew reaches my ears from elsewhere in the rubble. There *is* another creature trapped here.

I work quickly, tugging at the chunks of brick and concrete until I uncover the first. The shadowkind creature looks mostly cat-like other than a pair of gills that flap open for it to breathe, hidden beneath its shaggy gray fur. Or at least I assume it'll look cat-like when it isn't pouring out essence from several slashes in its lean body.

A blow from a chunk of concrete wouldn't have dealt

those narrow wounds. It wasn't only injured by the falling rubble.

The rogue shadowkind must have hit it with her claws or her wild power before the collapse.

Why would she hurt a little shadowkind being?

I scoop it up in my hands and press my fingers to the wounds. To my relief, I can tell the creature isn't too far gone to be healed.

I can save this being even if I couldn't the others earlier this evening.

Steadying my mind, I summon my icy power. Ever so carefully, I exude the chill into the creature—just enough to seal the flesh and stop the worst of the bleeding.

"Come with me," I murmur to it, as if I'm going to give it a choice, and carry it into the shadows.

As the darkness at the edge of the alley closes around us, the creature gives a little shake and seems to perk up. In the shadows, its wounds close even more quickly. I can feel its essence binding together into a more cohesive form.

After a matter of minutes, it squirms as if trying to crawl out of my arms back toward the heap of rubble. Another of those pitiful mews reaches my ears.

"Fine," I tell it, and pull us back into corporeal form. The shadowkind creature leaps out of my hold and scampers to a trash bin that's partly crushed, its lid held down by a few fallen bricks.

I knock those aside and open the lid to find an actual cat —mortal and bleeding crimson liquid from a shallow cut on its hind leg.

The shadowkind sort-of cat makes an urgent yipping sound. I lift out the mortal cat and set my hand against its wound.

I can't close that up as effectively as I could the shadowkind creature's injuries, but I can freeze the surface into a scab-like material that'll stave off more bleeding and numb the poor animal's pain.

As soon as I've finished, the cat wriggles out of my arms. The shadowkind creature immediately bumps heads with it and rubs their sides together.

"So you're best buddies, huh?" I say, bemused. I guess there isn't anything so odd about that if their natures are similar despite their differing origins.

The cat makes a throaty sound that the shadowkind creature echoes. They bound off down the alley with more vigor than I'd have expected after their recent trauma.

What if they re-open their wounds? I trail behind them with an uneasy sense of urgency.

They only travel a couple of blocks before leaping from a dumpster to a window ledge and then onward to a fire escape. I meld into the shadows again to follow them up to the third floor.

There, they both scratch on a windowpane. After a moment, an elderly human man slides the window open.

He clucks his tongue at the two creatures affectionately, obviously unaware that one of them isn't actually a cat. "Hungry again, are you? I spoil you two. Hold on."

He putters off and returns with two dishes full of canned tuna. Both cats chirp in approval and dig in without hesitation.

Clearly this ritual has been going on for a long time. And the man indulges them, to no benefit I can see to himself.

As he offers one cat and then the other creature a gentle stroke of the back, his gaze travels toward the site of the recent destruction. A frown darkens his face.

I don't need Peri's powers to know that he's worried.

Why wouldn't he be? The shadowkind being who's tearing up his city doesn't care who she hurts. She didn't even care that she nearly killed two creatures who were simply roaming through the city trying to survive, blameless in anything she could be angry about.

She wants to destroy everything.

I linger in the shadows, sitting with that knowledge. Letting it percolate through every particle of my being.

I can't say that Viscera is any less evil than the humans I've raged against in the past. She's *worse* than plenty of them. Certainly much more of a menace than this old man who enjoys offering food to stray cats and shadowkind.

Even I've hurt people who didn't deserve it, haven't I? I've been a jerk to most of the other shadowkind at the school. Peri sure as hell never did anything to deserve all the cutting remarks I've shot her way.

How is being angry an excuse if you savage so many beings other than the rightful targets?

If I've been this furious at humans for the acts only a few of them carried out… Wouldn't they be just as understandably enraged at shadowkind over the pain this one rogue is causing?

I ball tighter in my patch of darkness, stewing in those thoughts.

What am I supposed to do? I can't stop being pissed off over what happened. Maybe I can't be anything except a jerk.

Peri doesn't believe that, though.

At the memory of all the sympathetic words and gestures of trust she's offered me, my emotions tangle even more. But the image of her bright smile and the rainbow of colors that can gleam in her vibrant hair sends a reassuring warmth through the worst of my turmoil.

For moments here and there when I've been around her, I haven't felt like such a jerk after all. I've felt like I really was part of a team.

I shoved her away, again and again. But she's always been

there. Always been ready for me to get my head out of my ass.

She could blast my essence to bits if she really wanted to, but she'd rather hold out her hand to take mine, no matter how much I scoff and sneer.

This glowing spot in the middle of me was one more gift, one more sign of the faith she has that I'm more than the asshole I've acted like.

I've never thanked her for that faith. It's the sweetest thing anyone's ever done for me, and I've acted like it was an insult.

And she's so strong she's taken all my bitterness and still been able to speak in my favor just an hour ago. She never lets anything shake her generosity for long.

Why the fuck have I been fighting so hard against her? Because I didn't want to admit how much I've screwed up, as if I can pretend it didn't happen?

All the sanctuaries I've ever built have been made out of frigid ice. Peri's the only being I've ever met who I could imagine bringing them to life—and wanting to.

I need to show her. Somehow… I need to show her everything.

I set off through the shadows, following my sense of where I'm meant to be, where I can be most at home. Knowing it won't mean anything unless I can share it with her.

24

Periwinkle

We're heading back to the trailers when a waft of emotion reaches me. It washes over my body in a poignant mix of regret and longing, like chocolate so dark only the faintest sweetness laces through it.

It must be Hail, off in the distance—he's the only one of my marked men who isn't nearby. As the sensation saturates me from the inside out, the impression solidifies that he's longing for *me*.

I stop in my hurried trek through the shadows. Raze pauses, his presence looming large and impenetrable even in his ephemeral form.

"Hail hasn't headed back to the trailers yet," I say. "He's gone off somewhere in the city… I think he needs me."

The basilisk shifter bristles protectively. "Has he run into

Viscera on another rampage? We'll let the others know and—"

"No. Not like that. I think he just wants to talk. To have someone listen."

Raze is silent for a few beats longer. "Just to talk? The way he's looked at you sometimes… There's some kind of attraction between all of us with the marks, isn't there? Not because of the bond. It amplifies feelings that were already there?"

For me as well as for them, he implies but doesn't say.

I hesitate, careful of his own feelings. Raze might look like a toughie, but he's got a lot of marshmallow under his brawny exterior.

No jealousy or anger taints his vibe of concern, though.

I scoot closer to him so our essence brushes together like a shadowy embrace. "There is—and they were. But that doesn't mean— I'm not forcing anyone into acting on them. And even if you all *wanted* to act on them, I don't have to go along with that. You were here for me first. If you need more time—"

I get the sense of Raze shaking his head, as much as he has one in the shadows. A tingling warmth wraps around me on top of the pang of Hail's emotions, as if I've taken a long sip of sugar-laced tea.

"If *you'd* like it…" he says. "I can tell now how happy it makes you to get close to people. To enjoy all you can with them. And then you bring that happiness with you when we're together. I know you aren't abandoning me, so you shouldn't have to abandon anyone else."

He pauses, and a trickle of anxiety seeps through his comforting aura. "Hail hasn't always been kind to you."

"I know. But I think he's starting to let down all the defenses that made him snap and snark at everyone. Maybe I can peel off more of his prickles." I give Raze another nuzzle. "And if he decides to act like a jerk after all, I'll just leave."

"Then I have nothing to worry about. I'll tell everyone else that the two of you will be back later." Raze nudges up against me in return. "Be careful. We know there's at least one other being running around this city who *doesn't* care how much misery she causes."

"I don't think Viscera is likely to notice me if I stay quiet, but I'll watch out. I'll be back with you soon."

I flit off through the darkness toward my impression of Hail.

With night falling, more of the city is draped in shadow than not. I weave between the pools of light cast by the streetlamps and the beams sent out by car headlights, but there's lots of room to maneuver. The late-spring warmth lingers even without the sun.

The deepening thrum of Hail's emotions leads me to a city park. A large one, with a path branching off in several directions toward a playground, a sports field, and a large stretch of trees like a miniature forest.

I pass only a couple of humans as I enter, both of them hustling out of the park. People don't generally like to hang out in these natural spaces once night falls, I've noticed.

The atmosphere probably feels even scarier when some unknown threat has been smashing up their city.

I veer toward the trees. The pang of Hail's longing expands until it's squeezing around my heart.

Then it softens with a buttered roll sense of relief.

As I dart across the last stretch of mini-forest before the glade where Hail is waiting, he pulls his lanky frame to his feet. He turns toward me, his mouth twisting into a crooked smile.

Since he's taken physical form, I pull myself out of the

shadows too. The moment I'm visible in front of him, his smile stretches a little wider. "You came."

I gaze up at his coolly handsome face. "Of course I did. We're a team, aren't we?"

Hail's shoulders hunch slightly.

He looks at the ground. "I've never been very good at acting like a part of the team. I—I wanted to tell you that I'd like to change that. At least with you. You've been so patient and caring with me, while I treated you like garbage—"

I touch his arm to stop him. "It's all right. Well, treating me like garbage isn't all right, but I know you didn't really want to hurt me. You just have too many other feelings that keep clashing with each other and throwing you off."

He gives a hoarse chuckle. "Yeah, that's one way of looking at it."

His forehead furrows, but he doesn't look up. "I don't know how you can think I still deserve your concern. Or anything. You could tell me to get lost."

"What good would that do anyone?"

"You wouldn't have me hassling you anymore."

I let out a gentle huff. "You don't hassle me that much. And if you stayed away, I'd just wonder whether you were okay, what was happening to you—it wouldn't stop me from caring."

Hail's gaze jerks up to meet mine. He stares at me for a moment. "Why? Why me?"

I grope for the right words. "I mean, it isn't just you I care about. Obviously. And I think every being deserves to have someone looking out for them. But... I especially care because *you* care. It doesn't matter how much you pretend not to—I know you worry about the other shadowkind, and mortal animals too. That's why you've said so much awful stuff about humans. That's why you went off on your own today, isn't it?"

"I guess that's true. But even that…"

Hail trails off with a grimace and sits on a fallen tree that hasn't yet been cleared from the park woods. "Even that is me trying to make up for fucking up, in a way. It's not like I managed to protect anyone from getting hurt in the first place."

I sink onto the trunk about a foot away from him. "Why don't you tell me about it? I'd like to know what made you so angry that it's still tripping you up after all this time."

Hail's hands flex where they're resting on his knees. Then he reaches out and ever so carefully wraps his slender fingers around mine.

Despite his chilly looks and often icy demeanor, his touch is nothing but warm. More heat blooms beneath my skin, echoing the flare of desire the simple touch provoked in him too.

His grip tightens as if he's gathering his resolve. "It was… I don't know how many years ago. At least a few. When I first came into being in the shadow realm, I ran into another fae who'd been alive for centuries. He loved taking trips into the mortal realm—he spent most of his time there. He'd tell me stories of the grand forests and the creatures that lived in them, all the things that grow and thrive…"

Fondness and sorrow twine together with the memories he's sharing. They squeeze around my heart. "He meant a lot to you."

"Yes. And when he invited me to join him on his next venture mortal-side, of course I wanted to see this world for myself."

Hail drags in a shaky breath. "We came through a rift he'd used many times before. It was up in some northern region—he had wintry affinities like I do—and there weren't often humans around. He'd barely talked about them. Mostly he liked communing with the plants and the lesser creatures.

And that was good. But after he'd been showing me around the woods for a few days, we ran into a group of humans. Hunters—the regular kind."

There's an ominous note in his voice. I bristle instinctively. "What did they do?"

"We didn't realize they were there," Hail says. "They were hidden away in one of those shelters for hunting... We'd let out our full fae forms while we wandered around, so they didn't see fellow humans. They saw monsters. And they treated us like that. They started shooting, and then a few came after us with hunting knives and I don't even know what else—they were so determined to destroy us..."

I shift closer to him and tuck my arm right around his elbow. "They were scared. But that doesn't make it okay. Sometimes humans do awful things when they're scared. All kinds of beings do, I think."

"Yeah. It *was* awful. They came at Resin so hard he couldn't pull back into the shadows, and his essence was just pouring out of him. I didn't know what to do. I'd never seen humans before, or guns, or... I was injured and scared too, and I ran off."

He hangs his head. "They butchered him so badly he died. Just disintegrated into essence and blew away."

A suffocating surge of guilt, grief, and frustration rolls over me.

I lean into Hail as if I can absorb enough of his anguish to relieve the burden. "I'm so sorry. That must have been so hard for you, especially when you were totally new here, and he was such a good friend to you."

"Yeah." The fae man's voice comes out raw. "That's what humans are like. They just kill whatever doesn't fit their idea of what the world should be. We weren't harming anything, and they still—"

His jaw clenches. "I know you think most humans are

good at heart. And I'm not even saying you're wrong. But I've hardly seen anything except the bad. It's difficult to believe, no matter how much you argue it."

"I understand. I don't blame you for thinking that way." I might have believed the same things if I hadn't gotten to observe so many humans before the one who imprisoned me, if I couldn't sample the emotions roiling inside them and know the true flavors of their hearts.

I tip my head against Hail's shoulder. "Why didn't you just stay away from them? You ended up at the school—Rollick must have heard something that made him think you needed to be 'reformed.'"

Hail grimaces. "I didn't want to let the humans win. I had the idea—I *still* have the idea—that I could build a space in the human world, places for shadowkind to go where they'd be safe. Why couldn't we have our own parks and malls and theatres and… whatever? Which I guess Rollick is kind of already doing, although it doesn't seem as if he's pushed all that far into the human world, only a hotel here and there. I don't want people to be able to stop us from enjoying everything about this realm that we want to."

With each sentence, his voice gains strength. It reverberates with more passion than I can ever remember hearing from him.

"That sounds amazing! It's a wonderful goal. I'd like to see that too."

He glances down at me. "Of course you would. You always want every being to be as happy as they can be."

There's no dismissal in his tone, but he slides his arm free from mine. I'd regret the loss more if he didn't immediately wrap that arm around my back, nestling me right against his lean frame.

My pulse skips a beat and then thumps on at a giddy pace.

Hail strokes his fingers up and down my shoulder, summoning sparks through both my skin and his.

His words stay solemn. "I was getting ahead of myself. I didn't have the knowledge or the control to put on a good enough front and actually start building an empire. I kept losing my cool with the humans I had to interact with or be around. But getting a little revenge was never satisfying for more than a few seconds."

His arm tenses against my back. "They're so… everywhere, doing so many stupid things and not giving a fuck about anything other than themselves…"

I don't think it'd help to tell him how many things I've felt humans caring about. Even things that seem odd to me, like characters who are only drawings on TV screens or how many times a bunch of them can kick a ball across a field.

Hail started out with a wound in his heart when it came to mortal people, and it's tainted every observation he's made of them. How could it not have?

He bows his head again. His voice goes quiet. "Maybe I couldn't stop myself from acting out because I knew I'd never accomplish what I wanted to anyway. I couldn't even defend the one shadowkind who deserved it the most. How am I going to stand up for anyone else? Rollick would probably laugh if I told him what I'd like to do."

I slip one arm around his waist and lift my other hand to touch his jaw. "I don't think he would. I think if he knew all that, he'd have an easier time helping you adjust to the mortal realm. And then you could do all sorts of great things for other shadowkind."

"I haven't been great to very many of them either," Hail mutters. "I was so pissed off about being stuck at the school…"

He lifts his head abruptly. His eyes shine with the faint moonlight that filters into the glade. "But you saw right through my bullshit. You saw something worth believing in when I'm not sure even I totally did anymore. You're still here, after all the crap I've thrown at you."

A soft smile touches my lips at the awe that's in his voice and resonating through the bond between us. "It was just talking. When it came to the important things, you had my back."

He swallows audibly. "I can't promise I'm never going to get cranky or hostile again. There's still a whole lot I need to figure out. But I don't ever *want* to take it out on you, not like I have before. I don't…"

His voice drops to a whisper. "I don't want to break this bond. Being around you, feeling the things you feel—it helps me remember all the things that were really important to me."

The crème brulé sweetness of his admission shivers through me. I beam up at him, knowing my hair is beaming too from the pinkish golden light that tints his pale skin. "If you want to keep it, I'm happy to. Whenever your resolve feels shaky, you'll always be able to find me."

"You…" Hail makes a strangled sound low in his throat, and then his mouth is on mine, startlingly hot.

As he claims my lips, I kiss him back just as eagerly. The heat rushes straight to the apex of my thighs.

I press my legs together against the swiftly building pressure and clutch the front of Hail's shirt.

He groans and kisses me again before marking a scorching path along my jaw to my neck. "I screwed this up before because I couldn't wrap my head around what I wanted. I was stupid. I only want you. No one else at school ever *saw* me, not like you do. None of them glowed like you do. None of them were half as sweet." He nips the side of my neck. "My cream puff."

At the jolt of sensation, a gasp slips from my mouth. I tilt my head to give him better access. "You can be pretty sweet too when you decide to be."

Hail hums with a vibration across my skin. "I want to be, for you. Fuck, it's incredible being able to feel how good I can make *you* feel." He teases his hand across my breasts, and I press into his touch, chasing more pleasure from the caress. "Just like that. Just stay right here with me, Peri, and I'm going to take care of you so well."

A quiver of anticipation races right through my body. This shadowkind man has been hurting and harsh, but he's letting down all his defenses for me. He's letting me in like he never has before.

And I can feel how much it matters to him. Not only physical pleasures radiate through his nerves, but also tender wafts of affection that match his adoring words.

He tugs my jacket wide and eases down the neckline of my dress so he can continue his path of searing kisses past my collarbone. My voice comes out breathless but sure. "I'll always take care of you too. We look out for each other. A real team."

Hail makes a vaguely disgruntled sound. "You want the rest of them too."

Is that going to be a problem?

My chest tightens. "Yes. That doesn't have anything to do with how much I want you. But if you don't want *me* like that—"

"No," Hail breaks in roughly. "No, I couldn't ask you— It's who you are. Your essence came right out of you and connected you to all of us." He lifts his head to meet my eyes. "You're meant to be with us. You're meant to be with *me*."

My beaming smile comes back. "I am."

"And this bond, it isn't going away, is it? You're always going to belong to me?"

The hope in his voice cracks open something inside me with an even brighter glow. "As long as you want me."

He lets out an urgent sound. "Always, then. Never letting you go."

He drags my dress a little farther and closes his mouth over the peak of my breast, and then all I can do is moan. As he flicks his tongue over my nipple and sucks harder, I squirm against him. The need that's kindled between my thighs is becoming torturous.

Hail mutters another curse and teases his hand over my hip to the spot where I'm hungriest.

I arch into his touch with a soft cry. Bliss quivers through my veins with every stroke of his deft fingers.

"There's so much I want to do for you, with you." He steals another kiss as if he can't help himself. "But I don't think I can wait this time. I've wanted you too fucking much."

I nod vehemently. "Yes. Yes, please."

A little shudder ripples through his body. With his eyes smoldering, he eases me down on the log.

I blink in and out of the shadows so I can lie before him totally naked. There's something deliciously gratifying about the widening of Hail's eyes.

"Look at you. So fucking tantalizing." He runs his hands down my sides and peppers kisses across my cushiony belly, my broad hips, before swiping his tongue across my clit.

My body bucks to meet him. Hail hums, the provocative sensation spreading through my sensitive flesh. He laps and sucks as if I'm the tastiest delicacy he's ever devoured, until I'm shaking with the heady pleasure.

Before I've quite shattered apart, he pulls back with a strangled sound.

He wrenches at his slacks. "I'm going to fucking explode. Gotta take you with me."

He bends over me and claims one more kiss before he thrusts inside. His rigid cock slides so perfectly between my folds with their slick arousal.

Yes. I need this too, so much.

I clutch at his shoulder, at his increasingly rumpled hair. He plunges into me deeper and deeper again.

The sensations of fullness and the heated friction expand through my entire body. With every slam of Hail's hips, his own desire flares even hotter. Our joint sense of need swirls between us.

I rock to meet him, urging him to an even more desperate pace. Hail's breath turns ragged, but he still kisses my cheek and the shell of my ear.

His voice spills out with his panting. "Never want anyone else. Just you. Nothing could be as good as this."

He raises my hips to shift the angle of his thrusts, and I spiral even faster toward my release. A whine seeps from between my lips. Hail swallows it down.

He rams into me again and again and—

With a quavering cry, the pleasure sweeps me away. I tremble and clench around him, and Hail's chest hitches.

He hugs me close, racing closer to the edge with every plunge into me.

When he comes, I tip over the edge again with him, floating on the decadent flood of sensation that passes through our bond.

The glow on his chest flickers through his shirt. The matching spot on mine dances in turn.

Hail gathers me tight against him and rolls us so I'm on top of his much taller frame. He tucks my head under his chin.

"We're going to fix this, Peri," he murmurs. "We're going to fix everything that's gone wrong. I know that because I know you. There's no one else who'd stand a chance."

25

Mirage

Jonah, a couple of the shadowbloods, and Sorsha lean over the city map they've spread on the table in the mostly empty trailer that's become our operations room. The sites of our destruction-happy shadowkind's mayhem stand out in stark orange against the blueish buildings and gray streets.

They don't form any pattern to my eyes, only polka dots of chaos, but the others seem to be making more sense of it.

Riva swivels her finger around one neighborhood. "Viscera hasn't hit too close to this area yet, even though there are a lot of the taller buildings like the other streets she's rampaged through. I think she'd be even more tempted to take the bait here."

Sorsha nods slowly. The phoenix shifter only arrived a couple of hours ago, but we've quickly brought her up to speed.

She smiles a lot and cracks jokes even when the subject is serious, which I can appreciate. But there's a crackly, burn-y sense of heat around her even in her totally human-looking form that itches at my nerves.

Hail asked her if she couldn't just incinerate the crocodile-tailed woman, and Sorsha gave him a wry grin and said she'd have to have Viscera in her sights first. That is the part that's proven the hardest.

The rogue shadowkind is both pushy and slippery.

"How far away do you think the rest of us will need to stay from Peri for Viscera to feel comfortable showing herself?" Sorsha asks. "From what you've said, she's been awfully cautious since that first encounter where you managed to throw her off a little."

Jonah grimaces. "Unfortunately, I think we should keep at least half a mile back, spread out in different places and pretending we're focused on other things. But that's still close enough that we should be able to get there quickly when it's time."

Peri wanders around their cluster, peering between them at the map. Her voice shines as bright as ever. "This time we'll have it set up so I can signal all of you as soon as I see her. Then I'll keep her talking and calm her down as well as I can."

A deeper discomfort crawls under my skin. Peri is the bait we're hoping this maniac monster will take. We're sending her out there like a minnow on a hook, hoping the crocodile will bite.

Our Rainbow is much more stubborn than the arcs of light that streak across the sky. She insisted that we don't risk more devastation waiting to see if Rollick can track down another sorcerer whose powers might not help anyway.

I'm all for getting down to action, but what if Viscera decides she'd like to smash up shadowkind like she does windows and walls? What if she flattens Peri like she has all those cars before we can make it there?

Are we really putting our Rainbow at that much risk?

No one else seems to think there's a problem with sending Peri straight into the line of fire. Even Peri is taking it for granted that she should be dangled in front of this unhinged being. The emotions that trickle through our connection are all determination and pride, as if she thinks this is the best help she can offer.

Maybe it is. Maybe stopping Viscera is more important than her shiny presence.

It's not as if I can do enough to make it unnecessary to put her life on the line.

Restlessness twists through my chest all the way down to my gut. I pace in the back of the trailer as more details of the plan get tossed back and forth, but with each passing minute, my desire intensifies to tip over the table and shred the map into confetti that'll rain down over us.

That's definitely not going to bring a smile to anyone's face, let alone solve all this solemnness.

I need to burn off some energy before it wriggles out of me in worse ways.

No one's paying me any mind. It's easy to slip into the shadows and dart off toward the city without a word spoken to question my departure.

I can't sense anyone's actual feelings except Peri's, but an anxious vibe hangs over the city streets so thickly even I can taste it. The atmosphere quivers into me, setting my own nerves jittering faster.

Of course the humans are uneasy. A being they can hardly accept is real is popping out of thin air and playing wrecking ball with their city, and none of them have figured out how to stop her either. They have no idea where she'll appear next, or what—or who—she might hurt.

It must be like stepping across a frozen lake hearing the ice creak beneath you, hoping it won't crack. A game more precarious than any I'd like to play.

I watch various humans walk along the sidewalks—in a furtive rush, gazes flicking around them, eager to get back to relative safety behind solid walls.

Viscera's been smashing through walls too. I don't think they can feel secure even inside.

A familiar urge ripples through my essence. I might not be able to help catch the rampaging rogue shadowkind, but I can distract the humans from their worries. Provoke some laughter where before there were only clenched jaws. Remind them they can find little amusements even when a situation seems dire.

That's what every bit of my being craves. Why shouldn't I carry out the work every particle of me craves?

I slink along the edges of the buildings with my ears pricked. Muffled sobs carry through the pane of a basement window.

Peeking inside, I spot a child—a girl—curled up on her bed with her blanket tucked tight around her skinny frame. She's sniffling and staring at the window, but she can't see me in the shadows.

She's afraid of what might be prowling out here. The monsters human kids imagine in the dark have become much too real, even if the grown-ups in her life will be calling them terrorists and gangsters.

I'll show her the beings that lurk in the shadows aren't all cruel.

I wriggle past the pane and drop down into the patches of shadow on the floor.

What can I play with? My searching glance lands on a paper airplane, its nose a bit bent, sitting on a table in the middle of the room.

At a nudge of my powers, it lifts into the air as if with a sudden gust. The girl sucks in a startled breath.

I make the airplane dip and spin, whirl and bob, jitterbugging through the air. By the time it drifts all the way to the ground, the girl is muffling giggles rather than tears.

Pleased warmth flows through my being. Leaving her, I creep deeper into the apartment.

A woman in the kitchen has just poured herself a cup of tea. Steam wafts from the mug as well as from the spout of the kettle.

I impose a little of my will on the particles gusting into the air, shaping them into a vague figure that gives a jaunty bow. But the woman has already turned away from the counter, cupping the mug between her hands.

I switch my focus to the steam drifting from the steeping tea in the cup. The impression of a playful puppy emerges, bounding through the air and swinging its floppy ears—

The woman looks down and yelps. Her hands flinch around the cup. It slips from her fingers.

Scalding water sloshes across her legs and feet before the mug fractures on the tiled floor.

With a hiss of pain, she dashes to the bathroom. I gaze after her, my heart sinking.

I only wanted to cheer her up, but I ended up frightening her so much she hurt herself. How could what was so delightful to me be so terrifying to her?

No matter how much I play, I never know what effect I'll have.

A sense of helplessness as tight as if I was still trapped in one of the experimenters' cells closes in around me. I dive deep into the darkest shadow I can find, but the anguish follows me.

I only wanted to brighten these people's lives, take them away from their worries. Instead, I gave them more.

That's why I ended up at the academy in the first place, isn't it? Because I didn't know where to draw the line.

I *thought* I was being careful. I thought I could keep it low key enough.

Maybe I haven't gotten better after all. Should Rollick have trusted me to be on this mission?

Shame and fear mingle with my guilt. I ball myself even smaller within the swath of darkness, as if I can shrink enough that the awful feelings will no longer fit inside me.

Then, through the despair I can't contain, a thin glow seeps in. A faint sense of affection washes over me, smoothing the worst edges off my nerves.

I tense in confusion and then realize the feeling is reaching me through the spot on my chest that connects me to Peri.

She must have noticed my turmoil. She's reaching out to me—sending out the softest emotions she can to surround me in a gentle embrace.

Another current of loving reassurance drapes around me like a cozy blanket. I can almost feel Peri's arms encircling me the way I haven't let her touch me in weeks.

Every part of me aches to lean into her body, to soak up the tenderness she can offer for real.

But this distant caress is good too. She's with me even though I wandered off.

She caught my distress and is drawing me out of it without even needing to be in shouting range.

As the shame that gripped me melts away, a spark of excitement quivers to life at the center of me.

This—this bond that ties us together—it isn't chaining or caging me, is it? The mark Peri placed on me isn't anything like a shackle.

It's a safety line, there for me to grasp hold of if I careen out into stormy seas, so she can guide me back to firmer ground. And she always will, just like I will for her if she needs it.

Why have *I* been so scared of this closeness when it's the one thing guaranteed to ward off all my fears? How is it anything but delightful?

I laugh into the shadows and spring back toward the streets. Urgency resonates through my essence alongside the swell of relief.

Peri might need me for more than emotional comfort very soon. She's about to put herself directly in front of the most brutal shadowkind I've ever met.

If the emotions I'm picking up from her are accurate… she's setting off to position herself as bait right now.

26

Periwinkle

Here I am taking a perfectly innocent stroll down the city street. With my hands tucked in the pockets of my leather jacket, I amble along as if I'm simply enjoying the balmy spring weather and taking in the sights through the shop windows.

What a delightful tower of shoes! Let me pause and take a closer look.

And how about those pictures of burgers and fries, with colors so vivid you'd think they were radioactive? They're worth gazing at for a moment or two.

The slower I saunter, the more likely Viscera will notice I'm back in town and decide to strike up a conversation. Or pelt me with cars. I'm still not sure whether the warped higher shadowkind's reasons for asking about me by name were friendly or hostile.

She *was* asking for me, though, so I'm giving this bait thing my best shot. I should be reasonably eye-catching with my turquoise hair uncovered and my current sundress striped with an it-should-clash-but-doesn't combo of green and neon pink.

I just can't help feeling incredibly self-conscious with every step I take.

That's fine. I can grin and bear it so we'll finally get this destructive maniac subdued.

And if she does start hurling cars at me, I'll dive into the shadows like my butt's on fire.

I probably do look a little odd, because no one else is wandering the street so casually. A few people have showed up in taxis and practically sprinted into their places of business. Not many shoppers or restaurant goers frolic in the buildings behind the windows.

Viscera has never attacked this neighborhood, but she's got the whole city braced in fear of her next rampage.

We *have* to stop her.

Little twinges of uneasiness, salty-fishy as dried herring, ripple through me with every step. Those aren't only from the nearby humans. My awareness of my marked men has intensified with each moment that's brought us closer: my kiss with Jonah, my intimate collision with Hail, the tender compassion I extended to Mirage yesterday, which brought him back to our group for the first hug he's offered since I accidentally bound them.

It's as if we're even more connected now than we were before. Because we're all accepting this connection, whatever exactly it means, rather than struggling with it?

I still have no idea how any of this works. Which doesn't seem right, since I'm the one who made it happen. Shouldn't we come into existence with an innate understanding of how our own powers work?

Someone really should have a word with whoever's in charge.

After about a half hour of the most believable strolling I can manage without straying out of the streets we decided on, I start to whistle. If Viscera hasn't seen me, maybe she'll hear me?

My cheerful tune lilts through the streets. I'm not sure how in-tune I am, but I'm definitely audible. And who doesn't like the simple melody of "Twinkle, Twinkle Little Star"?

Well, I guess someone doesn't. A man opens a third-floor window just to yell at me, "Cut it out, you… you punk!"

He thinks I look like a rebel! Or at least, that was the most accurate insult he could come up with. I chose my outfit well.

I give him a jaunty salute. "Thank you!"

Once I've walked past his building, I pick up the tune again. I'm sure it's cheering up more people than it's annoying.

I cross the street and head around the block, my gaze sliding over the shadows. A few lesser creatures have ventured over to see what the odd but non-homicidal higher shadowkind in their midst—a.k.a. me—is up to.

I don't think any of them are from the strange rift. The energy I sense as I pass them feels more settled than the warped beasts ever do.

The sun rises higher. The shadows shrink, and I veer closer to the buildings.

Then a figure leaps down into the middle of the road twenty feet ahead of me as if she's popped out of the air.

Viscera lands hard enough to set off a minor earthquake. The asphalt cracks beneath her boots. She grins at the damage before lifting her gaze toward me.

Her form has shifted again, other than the crocodile tail

that seems to be her favorite appendage. Her hair sprouts from her head and down her neck in a style I think I've heard humans call a mullet. Her face has widened but her body has narrowed, making her look unnervingly top-heavy.

I don't think I'd want her to head-butt me.

"Periwinkle," she says. "You came back."

Her voice has morphed too, thicker and huskier than I remember it. Her tongue flicks over yellowed teeth as if she's imagining snacking on me.

I stay where I am, because more distance seems safer, and put on my brightest smile. At the same time, I picture her lunging at me and sinking those yellowed teeth into my neck.

A jolt of panic at the image resonates through my veins. I know my men have picked up on it from the surge of distress that echoes into me in return.

They shouldn't worry too much. This was how we planned that I'd signal them if I encountered Viscera—the most fundamental way we can communicate without using devices that might tip her off that I've sounded a warning.

I keep my voice bright too. "I did. It's a nice city. You've been here for a while now. Have you found anything you like about it?"

She snorts. "I like breaking it. That's the best use for all this human garbage."

Then she cocks her head as if waiting to hear what I'll say. As if she's actually interested in my perspective.

I dig up all the calming imagery I've practiced since I arrived at the academy. Pictures of blue skies with fluffy clouds and ocean waves lapping at golden beaches float through my mind. A banquet of serenity.

As I nudge a careful whiff of that vibe toward Viscera like I have with lesser creatures in the past—like I did with Mirage last night—a splash of chardonnay-sharp anxiety hits me from farther away. My sense of the men I've marked is strengthening more as they rush toward me.

They're awfully worried. Can't they tell she isn't hurting me?

I guess it's hard for them to believe I might not become a target of her joy of smashing.

I can't afford to redirect any of the soothing vibes I'm summoning to them. If I'm going to tame Viscera even a little, it'll take all my concentration. As it is, a jitter runs through my nerves at the urgency of their emotions.

I take a deep breath and focus even more narrowly on the peaceful scenes in my head. "There are definitely some things humans make that might as well be garbage. But I have seen lots of good things from them too. Like food. Have you tried eating any of the things they cook or bake?"

Does she even need to eat? Most shadowkind don't have to—at least not regular types of food. If they do need to consume something in the mortal realm, it's more ephemeral like my hunger for emotions or more animalistic like Raze's hankering for raw meat.

Another jolt of fear shoots through me, and I find myself gritting my teeth against a swell of my own uneasiness. The glowing spot on my chest jerks at my attention. *They're upset. You have to help them.*

No, I don't. This is the plan. They'll see I'm okay as soon as they get here.

Let them get here fast.

That last thought sets my nerves jangling at a higher pitch. My smile tightens a little around the edges.

Thankfully, Viscera is distracted by my question. "Food? It looks interesting when I splatter it across the floor or the walls. Why would you put anything like that sticky, mushy stuff in your body?"

"It's not all sticky and mushy!" I point out helpfully.

"There's crunchy and doughy and chewy. Some of it tastes pretty amazing. And clothes are great, too—you've put on some automatically, but there are all kinds of shapes and textures. Cashmere is so soft. So is silk!"

I think I'm babbling, but she hasn't broken anything yet, so that seems like a sign I'm on the right track. For good measure, I summon memories of cozy blankets and supple dresses wrapping around me.

Maybe those images can plug up the streams of worry that are battering me.

Viscera shakes her head with a swish of her hair, but her expression is still thoughtful. I dare to push my calming vibe toward her with a little more oomph.

The more I can lull her into a sense of complacency, the slower I can hope she'll react when my companions get here ready to fully subdue her.

She scoffs. "Clothes do nothing. They tangle and tear. Stupid stuff. And what about all these walls they throw up all over the place?" She waves at the buildings around us before motioning to the few cars parked on the road as well. "What about these hunks of metal that belch out toxic smoke?"

"There are some bad things about those," I allow. "But cars can get you places much faster than we can even travel through the shadows. That's pretty amazing. And the walls help keep in the warmth when it's cold out and the cold when it's too hot. They can hold all kinds of activities. You should watch a movie sometime! It's an incredible experience."

Viscera arches an eyebrow. "A movie?"

I nod eagerly and try to create a picture with sweeps of my hands. "There's a huge screen, and pictures move on it like a story, but it's made with real people and places so it feels almost like it actually happened. And they can make all kinds of amazing special effects like magic or explosions—I guess you'd like that part—"

I don't know if it's the mention of explosions—which does bring a gleam into Viscera's eyes—or if it's just the distance closing between my men and me, but the rising anxiety smacks into me even harder than before.

My breath hitches, and my muscles tense with the urge to spring in four different directions at once, to race to everyone's rescue.

They're mine. I need to protect them.

They're only upset because they think they need to protect me, I shout back silently, but my retort only amplifies the swell of emotions.

Sour sparks of anguish flare as my men sense my distress. My frustration sears hotter in turn.

Viscera frowns. "What are you doing, Periwinkle?"

I have to find my way back to tranquility—I have to balance out all this turmoil—I'm going to screw everything up—

That last thought crackles through all my good intentions, rattling me from head to toe. My men's answering concern floods me. My vision hazes.

And a spurt of the emotions churning inside me surges out and smacks into a nearby lamp post.

I've kept enough control that my lapse doesn't do any real damage. It only leaves a few dark scratches on the concrete surface.

But a cackle bubbles from Viscera's lips. "That's right! You want to blast it all too. Those mortals messed with us too much. This place wanted us and then it doesn't let us in, no matter how we shift. So we'll shift it to match us!"

A twinge of confusion breaks through my panic. "What are you talking about? Who messed with you? Where are you trying to go in?"

"All of them! Everywhere!" She tosses her hands in the air. "Pull us in and push us away. Make us twist and twitch. Never enough. Screw them! Let's smash and burn it down!"

"Wait!" I cry, but the anguish that wells up with my protest only eggs her on. She whirls around, her tail smashing through the nearest car window. With a spring of her sinewy legs, she hurtles on top of it and crushes the roof toward the ground.

In a matter of seconds, she's flung herself into one storefront and then another. More glass shatters; bricks crumble. The foundations groan as the buildings start to collapse.

Viscera shrieks with apparent glee. "That's enough for here! You can do the rest. So many streets, so much to wreck."

"No!" I gasp out, grasping at her, but she's already flitted away into the shadows.

I spring after her. If I can keep up with her, follow her, maybe…

But by the time I've made it two blocks down the street, I've lost all sense of Viscera. I pull myself back into physical form feeling as low as the dirt beneath the asphalt.

The vans and cars carrying the rest of my colleagues roar onto the street a minute later. My four teammates leap out and race straight to me, as if *I'm* the one who needs help.

"Peri?" Raze says in a fraught growl.

I swipe at my eyes. "It's my fault. I made her want to destroy things even more."

27

Periwinkle

Footsteps crunch through the gravel next to the trailer I'm huddled under.

A wry voice carries into the thicker darkness. "Do you want to come out and talk about it, Peri, or would you rather I pretend I can't tell you're hiding in the shadows."

It's Sorsha. The phoenix shifter helped us a little in handling the first weird rift we found, but I don't know what she can do about this. I couldn't even get her in a position to tackle Viscera with her fiery powers.

On the other hand, when she says it like that, I do feel kind of ridiculous staying tucked away under here.

The men I marked are spread out through our fake movie set, pulsing concern and their own flavors of guilt, as if *they've* done anything wrong. How could they have when they didn't even get close enough to Viscera to invite her to dinner, let alone capture her?

I don't know what to say to any of them. I'm not sure I want to hear what they'd say to me.

And while I'm shying from my failure, Viscera might be turning yet another part of the city into her violent version of vigilante art.

Talking to Sorsha definitely couldn't *hurt*, could it?

Shaking off my reluctance, I emerge from the low crawl space and the shadows one after the other.

Sorsha looks me over, taking in my now standard outfit of leather jacket and vividly colored dress, the twist of my mouth, and my drooping head where my hair flickers shades of bruise-purple and sickly yellow into the dusk.

"What do you want to talk about?" I ask, as if I don't know.

Can ignorance still be bliss if it's feigned? It seemed worth a try.

She cocks her head with a swish of her bright red ponytail and motions to me. "Let's take a walk. Sometimes it's easier to think when your legs are moving to get your mind moving too."

I haven't heard that theory before, but it sounds reasonable. And I'm relieved that she walks onto the field in the direction away from the trailers rather than toward the men I've been avoiding.

"From what I've gathered, this isn't the first time your powers have gotten away from you and had a negative effect," Sorsha says after a moment.

My grimace deepens. "No. But I thought I'd gotten so much better at controlling that part of my nature. I don't know why it happens in the first place, and then It was *so* important that I keep Viscera there and calm… and I still couldn't do it."

"It wasn't all on you, though. No one managed to catch her."

"I was the one the plan depended on. And…" I swallow hard. "It all comes down to me. My powers connected me to the rest of my team, and all those bonds do is mess us up. It's like… like the shadowkind creatures we saw that merged into each other when they warped. They couldn't function properly because they were tripping over each other, and they couldn't pull themselves apart…"

So Hail had to put them out of their misery.

"And I wanted to stop Viscera so badly that I made her even more eager to break the city," I finish. "One more way I threw everything out of whack."

Sorsha hums to herself. She extends her hand palm up, and a flame flares into being above her skin. "Did I ever tell you about the time I nearly burned up the entire world?"

I stare at her. "No. Why would you do that?"

I don't remember reading anything about the phoenix in the records about problems between shadowkind and humans… but Rollick does seem to be friends with Sorsha, as much as the formidable demon has friends. Maybe certain details got strategically left out of the shadowkind history books to protect those who'd be implicated.

She laughs, the sound as dry as the air. "I didn't exactly *want* to. Not really. But that's what phoenixes are meant to do—flame out and be reborn. And when you're a rare, unstable, unprecedented hybrid human-shadowkind who's also a phoenix, it turns out you could be powerful enough to take an awful lot of what's around you down with you. Unfortunately, the rest of the world wouldn't automatically rejuvenate."

I try to picture the smiling, upbeat woman beside me hurling destructive fire at everything around us. My brain cannot process the image. I'll just have to take her at her word.

"But you didn't," I say.

"Obviously, or this place would look a lot more charbroiled. But here's the thing: you didn't burn down the whole world either."

I can't stop a giggle from popping out of my mouth. "I couldn't even if I did want to."

"That's the whole point, though, isn't it?" Sorsha arches an eyebrow at me. "You're beating yourself up over doing a little damage, but you could have powers capable of a whole lot worse. You're hardly the most dangerous shadowkind out there. Your mistakes aren't that horrifying. You've got plenty to be grateful about."

She snuffs out the fire beneath her fingers.

I can see what she's getting at, but her story doesn't comfort me much. "It's not just about the damage I did. It's the damage I didn't stop from happening. Ever since I came to the mortal realm, I've hurt *so* many people without meaning to, and every time I have the chance to balance things out… No matter how much I try to only bring people happiness, more things go wrong. The men I care about can't use their own powers effectively because our emotions get all muddled now. How many more people will Viscera hurt because I couldn't stop her—and maybe riled her up more?"

Sorsha considers me for a few moments with a pensive expression. "I might have a few ideas about that too. Let's head over to the Everymobile. We've gotten our thoughts moving around plenty. Now I think the conversation needs drinks."

Having something filling my throat other than uncomfortable words sounds good to me. Especially when my feet are starting to twinge with familiar aches.

As Sorsha leads me to the hulking vehicle parked down the road from the trailers, she slings her hands in her pockets and murmurs a couple of lines of a song I can't make out. Then she glances over at me. "How are you normally thinking about your powers, Peri? And, well, everything else around you? What do you mean by 'balancing things out'?"

I grope for the right words to explain. "I've had so many accidents, and the sorcerer who held me captive forced me to use the harmful side of my powers to blast people *he* wanted to attack. I feel every single being I hurt. I have… sort of a list, in my head, of the total number. Whenever I can make someone feel happy instead, I can knock that number down."

"I assume you'd eventually like it to be zero."

"I'd like it to be in positive numbers. More happiness than hurt." Imagining that brings a bittersweet ache into my chest—the joy I'd feel if it happened, the fear that I'll never get even close.

Sorsha nods. "So you're always trying to make people happy and encourage other positive emotions."

"Yes. I don't know why it's so hard."

"Probably because both human and shadowkind beings are too damned complicated."

Before I can ask what she means by that, she opens the door of the RV we've just reached. It swings out with a jangle like a phone ringing in an old movie and a brief flash of rainbow strobe lights.

I peer at the doorway. "What was— Does it normally do that?"

Sorsha laughs and beckons me inside. "The Everymobile has been with us through a lot of adventures. Even passing through normal rifts into the shadow realm leaves it a little warped—in interesting rather than dangerous ways. Usually."

The RV's front room holds a tiny kitchen across from a padded bench that forms a semi-circle around a narrow table. Some of the cushions are a neutral beige; others sparkle with a silver gloss. A pinwheel spins on the ceiling between two light fixtures.

I sit down at one end of the bench, and a little green

creature comes hurtling out of a doorway at the far end of the vehicle. It looks like… a tiny dragon?

The shadowkind creature freezes at the sight of me and lets out a squeaky sort of grunt.

Sorsha clicks her tongue at it. "Now, Pickle, you know to be nice to guests."

The little dragon studies me as if sizing me up. It's so cute I can't help smiling, even though I'm not sure there's anything nice about the trickles of smoke that puffed from its nostrils.

All at once, the creature flings itself onto my lap and flops there. I rub the smooth green scales on its back tentatively, and it gives a raspy rumble that's almost like a purr.

Sorsha grins. "There you go, already making friends. Now let's see…"

Grabbing a mug, she turns on the tap at the kitchen sink and makes a face at the sand that hisses out. She turns the faucet off, waits a few seconds with her foot tapping, and tries again.

This time water burbles into the sink, but apparently that's not what she wants either. She gives it one more try, and on the third gets a gush of steamy, dark brown liquid.

When she sets the first mug in front of me, the scent that reaches my nose immediately soothes my nerves. "Hot chocolate! I need a sink like that."

"If only it came with different faucets for every flavor." Sorsha sits across from me, cradling her own mug. "Before we talk about how to fix your problem, let's touch on how I solved mine. How do you think I managed not to burn the world down?"

I pause. "You… decided you liked it better when it isn't charbroiled?"

She barks a delighted laugh. "I guess that's the gist of it.

But I think you know that with these things it isn't as easy as deciding, or you'd just decide never to hurt anyone."

"True."

"Back then, my fire would flare out of its own accord when I was angry or upset. Kind of like for you, when the destructive energy comes out of you."

I perk up. Maybe she can help. "It is like that. It builds up inside me until it explodes."

Sorsha turns her mug between her hands. "I used to try to hold the fire in. Ignore the anger, suppress any stress that might stoke it. But then humans did something really horrible to someone I love, and the rage took over. That's when I almost burned everything down. The anger had already burned away every other consideration inside me."

I knit my brow. "So how did you stop being angry?"

A soft smile touches the phoenix shifter's lips. "I had help. Other people I loved called out to me and broke through my anger. I remembered all the things I *didn't* want to destroy. Afterward, I realized that part of the problem was that I'd tried so hard not to give in to my anger at all. I bottled up so much, got so scared of what I might do with my powers, that I only added to the stress I was under."

"And you've never gotten to that point again?"

She shakes her head. "Sometimes I want to use my fire. Sometimes I *need* to. There are things in this world that need to be destroyed, and things that are going to hurt whether we like it or not."

Every particle of my being balks at those words. Sorsha contemplates my expression. "You don't like accepting that fact."

"I don't think we should have to," I say. "Why *can't* people only be happy? Why does there have to be so much pain?"

Her tone gentles. "I think too much of anything can be a

problem. From what Rollick's told me, you blast out energy when you get overly excited too, don't you?"

A shamed flush heats my cheeks alongside a flicker of orange through my hair. My gaze drops to the tabletop. "Yes. It's either way. That's how the bonds happened too. Whenever the emotions inside me get too big to contain, something bursts out. That's why it's so hard."

Sorsha lets us sit with that thought through a sip of her hot chocolate. "I'm just wondering… What if the reason you yo-yo back and forth between those extremes is because you're thinking of *everything* in extremes?"

I frown. "What do you mean?"

"You see happiness as the only acceptable emotion. You try to avoid pain and sadness at all costs. If you're always pushing in one direction, it makes sense that it'd be easy to stumble too far that way—or to rebound too fast in the other direction. Like a vicious cycle, always swinging around from one side all the way to the other, when the safe space is in between. A little happy, a little sad. A little pleasure, a little pain."

My fingers clench around the mug's handle. "But if I let both happen… how am I ever going to make up for all those people before?"

Sorsha lifts her shoulders in a shrug, but the vibe she gives off tastes like sympathy rather than disregard. "Maybe you won't. I don't know if I've helped more people than I accidentally hurt before I got a handle on my powers. I just know I'd have hurt even more if I hadn't sorted myself out. Is beating yourself up for things you couldn't control in the past making it easier to do good in the world right now?"

The question hits me like a punch to the chest. For a second, I can't breathe.

"No," I admit. All the anguish, all the guilt—it's tangled

up inside me, searing sharper and hotter whenever anything else upsets me.

What would it be like to go forward as if with a plate washed clean? To believe that only what I do today and tomorrow and every day after that matters, not what happened before?

It's hard to imagine that too, but a strange flutter passes through my pulse when I try.

I thought the problem was that I couldn't keep the men I've marked happy enough, that I was passing on too much distress and failing to soothe theirs.

What if… what if I *have* been fighting the parts that are scary or uncomfortable too much? What if we all should look at what we actually have, good and bad?

We might find out we can make more of ourselves than we realized. We are still a team.

The thought brings up a memory of Viscera's vicious grin. I tried so hard to calm *her* down and turn her toward happiness rather than rage…

I sit up straighter, so abruptly Pickle startles with a disgruntled chirp. "I think I might know how we can bring Viscera in."

28

Periwinkle

When I've finished explaining the gist of my plan to the full group in the yard of the fake film set, Drey raises his eyebrows. "You want us to stop the crazy shadowkind who's going around destroying things… by destroying more things?"

Riva elbows her shadowblood mate. "Hush. It's not like anything else we've tried has gotten us far."

I twist my hands in front of me. "I don't want to ruin anything that's important to the people in the city. I figured we could find an area that's mostly abandoned, or maybe evacuate the buildings… No one should get *really* hurt because of us."

Rollick cocks his head. "I can identify a stretch where all the buildings would be covered by insurance, and we could start there. But clearing the areas out will be a bit of a hassle."

The demon is the one I most need to convince, the one who's calling the shots. If he doesn't believe in this plan, nothing anyone else says will matter.

I gather the confidence that came to me during my talk with Sorsha. "Viscera enjoys destroying things. She's talked as if it's expressing herself, making her mark on the world, showing who she is—as strange as that sounds."

"Strange does as strange is," Mirage remarks in a wry tone.

I offer him a small smile before turning back to Rollick. "Anyway, we've spent all this time attempting to calm her down and stop her. But that's basically us saying that she isn't okay the way she is, that we think there's something wrong with her."

Hail coughs and raises his hand. "After everything, I for one would like to support that idea."

Raze lets out a faint growl, but I just roll my eyes. There was no hostility in the winter fae's comment.

And besides… "That might be true, but *she's* not going to like us making her feel deficient. Why should she listen to us, trust us even a little bit, when we're trying to change her? Trying to make her act the opposite way from what feels right to her?"

Jonah frowns. "So then by dealing out a little destruction ourselves… we make it seem as if we understand?"

I nod eagerly. "When I let out that bit of my darkness, she got all excited. She thought it meant I was on her side. If a bunch of us start smashing up part of the city, it'll catch her attention. And hopefully it'll make her feel like we have the same ideas she does, so she'll be comfortable enough to join in."

"And then we catch her," Raze says.

"Yes. The main problem has always been getting her in a

place where the rest of you can actually reach her. All we need is to create a scenario where she'll show up."

Rollick runs a finger across his lips. "You know, that's a warped enough idea that it just might be exactly what our warped shadowkind needs. Let me put the pieces in motion, and we'll see if we can't have our destruction ground ready sometime tomorrow."

He turns with a beckoning gesture toward his assistants, who scurry after him. He's already rattling off instructions before they disappear around one of the trailers.

The shadowbloods follow him, probably to see if they can pitch in too. Sorsha salutes us before heading back to her RV with her men.

My own lovers stir around me. An unexpected jolt of panic shoots through me at the thought that they might walk away.

They must pick up on that emotion, because Hail stops in his tracks and Mirage swivels back toward me.

I give them a hesitant smile. "There are some things I'd like to talk about with all of you. I think it'll be better if we're all together… Since we are all stuck together, whether I meant that to happen or not."

Jonah glances around at the other men. His lips curve into a soft smile of his own. "I think we're all okay with being 'stuck' now, Peri. What's on your mind?"

The shadows draped across the yard between the trailers remind me of how easily other beings could listen in on our conversation. "Is there somewhere we could go that'll be just the five of us?" What I want to say feels too private for an audience.

"Sure." Jonah motions for us to join him. "I have the one trailer that's been my home on the road. No one will bother us in there unless there's an emergency."

"Maybe we'll get a whole twenty-four hours without

one," Hail mutters, but he saunters along with the rest of us without complaint.

Jonah's trailer is set up like a tiny apartment—not too different from the RV, but all one rectangular room. A bed fills most of one end, a table and benches the other. In between, a couple of small dumbbells sit on an exercise mat. A suitcase that must hold all the clothes he brought with him from the school is tucked in the corner, a book lying next to the neatly made bed, but those are the only real signs that anyone's actually living here.

It doesn't really feel homey, but this conversation is about the men around me, not the space we're occupying.

When we've all filed in and Jonah has shut the door behind us, he seeks out my gaze. "What's on your mind, Peri?"

"We're going to help with your plan, of course," Raze puts in, and glowers at the other men as if daring them to argue.

Hail snorts. "A chance to rain a little hell on the city while also completing our mission? How can I resist?"

He says it with a sarcastic edge, but I know he does like the idea at least a bit. Even if he's changed his mind about Viscera, the resentment he's carried toward humans isn't going to vanish in a day.

Mirage shakes himself with a flick of his ears from his hair. "I can make it look as if we're smashing more than we really are."

"That's not a bad idea, but I think it's the real smashing that's going to catch Viscera's interest." I drag in a deep breath. "But I didn't want to talk to you about her. I wanted to talk about me—you—all of us. I've been so concerned about how you were handling these bonds that *I* haven't been handling them very well."

Raze's gruff voice turns gentle. "You haven't done

anything wrong, Peri. You've been so patient with us while we were being asses about it." He shoots his glower specifically toward Hail.

I shake my head. "The thing is, you deserve more than patience. I shouldn't have treated you like the way you were reacting was a problem."

I swallow and reach way down to the glimmer of peace I found when I was talking with Sorsha. "When we've felt angry or upset or scared or stressed… that isn't a problem. Maybe it's caused by a problem, but I shouldn't be trying to be happy or making all of you happy all the time. That's not possible… I'm not sure it'd even be *good*."

Mirage reaches out to twirl a lock of my hair. "Hard to know what happy is if you don't have any other colors for contrast."

"Exactly."

I set my hand on Raze's arm, holding his gaze. "It was totally okay for you to feel nervous about getting closer to me and worried that you might hurt me. It makes sense that you have awful feelings about the mistakes you made in the past. That's part of who you are. I can't erase that, and I can't expect you to. You shouldn't think it's wrong. We'll just make sure there are lots of brighter feelings in the mix too."

Raze's voice gets rougher. "You definitely bring those."

I turn to Mirage next, taking in the twist of his smile that matches the splash of apprehension trickling through our connection. "Of course you were hesitant to open up about anything serious when you've been through so much pain. And being scared of getting trapped again is part of what keeps you safe. I can respect that just as much as I enjoy all the ways you light up our lives."

Mirage's fox ears flick out again, and this time he lets them stay as he strokes the back of his fingers over my cheek. "I don't bring as much light as you do, Rainbow."

I beam back at him. "I think you do, just different kinds."

My attention veers to Jonah, whose stance has become a little awkward. I step toward him and take his hand to twine our fingers together.

When I look up into his eyes, he doesn't shy from my gaze.

"I shouldn't have tried to argue with you about how we could be together. You know what feels right to you, and your conviction has gotten us through a lot of troubles already. And I won't try to talk you out of the things you're insecure about. I'll tell you how I see it and give my point of view, but I know no one can be sure and steady all the time, no matter how good you are at being that person."

Jonah's fingers tighten around mine. "I'm glad I'll have you to hold on to when my confidence starts to waver."

"Me too." I bob up on my toes to kiss his cheek and then let him go so I can face the last of my marked men. The one who's hurled the harshest emotions at me.

Hail stares back at me, his posture rigid. An ache forms in my chest at the taste of uncertainty that laces his instinctive defiance.

Even after everything I've said so far, he isn't totally sure I won't reject him. Or some part of him, anyway.

"I see now why you were so upset—so upset that you couldn't help turning on people," I say softly. "I should have given you the space to decide whether you could trust me rather than pushing for you to be friendly. Some things you said might have been uncalled for, but there's nothing wrong with all the anger in you. It just shows how much you care."

Hail blinks. Then he slips his hand around my elbow and tugs me into a hug, my head tucked under his chin. "I only want to be angry *for* you from now on, Cream Puff. Never at you."

I hug him back, but I don't let him distract me from the point I'm trying to make. "It'd be all right if you are. Because… sometimes I make people angry."

I ease back and glance around our circle. These words are the hardest. "Sometimes I get nervous or overeager and say things that bother people. Sometimes I feel hurt or totally frantic. That's okay too. I'll never reach a place where I'm always happy. And pushing too hard for it only turns the joy too intense when it comes. What's important is that I keep working on finding my own balance of all the things I end up feeling—and taking action the best way I can."

Hail raises an eyebrow. "So where do we go from here?"

I spread my hands. "I don't know. I guess we just keep figuring it out as we go. I only wanted you all to know that I see everything that makes each of you *you*. I want all of it. Sometimes I might get sad or frustrated, but I'll still be here for you. None of it is wrong."

I pause, and the rightness of the emotion swelling inside me spills onto my tongue. "I love all of you, for everything you are, with everything I am."

That love pours out of me, and a matching affection flows out of my men to meet it. Warm and comforting, savory with a hint of sweetness, like the perfect cream soup.

My hair lights up with a pink sheen. The marks on all four of my men's chests glow brighter too, strong enough to seep through their shirts.

But it's not the searing white shine from when I first marked them. No, now it's the vibrant bluish-green of my turquoise hair, halfway between darkness and light.

All the joy we've found with each other and all the pain, melded together the way our essence seems to be.

The men glance down at themselves with a start, but awe and delight mixes with their surprise. Hail grazes his fingers over the spot and then looks at me.

My own mark has lit up with the same hue. The connection, the bond, twines between all of us. Joining us together as a team.

Maybe even a sort of family.

Raze moves first, his sinewy arm sliding around me. As he presses his mouth to the top of my head, his brawny frame lines up against my shorter, softer body.

A waft of devotion that's got a lot more spice to it tickles over my tongue.

"Our Glowbug has shown us how much we mean to her," he says in a rumble. "I think we should show her just how well we can work together to adore her."

Hail's eyebrows arch higher. "*All* of us? At the same time?"

His tone is dry, but a flare of his own heated desire tingles through me.

"Why not?" Raze nuzzles my temple. "We're all joined together through her. We can accept each other just as much as she accepts each of us, can't we? I want to see every part of her lit up the way no one but us can manage."

Jonah wets his lips, but he stays where he is. "I'm not sure —Peri and I have barely done anything—"

I smile at him. "Whatever you want to do, whether you're comfortable with Raze's idea or not, it's all okay."

Mirage lets out a light chuckle. "But you can feel it, can't you? How much *she* wants it? Rainbow, you always taste delicious."

The fox shifter closes in at my other side and nibbles the shell of my ear. At my pleased gasp, more carnal hunger flares in all four of my men.

"I can feel you so well," Hail says with a kind of wonder. "Even clearer than before. Every response. Everything that gets you off."

He strokes his hand around the curve of my breast before

flicking his thumb over the nipple. Pleasure sparks through my flesh alongside my noise of approval.

Jonah eases between Hail and Raze and trails his fingers from my jaw down my neck to my shoulder. As my pulse jumps giddily at his caress, he inhales sharply.

"You do want this," he says, and it's not a question. He must be able to sense how much the idea of being adored by all four of my men at once thrills me.

I tease my hand down the front of his shirt. "I've never even gotten to have you yet. It's not too much?"

"No," he says in a raw voice. "No, I think it's perfect."

Then his mouth is crashing into mine, and the thrum of affection and desire drowns out the rest of the world. All I can feel now is that delicious heat flooding my body inside and out: Jonah's kiss, the other men's caresses, all the ways their bodies encompass mine.

Hail slides his hand beneath my jacket, and Raze helps him peel it off. The winter fae tugs the strap of my dress down my arm so he can dip his hand beneath the fabric and cup my breast skin to skin.

He hums to himself. "Peri is so dedicated to appreciating every part of us. Maybe we should see how many different aspects she can enjoy. Sometimes the heat"—he nips the crook of my jaw with a wash of hot breath—"is even more potent with a little chill mixed in."

With those last words, he sends a tiny flare of frost over my nipple. The shock brings a gasp to my lips, and the warm stroke of his thumb following it sets off an even sharper jolt of bliss.

Raze lets out a rumble that reverberates into me where our bodies are pressed together. "She liked that. Do it again."

Hail shows no sign of annoyance at being ordered around. With a cocky grin, he dips his head to close his mouth around the tip of one breast while reaching between me and Jonah to give the other his thrilling cold-and-hot treatment.

Raze sets his hand on my belly, just above the spot where I'm aching most. "Maybe we should all find our ways to give Peri everything we have to offer. Would a little fierceness make the tenderness sweeter?"

He draws his fingertips across my dress, the claws he's extended drawing little lines of not-quite-pain across my abdomen through the fabric. Sparks quiver over my skin. When he smooths the spot over with a gentler caress, a whimper slips out of me between my kisses with Jonah.

Mirage chuckles. "Our Rainbow wants to enjoy every color." He trails his hand over my hip and squeezes my ass. "I can be right here with you, staying grounded together. And I can send you soaring far away too."

A tremor of his supernatural power passes through my mind, and all at once I do feel like I'm soaring—as if my feet have floated off the ground, my body drifting in a buoyant breeze.

As my breath catches with my surprise, Mirage pulls me out of the illusion with another provocative squeeze. A heady shiver ripples through my nerves.

Raze teases his claws across my belly again, dipping almost to my sex. Hail laps a chilly streak across my nipple and then sucks the peak of my breast into his scorching mouth.

The dueling sensations drench me with pleasure. My hips sway with kindling need.

Jonah wrenches his mouth from mine but doesn't go far. His voice is taut with his own desire. "I want to make you feel as good as possible, but I don't have the same kind of powers they do."

I clutch the front of his shirt. "I don't need you to.

Maybe we can find a way to play with your sorcery later. Right now… just *having* you is lots of novelty in itself."

With a rough sound, he closes the short distance between our lips again.

Raze curls his fingers right between my legs, and I can't help squirming into his touch. He hums. "I think she really did mean *right* now. Let's get her to the bed."

I drag Jonah by his shirt, not that he resists. When I nudge him onto the mattress, he sinks down, watching me like a starving man faced with his first meal in days.

I'm too impatient to bother with a full undressing. I reach for the fly of his slacks. As I yank down the zipper, Hail tugs off my panties with contrasting streaks of heat and cold trailing from his fingers.

Jonah's longing washes over me, as sweet and rich as the most decadent caramel pie. Drinking it in, I straddle his rigid cock.

He tugs my mouth back to his. Our groans mingle as he presses into me.

Yes. This is where I'm supposed to be. This is how close I'm meant to become with all of my men.

I ease down, taking Jonah even deeper. When I lift my head to rock more forcefully over him, Raze leans in to steal a kiss of his own.

The basilisk shifter yanks my dress higher on my waist. "Mirage, do you think you can make her doubly satisfied?"

The fox shifter grins and teases his fingers over my back entrance. "If Peri would like that… Oh, yes, she would."

I couldn't suppress the flare of excitement their suggestion provokes if I wanted to—which I don't. I tip forward over Jonah, who massages my breasts to delicious effect while Mirage gets into position behind me.

Hail folds his arms over his chest. "What am I supposed to be doing?"

I look at him standing there, and an even giddier desire expands through me with the press of Mirage's erection into my tighter hole. "Come here."

As Mirage fills me as completely as Jonah has, my eyes roll back. Bliss radiates into every particle of my essence.

With a shaky breath, I manage to gather myself enough to yank at Hail's pants.

He helps, his own cock springing free. I lick my lips and lean over to wrap my mouth around its rigid length.

Hail's breath stutters. "Fuck *me*."

Raze's guttural laugh is nothing but joy. "She's certainly doing that. Give her a good rhythm there. Don't bruise her lovely throat."

"Never," Hail swears, his fingers tangling in my hair.

I wind my tongue around his shaft, even hotter than the rest of the heat he brought to bear, and rock with Jonah and Mirage as they plunge into me together. With every thrust and every trace of salty arousal that laces my mouth, my heart thumps faster. Pleasure sweeps through my veins and rushes along our joint connection.

It swells between us so swiftly I'm tossed to my peak with a shock crackling through my body. The ecstasy ricochets between me and my men, their delight expanding alongside my own, until we're moaning in symphony.

Jonah spills himself inside me. Mirage bows over me moments later with a frantic panting. Hail yanks his cock from my mouth with a spurt over my chin.

A wicked gleam lights in the winter fae's eyes. He leans in and licks his cum right off my face.

A fresh thrill races through me, stirring another surge of hunger.

Mirage draws back with a final caress of my back and glances slyly at Raze. "I think she might need even more satisfying."

Jonah kisses me hard, heedless of the lingering flavor of the other man on my mouth, and eases aside. The next thing I know, Raze has swept me up in his arms.

As the massive man lays me out on the bed beneath him, he blinks away his clothes. I splay my legs instinctively, welcoming him in too.

With the drive of his thickness into me, I careen back toward my previous heights. I spiral upward faster and faster, driven by the prick of Raze's claws down my spine, the nip of his basilisk fangs against my neck, and the comforting swipe of his tongue to balance out the spark of pain.

As I come for the second time, my hair and the glow on my chest flare together, pink and turquoise, both pulsing with love. The emotion fills the room, emanating from all four of my men in tandem.

I'm not sure where our path together will lead us, but for the first time, I know we're heading in the right direction.

29

Raze

In the first faint light of dawn, a twinge of hunger prickles through me.

Not the exhilarating craving to pull Peri out of the shadows where she's been dozing and make her moan all over again—although there's also a little of that desire tingling in the background of my existence, as there almost always is.

No, this is the darker, bloodier hunger I'd rather never existed.

If I don't eat raw flesh soon, I won't be able to concentrate on Peri's brilliant plan.

No one else on site is alert to notice me slink out of the trailer through the shadows. At least, it appears that way at first.

I've only made it about a hundred feet from the makeshift film set when I sense my lover floating after me through the shadows.

I whirl around, tension I don't want to unleash at her jittering through my essence. "What are you doing?"

Peri sidles closer with an air of curiosity that carries through our deepened bond. "You're going hunting, aren't you?"

I can't stop my voice from turning gruff. "I need to eat. I don't want to screw anything up today because I wasn't at my best."

A flicker of confusion quivers through her curiosity. "I wasn't saying you shouldn't. I'd like to see how you do it. If that's all right."

Even more tension coils inside me. "Why would you want to see that?"

She nudges me gently through the shadows. "I told you I love every part of you. I'd like to know as much about you as I can. I promise it won't upset me. I understand that you're going to have to kill an animal. That's how you're built. You shouldn't have to hide it."

I waver in indecision, but the warmth of her presence and her words melts most of my hesitation. Only Peri could turn vicious bloodshed into an act of adoration. "If you're sure… I was planning on being quick about it. I just need to find viable prey."

"I'll stay quiet and out of your way. Don't worry about me."

Easier said than done. Although when I start forward across the patchy field again, the twisted feelings inside me have softened.

This *is* who I am. I've never had any choice about how I fuel myself.

If even Peri, who's spent so much time trying to spread contentment, can be okay with that part of my nature… why should I fight it?

I prowl across the terrain near our work site for several

minutes, careful not to venture too far. Peri's with me now, but she can't roam very widely without putting herself and the men I share her love with in pain.

Finally, my predator senses snap to alertness. I glance around to confirm there are no humans nearby to notice me and then emerge into the early-morning sunlight in my basilisk form.

A flick of my tongue to scent the air confirms what I already suspected: there's a wild rabbit nearby.

As I creep closer, my clawed feet padding across the ground ever so quietly, I spot it. The brown-furred creature is nibbling on some grass not far from a hole that must be its burrow.

It won't notice my scent. I'm not a natural predator in these parts—and my body gives off a different impression than a mortal predator's would. Besides, I don't have to get all that close to claim my meal.

I approach even more slowly. When I'm still several paces away, I pause and concentrate the searing energy behind my eyes.

Kill. Kill. Kill.

My eye sockets sting with the energy piercing through them. The rabbit jerks in a sudden spasm and topples over on its side.

Before it's even hit the ground, I'm lunging forward. The part of my brain that craves fresh meat also craves the thrill of the pounce, even if I temper the violence by ending the creatures' lives before I tackle them.

There's no reason why my hunger should put them in more pain than necessary.

My claws rake through the furry pelt. My jaws snap around the muscles inside and wrench free globs of meat.

The bloody flavor saturates my mouth with a strange swell of satisfaction mingled with shame.

Maybe not quite as much shame as has gripped me before, though.

Peri materializes while I'm crunching down the bones. I freeze for a second, but as she promised, there's no anguish or consternation in her expression or the emotions that waft through our bond. She has an unusually thoughtful air.

"You used your killing gaze on the rabbit," she says. "It was already dead before you jumped on it."

I lick the last droplets of blood from my jaws and straighten up into my human-like form, willing the green contacts to appear alongside my clothes so my natural eyes are covered. "I always have, once I figured out that I could. It makes the process easier for both me and the prey."

Peri nods. "You don't like them to suffer any more than they have to."

"Of course not."

She smiles at me, so bright my heart skips a beat. "You see—there's nothing cruel about you."

I don't know how to answer that statement.

As Peri's gaze slides back toward the trailers, a shiver of anxiety travels into me from her.

I frown. From the timing, I don't think that emotion had anything to do with my hunt. "What's wrong?"

"Oh, it's nothing—"

Peri cuts herself off and shakes her head, momentarily abashed. "I shouldn't say that. It isn't nothing. It isn't good for me to pretend I'm only happy and calm when I'm not."

She seems to gird herself. "I'm nervous about what we're going to do today. We need to bash up a bunch of things that belong to mortals… What if it doesn't bring Viscera to us after all? If it does bring her, what are we going to do with her? Just kill her?"

The uncertainty in her voice makes my gut clench, but I

want to be honest with her too. "That might be the kindest thing we can do for everyone involved."

"I know. I guess that's partly why I wanted to come with you. To see how killing can be for a good reason too. But I'm not sure it stopped me from being nervous."

She rubs her temple and then shoots me a softer smile. "But that's okay, right? It's normal to be nervous. That doesn't mean the plan is wrong. We have to do *something*. I don't want to let her keep wrecking the city either."

I tuck my arm around her shoulders for whatever comfort that'll give her, as hard as it still is for me to comprehend that I can comfort anyone. "That's why we're doing it. It's a very smart plan. How we deal with her… A lot of that is her decision. She messed up other people's lives. She can't really complain that we're not allowed to do the same in return to stop her."

Peri perks up. "That's a good point! She made the first choice, not us."

She pauses before cocking her head at me. "I was wondering something, though."

Her tone is light enough that I raise an eyebrow. "What's that?"

"The power you can send from your eyes—and the poison from your skin—does it *have* to be strong enough to kill?"

I knit my brow. "That's what it's supposed to do."

"But do you think there's a way to rein it in so that you only knock the target unconscious or similar? Pull your punch a bit? Like… a lot of poisons are only deadly if the dose is big enough. Less and it simply slows you down or makes you sick."

The question stirs up all kinds of feelings I don't know what to make of: denial and doubt with a gleaming thread of hope winding through them. "That's true. I don't know if it'd work that way for me. I've never tried."

Peri presses a kiss to my jaw. "Do you want to? I can do my best to help—to balance out the aggressive impulses that drive your instincts."

I can tell she'd be fine with me refusing… but the hope expands as I consider the possibility. "All right. Let's see what happens."

How well can I not-quite-kill something?

We dive back into the shadows where we can scout for new prey discreetly. I stalk across the landscape, avoiding any signs of human occupation.

I definitely don't want to experiment with the deadliness of my killing power on that kind of mortal being.

Over by a stand of spindly trees, a few sparrows are hopping around. They wouldn't make much of a meal, hardly a mouthful, but I'm not aiming to eat them.

As I pull myself back into physical form, Peri follows. She rests her hand on my arm. "We'll do it together. I can feel when you're focusing."

I swallow thickly and blink away the contacts I automatically conjured. The sparrows peck at whatever seeds or bugs they're snatching off the ground.

They consume other life, just like I do. I don't resent them for it.

Just like Peri doesn't resent me.

Why have I let my needs bother me so much? Is it possible I could have found new, less harmful dimensions to my powers all this time, if I hadn't shied away from using them unless I absolutely had to?

There's only one way to find out.

I pick a sparrow and narrow my eyes. As the stinging sensation forms behind them, a waft of moderating reassurance flows from Peri.

I'm in control. I can decide how much harm my power inflicts.

Just a quick smack of the brain, enough to dim the lights. Leave all essential systems functioning. It shouldn't be that hard, should it?

A slight pull of my punch, like Peri said.

I clench my hands and let a brief flare of my power burst from my eyes.

The sparrow flops over. Its companions startle and flit into the branches of the trees.

With my heart thudding at the base of my throat, I rush over to check the little creature.

As soon as my hand closes around its feathered body, I can sense the pulse still thrumming at its core.

A grin leaps to my face. I glance over at Peri, my relief radiating into her and mingling with the sunny pride glowing in her hair.

Who would have thought my power didn't make me an unmitigated killer after all?

Peri would have thought. She watched and she saw me like no one else ever has.

"I did it," I say. "*We* did it. Let's keep practicing. I want to be as ready as possible when we see Viscera again."

30

Periwinkle

As we emerge onto the street Rollick picked out to stage our acts of destruction, one thought sits heavy in my mind. I look at my companions—the four men who've embraced our connection, the six shadowbloods, Sorsha and her men, Rollick and his various assistants—and my heart sinks.

If my plan works and we tempt Viscera into showing herself, we have more than enough power between us to destroy *her* in a matter of seconds. But as much as I hate the damage she's done to the city, more violence was never my goal.

All of these people gave me a chance—multiple chances. If we had a competition for who's done the most harm to the human world in total, I bet I've been responsible for more than Viscera has. I mean, I did have a head start of several years.

"Hold on," I say.

Everyone's gaze veers toward me. Rollick motions for me to go on.

I draw my short frame as tall as I can in the warm morning sunlight and aim for a voice that's more determined champion than cream puff. "I don't want to murder her if we don't have to."

Sorsha's mouth twists. "It isn't exactly murder when it's in defense of other people's lives, Peri."

"I know. But the point is, I don't want to see any more beings die if we can help it. She's messed up from the weird rift. We don't know if there might be a way to get through to her once we're not chasing her around the city."

Jonah speaks up in his reassuringly steady tone. "Peri's right, for more than one reason. Viscera is the only higher being we've encountered so far who came out of one of those new rifts—the only warped shadowkind we could talk to. If we can convince her to talk with *us*, she might be able to tell us things that could fix the whole problem of the rifts."

That is also a good point, probably a better one than my appeal to emotion as far as Rollick is concerned.

A smile touches my lips. This is why the bonds we've formed are a good thing. We really are stronger, smarter, *more* when we're together.

A whole food court of buffets with all the flavors any of us could need.

Raze nods. "I've been experimenting… I might be able to paralyze her with my powers rather than outright kill her."

Hail's eyes brighten. "She didn't like the wind I conjured before. I can whirl a bunch around her to help trap her. And add some ice to the mix if I need to."

Mirage lets out a burst of laughter. "And I can reach right into her head and tweak her thoughts. Make her think she's still free when she's really caught. Maybe then she won't fight?"

Rollick's expression looks skeptical. He exhales in a sigh. "All right. I can't say I'm hopeful about your odds, but you have plenty of backup. I'll be here—and Sorsha's crew and our shadowbloods—to strike the final blow if it comes to that."

He gestures to everyone he mentioned. "Be prepared to surround the rogue shadowkind and take her down immediately if Peri's team can't contain her."

The uncomfortable weight lingers in my stomach, but his acceptance is the best outcome I could hope for. We aren't smashing up part of the city just for kicks.

We have to take the opportunity to stop Viscera completely, however we need to in the end.

Jonah passes me a steel bar while holding on to one for himself. Unlike most of our allies, we don't have powers that lend themselves easily to bashing and breaking. I'd rather not turn myself into a volcano of emotion just to carry out our ploy.

I extend my awareness as far as I can reach it through the strip of storefronts we've chosen. Not a single splash of human emotion reaches my senses.

"The buildings are all clear," I tell Rollick. "Everyone's gone."

He sweeps his arm toward our surroundings. "Then let's begin!"

We don't want to ruin the whole street all at once. We need to leave time for Viscera to notice the commotion.

That's not a problem for me. I march up to the front of a clothing shop and whack the display window with my bar, but all that I get for my effort is a crack in the glass.

Frowning, I hit the pane harder. More cracks form.

With my third strike, the glass crumples in a shower of shards.

An unexpected sense of satisfaction ripples through me. There's something almost… exhilarating about making something fall apart. Maybe just being able to exert enough power to do it in the first place?

But I can only feel that way because I know no one is getting hurt because of what we're doing. The store owners will be able to recover from the damages with the insurance Rollick talked about.

Viscera is going around trying to harm everyone as much as she can.

Not just for the sadistic enjoyment after all, though. She's sounded angry, frustrated… almost betrayed.

Pull us in and push us away. Make us twist and twitch. Screw them!

Who was she talking about? That thing about pulling and pushing sounded almost like the impressions I get from the strange rift… but she's not rioting at the portal.

As I batter my bar against the window frame, leaving dents in my wake, my companions bring their own powers to bear. Raze snarls and flings a mailbox across the street with a swing of his fist. Hail sends a shower of piercing ice pellets at the upper windows of the buildings, the frigid chunks smashing through the glass and thudding across the floor inside.

Mirage has shifted into fox form. He cavorts through the street, all five tails swishing behind him, scratching up paint and tearing posters from the telephone posts with his teeth. Jonah shatters the pane on a shop's windowed door and kicks the metal frame for good measure.

Matching trickles of exhilaration and an airy tang of relief stream through our connection. The tension that gripped my men for most of the past few weeks is seeping away with every slash and bang.

Maybe they've needed a chance to let it out. All our own frustrations and fears can be poured into this unnerving act.

Just how much emotion is Viscera trying to conquer with the way she rampages around the city?

Unless I'm being too optimistic in my interpretations, and she's simply psychotic to the core.

She did freak out about the wind that one time. She isn't impervious.

We have to find a way to get through to her, a crack to open up so we can reach a part of her that cares about more than just spewing harm, however deeply it's buried.

Farther down the street, Sorsha's winged giant of a mate and the one who's turned into a huge, eerily glowing dog smash more windows. The phoenix shifter sends spurts of flame inside that light up the shop furnishings.

Zian rams his shoulder into a telephone pole and sends it toppling across the street. Riva dashes to and fro, wrenching fixtures off the fronts of the buildings and hurling them toward others.

There's no sign of Viscera so far. I ease farther down the undamaged part of the street and break another window with a couple of determined swings. Then I smash the front of a newspaper box for good measure.

How long will it take the rogue shadowkind to pick up on the destruction being waged without her?

What if she *doesn't* notice?

It'd be just great if she's decided to snooze on her self-appointed job now.

A few of the shadowbloods cross the street to tackle the shops along the other side. Mirage joins them, shifting into humanesque form and swinging from one store's awning until it tears.

I stretch out the carnage by hitting every shard of glass still clinging to the window frames. They fracture off into tinier fragments like spiky snow.

When I've completely cleared the two windows I destroyed, I walk to the next shop. Cakes dolled up with elaborate whorls of pastel icing pose on the other side of the glass.

My stomach lurches as if I'd just swallowed one of those cakes whole.

They're so pretty. It doesn't seem right to bash them up.

Maybe if I smash the window *carefully*, I can manage not to get any glass in the fondant?

I'm raising my bar to make a valiant attempt when a surge of emotion hits me from out of nowhere.

A treacly mush of anguish clogs my throat. My head jerks around.

The sensation isn't emanating from any of my marked men or my other companions. None of my allies are over in the direction the unnerving flavor is wafting from.

I think the source is close, though. It tastes… maybe only a block or two away.

Did I miss a civilian in my initial search, or has a human ventured nearby that Rollick's people weren't able to redirect?

The swell of misery hits me harder. Whoever it is, they're definitely not having a good day.

I lower my bar, hesitate, and then slip away into the shadows.

I'll go take a quick look. There's no reason to distract everyone else from our mission. If Viscera does show up and most of us have abandoned our rampage, she might leave again without revealing herself.

Of course, there are four companions I can't help signaling inadvertently. I've only made it around the corner when I sense my three shadowkind men rushing toward me through the shadows, with Jonah loping along on the sidewalk behind me.

When I pull myself into physical form, the men follow me.

"What's going on, Peri?" Raze asks. "Why did you leave? It feels like something's upset you."

"Someone else is upset." I motion toward the neighborhood ahead of me. "I'm just making sure we're not accidentally causing more harm than we meant to. You don't need to come."

Hail makes a dismissive sound. "Like you said last night, you're stuck with us now, Cream Puff. Where you go, we go."

I don't think I phrased it quite that way.

Mirage whirls around us with a swish of one of his tails before it vanishes. "We can see more of the city and keep our Rainbow safe."

I don't think I'm in any danger, but at least they can help if the person I'm sensing needs more than I can offer on my own.

"All right," I say. "But be gentle. We don't want them thinking we're terrorist gangsters from outer space too."

As I hurry onward, the anguished sensation spreads up my throat and down to my chest to squeeze at my heart. It's coming from just around the next corner… Somewhere along this next street…

Right above me.

As my head snaps up toward the shifting impression, a gangly figure with a mane of silver hair careens onto the street inches away from me. I stumble backward, and my men press closer around me.

The miserable feeling vanishes, replaced by apple-streusel amusement as Viscera aims one of her jagged grins at me.

"So you did come," she says, poking me in the chest. "You acted like you wanted to tear the city down, but as soon as you thought someone was bothered about it, you came running."

She tricked me—she figured out my ability and used it to catch my attention?

My gut squirms with disappointment, but that's okay. It's okay that I made a mistake.

Because my plan still brought her to us.

My voice bursts out of me. "Hold her!"

Raze's green contacts dissolve, revealing the full ominous black of his basilisk eyes. As he fixes his gaze on Viscera, a chilly wind whips up from the ground, sending a flurry of snowflakes swirling around her.

Jonah lifts his voice, sorcerous syllables thrumming as they spill off his tongue. Mirage spreads his arms like he's a magician in a stage act, although I know the illusions he's going to create will feel much more real than that.

And I cast out all the soothing emotions I can summon: keeping Raze's most aggressive urges in check, boosting Jonah's confidence, wrapping Hail in gratitude, encouraging Mirage's energy. Dampening Viscera's desire to fight us as well as I know how.

It doesn't appear that I'm affecting *her* all that much. She's still got plenty of fight.

She yelps in an uncharacteristically squeaky voice at the gusting of the wind against her clothes, as if she's been transformed into a bath toy. Her arms and tail lash out and jerk back toward her body with a tremor of revulsion.

Then her movements slow.

Is Raze's power starting to paralyze her?

My hopes lift. Excitement shivers through my veins.

We're really doing it. We've caught her; we're containing her without hurting her.

I don't know how much Jonah's sorcery and Mirage's mind-warping abilities are subduing her as well, but the combination of all of us working together is more powerful than I dared to imagine.

Now what do we do with her? Can we risk one of us stepping away to alert our other allies?

I don't want to throw off the balance that's let us finally contain her.

Maybe it's that momentary prick of uncertainty that sets us off-kilter. Maybe Viscera was only going still so that she could gather her strength for one larger effort.

Whatever the case, before I can suggest our next step, she thrashes against our hold even harder than before.

Raze winces, a blink of his eyes diffusing their power. Hail sends his blizzardy wind roaring even harder around the rogue shadowkind, but he's only focusing on her sides.

Viscera shudders and shakes her head, and Mirage's head twitches in turn. Then she's springing straight upward like a rocket.

She leaps free of the whirlwind that only extended a few feet above her head and flings herself farther down the street. As she races away from us, her boots clack and sizzle against the asphalt, punctuating the cackle of her laugh.

"You think you're tough?" she hollers back at us. "You're not stopping me, not ever. Let's see how many humans I can bring crashing down while you try."

31

Periwinkle

Raze hurtles after Viscera first, shifting into his full basilisk form as he charges. His black eyes glitter— but the rogue shadowkind vanishes into a patch of shadow.

"Keep after her!" I shout. "And we have to let Rollick and the others know somehow."

Jonah waves the rest of us onward, his eyes wide. "I—I might be able to signal them with my sorcery. Just go. If one of you can pop out of the shadows here and there so I can see you, I'll follow as well as I can."

I leap into the nearest patch of darkness and flit through the rivulets beneath cars and street fixtures in the direction I can feel Raze giving chase. Hail and Mirage race up beside me.

Mirage flickers in and out of the shadows just before we veer around a corner. Jonah's feet pound across the sidewalk after us, a slew of sorcerous syllables tumbling out of his mouth between his breaths.

Even in the shadows, I'm not much of a sprinter. As I push myself to stop the distance between Raze and me from widening, the strain reverberates through my essence.

Hail lets out an unusually gentle chuckle. "Come on, Cream Puff. We're not leaving you behind."

His presence tugs at mine, urging me along as if he's swung me onto his back. As our energies mingle, we surge forward even faster.

Mirage lets out a yip of excitement and dashes alongside us, but splinters of tension radiate off him. We all know that Viscera can't have anything good in mind.

Should we have killed her to begin with? If I'd let Raze inflict the full power of his gaze or Hail freeze her while she was briefly trapped, this fight would be over.

But I'd have needed to live with that decision for the rest of my life. It's hard to say I regret trying to choose compassion.

Whether I find myself regretting it an hour from now will depend on what she does next.

We're still lagging behind Raze, but not by much. Jonah's breaths have faded to a distant panting, but I can hear him loping after us.

However his sorcery tugged at Rollick and our other shadowkind allies, I hope they felt it. I hope they understood what he meant.

We swerve down another street—a wide one lined with cars. Several blocks up ahead, the two- and three-story buildings give way to towering apartment buildings and skyscrapers.

My stomach drops. Oh, no.

Is she going to bash up one of those places—bring down

a structure that's holding hundreds, maybe even thousands of people—all in one go?

She said she was going to bring as many humans "crashing down" as possible. *Is* she powerful enough to collapse an entire high rise?

The chill that washes through my essence has nothing to do with Hail's wintry affinities. I don't want to have to find out the answer to that question.

"Faster!" I cry, willing my being forward with everything I have. Hail grunts, but he manages to rush on with a tiny bit more speed.

What if we can't stop her in time? Even if we catch up with her at whatever building she plans to target, I don't know if we can subdue her on our own. We might not even get another chance to kill her if she stays in the shadows.

No, I can't let my doubts rattle me. We held her in place before, if not for long. We don't have that much experience at combining our talents, but we're only going to get better.

I believe in us.

Even as I think that, Viscera blinks into view on the road a couple of blocks ahead of us. A car honks and swerves to avoid her. She dives back into the darkness beneath one of the parked vehicles... but not before I make out a flicker along the edges of her physical body.

A few plumes of black essence trail from the spot where she vanished.

My gut twists itself into a knot. "She's starting to disintegrate. Like the creatures Rollick captured did."

How long does she have before she completely goes up in smoke?

We still have to put an end to her reign of destruction now. It might take a day or two before the warped effects completely overtake her.

We don't know how long ago the process started—it

could have been creeping over her since yesterday, or it could have begun this very moment.

Whatever's happening to her, it appears to be messing with her self-control. Several seconds later, she wavers into physical form again with a ripple that passes through her body before it fully solidifies.

My pulse hitches. Before I can think better of it, I throw myself out of the shadows too, springing on top of a car—without smashing it, of course. I have manners.

"Viscera!" I holler. "Your body is starting to fail because of the rift you came through. You'll *die* soon. But we can try to help you!"

I can't say I'm surprised by her snort in response. "You don't know anything, Shiny Girl!" she shouts back, and manages to slip into the shadows again just as Raze bursts out of them.

More cars honk. Tires screech as an SUV collides with the back of a pickup truck.

With a growl, Raze lunges after Viscera. Pedestrians along the street gape as his tall, sinewy body ripples with basilisk scales.

The rogue shadowkind is bringing out the predator in him, and he's so focused on catching her that he can't concentrate on his form.

We're charging past the high rises now. Just a couple of blocks up ahead looms the tallest of them—that glinting structure of mirrored windows and smooth steel that Rollick said the city's people are particularly proud of: The Diamond Victory Tower.

It stands out like a single candle on a birthday cake. One I can't help thinking would be awfully tempting to blow out —or over, if you're so inclined.

Certainty sinks into my essence that Viscera must be

aiming for it. Taking a deep breath, I plunge into the shadows and hurtle onward.

I've just come up on her last location when she pops into being at the base of the looming tower.

As she appears, her figure morphs. Her hair shrinks again, deepening to an unusual grayish-mauve hue. Her biceps bulge.

Which gives her all the more power to ram her fist into the polished marble wall next to the glinting lobby doors. Supernatural energy warbles alongside the impact.

A flinch ripples through my essence even in the shadows.

"Stop her!" I call out, not even sure who I'm talking to.

As I speed the last short distance between us, Viscera pummels the skyscraper again. Then her skin seems to shudder.

The outline of her body wobbles with a momentary translucency, as if she's turning into gelatin from the outside in.

For the first time, a dash of coppery panic reaches me— sharper than the stew of bewildered uneasiness that's wafting off our mortal audience.

Viscera's expression hardens, but I know what lies behind her fierce mask.

She's scared of what's happening to her.

Raze materializes a few feet away and tackles her without hesitation. Viscera's screech suggests he's exuded some of his basilisk poison.

Her body flickers again, and she slips through his claws as if she's made of mist.

I sway to a stop a couple of buildings away, my breath rasping and my feet radiating an ache up through my ankles.

It takes a massive effort to push the words from my throat. "Viscera, please! You're going to fade away. All you have to do is stop fighting us and stop breaking things. I swear we'll do whatever we can to make sure you survive."

She wavers right through a parked jeep and ducks under it when Raze pounces, but her voice peals out from the space beneath as if she couldn't meld with the shadows. "What good is a promise from a weakling like you?"

"That 'weakling' convinced the rest of us not to kill you in the first place," Hail snaps. A frigid wind whips down the street, shoving aside the stunned pedestrians and warbling around the jeep. "You already owe her the life you still have."

Mirage makes a brusque sound of agreement, circling the vehicle. "Our Rainbow isn't weak. She's *kind*."

"Who the fuck wants kindness?" Viscera bolts for the tower just as Raze wheels to leap at her under the jeep. She batters the panes with her fists again. "Nothing in this place was kind to me. It called me and now it won't let me in."

She's opened up spidery cracks all through the marble. With each new blow, the gaps spread wider. The bands of steel around the panes shudder increasingly visible indents.

How much more will it take before the foundation itself starts to buckle?

I'd suggest that if she wants to go inside, trying the door would be a good start, but I don't think that's what she means. What is she so furious about?

As Viscera wrenches away from Raze's clawed hands again, a guttural sound reverberates from her throat. Her frustration smacks into me, harsh and acerbic as pure wasabi.

"If this realm is going to break me, I should get to break as many other things as I can on my way out," she shrieks to the street at large. "It should all fall down!"

I guess there's a certain logic to her approach, but I don't have to like it.

My men can't seem to contain her fury, though. Her

increasingly warped and wavering form is working to her advantage.

If we can distract her until Rollick and the others get here… Maybe I can keep her talking.

"How is it breaking you?" I ask. "Why did you even come through the rift if you don't like it here?"

She grunts through clenched teeth. "One pulled me, one pushed me—there was supposed to be a home. Everything together. But nothing's mixed right. I don't fit. It doesn't work. So we'll all shatter apart!"

She slams into the side of the tower with even more force and a metallic groan.

Pulling and pushing—like she said before. Like the dissonant energy from the rift.

I don't understand what she means about the rest of it. What was supposed to be mixed? What doesn't work?

It occurs to me that she might not even know. But I can't help trying again. "There are places here that could be home. We could find somewhere that you fit. If you'd just stop and—"

"It's too *late*," she screams, cutting off my plea, and whips away from Raze before bashing her shoulder against the other side of the doorway.

Jonah reaches us, his breath rasping from how fast he was running to keep up. His voice comes out ragged but firm. "The others are coming. I can feel it. I just called out to Rollick and Sorsha's men with my sorcery again." He lets out a short laugh that doesn't hold much humor. "Let's hope they forgive my intrusion."

"How far behind us are they?" I ask.

He shakes his head. "I don't know."

Viscera darts around Raze's next lunge and aims a roundhouse kick at the apartment's shiny face. When her body shivers with filminess, Hail's wind makes the edges of it jitter even more.

Streaks of her essence darken the air. She groans but keeps swinging.

My thudding heart lodges in my throat. "They might not get here in time. We have to make sure she doesn't send this whole building toppling over."

So many people inside. So many lives hanging in the balance.

Viscera's next blow knocks off a whole chunk of marble and bends the steel sideways. Sparks fly from her fists as she throws them even faster.

Fear and horror knot in my chest… but stronger than them is the swell of determination that rises up inside me.

Yes, I'm afraid and horrified. I'm pretty sure the situation warrants it.

I'm also grateful for the men who've followed me this far, spoken in my favor, and listened to my pleas. I hate what Viscera is doing, and I love my companions who are braving her rampage with me.

All those emotions, good and bad, twine together inside me into something even more powerful than the flare of darkly vengeful energy I spewed at my former captor or the blazing glow that seared marks into my men's chests.

We're stronger together, and everything I can feel is stronger if I don't deny any of those feelings.

My power surges beneath my skin. I yell as loud as I can. "Surround her!"

Because they understand me, because they trust me, my men spring into action. Jonah dashes toward the apartment building. Raze settles into a tensed pose at its other side, beyond Viscera. Mirage and Hail close in, Mirage leaping onto the hood of a nearby parked car.

I focus on the blare of emotions inside me and let them pour out.

The light that erupts from me now doesn't blaze but beams. It shimmers the same turquoise shade as my hair, as all our marks did last night when I declared my love.

It streams between all of my men, joining us by our marks in a ring.

A ring Viscera is now inside.

When she flings herself at the building, the glowing torrent between Jonah and Raze tosses her back. They step forward, driving her farther away with the thrumming light.

I keep pouring more out, giving them and her everything I am. Every bit of hope and denial, joy and anger I have in me, resonating stronger as those feelings are echoed by the men I'm connected to.

"What the fuck are you doing?" Viscera shrieks.

She hurls herself at one side of the beaming ring and another, but the currents of energy just bounce her back. When she propels herself toward the sky like she did with Hail's wind, a turquoise sheen curves over her head, nudging her back down.

We're doing it. We're really doing it—the five of us together, penning her in, preventing her destruction.

But any dreams I might have of Viscera surrendering and accepting whatever help we can give dwindle with each cry that leaves her lips, each blow she aims at my men only for the glow to deflect her. She spins in the center of the ring, seething so visibly I wouldn't be surprised to see steam gusting from her ears alongside the essence wisping from her skin.

How long can our combined power hold her when we haven't even really touched her?

My horror at the destruction she's dealt out peels back

like a bitter rind. Inside lies a kernel of something tarter and more poignant.

I had us stage a spree of violence to pretend we were joining her rampage. Can I accept what she is and what she's done for real, not just as a ploy?

She's been cruel and brutal… because she feels as if she was tormented first. Because she wanted to fit in here but couldn't.

Isn't that what we all crave, in our own ways? Her recipe of wanting cooked up a storm of devastation… but I'm not sure she's the one who wrote it.

My voice comes out gentler than before, pitched just loud enough for her to hear. "I'm sorry. It makes sense that you're angry—that you'd want to break everything."

Viscera falters in her flailing. She stiffens on a patch of road, staring at me. "What are you doing now?"

I swallow hard. "Telling you that I can see how hard it's been. This is the way you were built. There was something you needed that never came. It must be so painful. I wish I could take that pain away, but it isn't wrong for you to feel it."

Her eyes widen. Her stance seems to deflate, but the next shudder that runs through her stocky body looks like a release.

"I thought I belonged here," she says. "It was all lies."

As she holds my gaze, her form spasms. More shadowy essence billows off her.

She hisses a breath through her teeth and squeezes her eyes shut.

And then she seems to detonate.

The burst of fractured essence slams into our barrier of bonded emotion. We all rock on our feet, my heels stinging harder with the impact.

I catch a flare of concern from Raze, but the basilisk

shifter holds himself in place, knowing it's riskier to break our circle than to let me hold my own.

Darkness flares across my eyes. An ashy taste fills my mouth.

When I blink the haze away, the shadowkind woman is gone. I can't sense her fraught emotions anywhere nearby.

Her essence has dispersed into the world, never to reassemble.

A pang shoots through my heart. She wanted to destroy this city on her own terms… and she decided to go out with a bang herself rather than have the choice taken from her.

Did my acceptance help *her* accept what she assumed had to be her fate rather than continuing to rail against the rest of us?

I'd like to think I gave her some tiny bit of comfort in the end, but a lump stays lodged in my throat like I've tried to swallow a walnut whole.

Jonah meets my eyes from across our shining ring. "There was nothing else you could have done," he says, speaking to the guilt that's started to creep in. "I wish we could've snapped her out of her madness too."

I dip my head, and just then a whole crowd of shadowkind materialize around us in tandem with the familiar screech of a van's wheels.

While the shadowbloods pile out of the van, Rollick strolls over to my glowing ring. I pull the energy back inside myself, a flicker of embarrassment passing over my face and my hair.

The demon clicks his tongue. His tone is all dry amusement. "I wonder if you're ever going to stop surprising us, Periwinkle."

"I hope not," Mirage says, throwing his arms around me in an emphatic hug.

As my other men hurry over to surround me, Rollick

takes in the rest of the scene. "I gather our rogue shadowkind is no longer a concern. You have left me with another large mess to clean up, though."

I can't tell if he's actually upset. "Sorry?"

The demon aims a crooked grin my way. "At least it should be the last mess—in this city anyway."

32

Periwinkle

After my marked men and I have given a full account of our confrontation with Viscera, Rollick stands in the trailer meeting room for a while tapping his fingers together, his face set in an expression I can only call bemused.

"So you subdued her with the power of love and acceptance," he says finally. "Should we expect you to start farting stardust and rainbows next?"

I can't stop myself from glancing over my shoulder as if such a deluge might already have started without my noticing. "Um, I think maybe… maybe this is what my power was always supposed to be. The way I can send out energy, at least. It felt *right*. I just needed to find the right people to bring it out of me."

The people who could make me see how multi-faceted

love really is—not just happiness but every other fraught emotion that comes into play when you care that much. And accepting all of it as a valid part of the whole.

Accepting all that *I* am.

I'm sure I've seen this sentiment on an inspirational poster some human made, but that doesn't mean it's wrong: I had to love myself before I could be what I needed to be.

Mirage grins. "She doesn't need to *fart* rainbows when she can already shine one out of her hair."

I give him a playful kick under the table, but my thoughts have veered to more serious matters.

"Viscera is gone, but there could be more warped higher shadowkind like her who'll come through the new rifts. The lesser creatures are still a problem. They can do so much damage… and it isn't fair to them that they don't have a chance at a real life before they break apart. From some of the things Viscera said, it sounded almost like they're being compelled here, which would make it even less their fault."

Rollick frowns. "What did she say compelled her?"

"She wasn't really specific," I have to admit. "She just kept talking about being pulled and pushed, about how there was supposed to be a place for her but it was a lie."

As his frown deepens with concentration, Sorsha cocks her head where she's leaning against the wall. "I wonder if you could close up these rifts. Your lovey-dovey power contained Viscera better than anything else we've seen. If there's some way to apply it to the portals…"

My heart leaps. "I'll try anything. I just want everything to go back to normal."

Whatever normal will look like now that I have my powers under control and four men I adore who are just as devoted to me.

I can't imagine yet exactly how that will be… but it

should definitely be a juicier version of life than any I've experienced so far.

Rollick seems to shake off his apprehension and nods. "We'll start experimenting right away. I've also established contact with another sorcerer who's on her way and may be able to help Jonah rein the creatures in better while they're still coming. And—"

One of his assistants pops out of the shadows with a gasp of ragged breath. "The rift!" she cries out. "I don't know—it's doing *something*—you have to see."

We all scramble to our feet. As we rush out into the makeshift film set's yard, my stomach lurches like I'm on a teeter-totter.

We don't need to hustle over to the factory the rift was floating by. Even from here, half a mile away, I can see the portal now.

The wavering swath of air has stretched up and out, distorting several factory buildings beyond it and the more distant skyline of the city. The artificial lights that gleam brighter as evening starts to fall are quavering when seen through its surface.

The rift expands farther with every thud of my pulse: wider, higher, thicker. It was already huge, and now it's at least a hundred times larger than the biggest portal to the shadow realm I've ever seen.

Rollick curses under his breath. His jaw tightens as if he doesn't like what he's about to say. "Stay here. We don't want to risk getting any closer. We'll just have to wait and—"

His phone starts ringing. He cuts himself off to yank it from his pocket.

At the same moment, a thicker warbling of energy passes through the air, as potent as if I'm standing right in front of the rift rather than far off down the road. The portal's hazy outline surges farther even faster, swelling across the terrain and up toward the sky like a tidal wave.

And then it crashes.

The immense rift topples over, belly-flopping across the entire sprawl of the city in a spew of shadow.

ABOUT THE AUTHOR

Eva Chase lives in Canada with her family. She loves stories both swoony and supernatural, and strong women and the men who appreciate them.

Along with the Pack of Outcasts trilogy, she is the author of the Royal Spares series, the Rites of Possession series, the Shadowblood Souls series, the Heart of a Monster series, the Gang of Ghouls series, the Bound to the Fae series, the Flirting with Monsters series, the Cursed Studies trilogy, the Royals of Villain Academy series, the Moriarty's Men series, the Looking Glass Curse trilogy, the Their Dark Valkyrie series, the Witch's Consorts series, the Dragon Shifter's Mates series, the Demons of Fame series, and the Legends Reborn trilogy.

Connect with Eva online:
www.evachase.com
eva@evachase.com

www.ingramcontent.com/pod-product-compliance
Lightning Source LLC
Chambersburg PA
CBHW061227310726
48971CB00007B/1968